I0627575

Also from Indigo Sea Press
Novels by Bud Fussell

Scoundrel
Mixed Emotions
Shepherds
Serendipity

indigoseapress.com

Redemption?

By

Bud Fussell

Deep Indigo Books
Published by Indigo Sea Press
Winston-Salem

Deep Indigo Books
Indigo Sea Press
302 Ricks Drive
Winston-Salem, NC 27103

This book is a work of fiction. While many of the geographical locations are real, the names, characters and events are either a product of the author's imagination, fictitious or used fictitiously. Any resemblance to any event or person, living or dead, is purely coincidental.

Copyright 2013 by Bud Fussell

All rights reserved, including the right of reproduction in whole or part in any format.

First Deep Indigo Books edition published
December, 2015
Deep Indigo Books, Moon Sailor, and all production design are trademarks of Indigo Sea Press, used under license.

For information regarding bulk purchases of this book, digital purchase and special discounts, please contact the publisher at
indigoseapress.com

Cover design by Stacy Castanedo

Manufactured in the United States of America
ISBN 978-1-63066-205-9

CHAPTER ONE

The newlyweds held hands as the big 707 roared down the runway, and in a minute they were airborne. The climb was so steep; it felt as if they were going straight up. The lights below were so beautiful, it was hard to imagine that somewhere down there was where they lived, as did their family and friends.

Pretty soon after the wheels were up, Chuck, the pilot, announced on the speaker, "Well, folks, we're on our way. We're climbing to an altitude of thirty-three thousand feet, and according to the weather people, we should have a very smooth flight. Just relax, and in a few hours, we'll be landing in Paradise. It's such a clear evening, if you'll look to your left, the lights coming into view are the lights of Nashville. Beautiful, aren't they?"

As soon as they leveled off some and the seatbelt light went off, Monty asked Joan if she would like a glass of champagne. She asked, "Are you going to have one?"

"Yeah, let's drink a toast to our new life together. I really don't know much about champagne and those kinds of things, but it looks like Don went all out because this is French champagne, and I think that's supposed to be good."

He poured the bubbly in two glasses, then bent over and kissed Joan before they clinked their glasses together. "Here's to us. May our marriage be perfect, and may our love only grow stronger."

Neither one particularly liked the taste of the champagne, but since they felt as if it were what they were supposed to do, they finished the bottle. Since neither one of them were drinkers, the alcohol went to their heads. They were both feeling really amorous, but since neither of them had ever been with anyone sexually before, both of them were afraid to bring up the subject of going to bed.

Monty asked, "Would you like to see a movie?"

"You mean on the plane?"

"Yeah."

"Yes, I'd like that. How do you do that on the plane?"

"The plane is equipped with a gizmo that plays movies as well as music, and there is a pretty good movie library on board. Some of them are old, but they're good. Look these over and pick one out."

1

Joan looked through the selection and said, "Let's watch *The Graduate*. I know it's old, but I never did get to see it."

"*The Graduate* it is." Monty put the cartridge in the machine, pressed a couple of buttons, and the movie started. "Let's sit on the sofa, want to?"

Joan got up and moved to one of the plush sofas, and Monty sat down beside here. He put his arm around her shoulder and between kisses, they enjoyed watching Anne Bancroft seduce Dustin Hoffman.

About midway through the movie, Chuck came back from the flight deck. "I thought you guys would be in bed by now. What are you watching?"

"*The Graduate*," Monty said.

"I saw that. It's a good movie. That Mrs. Robinson is something, isn't she?"

Joan said, "She sure is."

"Monty, I forgot to tell you before we took off that your Dad wants us to land at LAX and re-fuel. Fuel is so much more expensive in Hawaii than it is on the mainland, it will save quite a bit of money if we fill up at LAX. That way, we will have plenty of fuel to get us to Honolulu International and back to LAX, where we can re-fuel on the way home."

"What time will we get to Los Angeles?"

"Approximately two a.m., Chattanooga time. That's eleven p.m., Los Angeles time."

"What time will we get to Honolulu?"

"We should be on the ground in L.A. for about an hour; then, it's about four hours from L.A., so that means we should arrive in Honolulu around four a.m., Hawaii time."

Monty said, "Man, I guess I didn't realize we were going to get there at such an inconvenient time. Our flight to Lanai isn't until ten o'clock, and I hate to check into a hotel for just two or three hours. I guess this is a good example of poor planning."

Chuck suggested, "Monty, you've got a perfectly good bedroom here on the plane. Why don't you guys go to bed en route and sleep until seven-thirty or eight o'clock. Your bedroom is totally private and soundproof, and you could get several hours rest before you have to board the commuter plane. Bob and Pat and I are going to crash on one of the bunks until time to go check into our hotel, and we could get you up in time to catch your flight. We'll even make a pot of coffee for you to wake up to."

"That's a good idea. What do you think, Sweetie?"

"Let's do that. If we don't, we'll be dead tired for the whole day, and I want to enjoy every minute of our stay in Paradise."

Monty asked, "Are we about two hours from LAX now?"

"Something like that."

"Okay. Sounds like a plan. Thanks for the suggestion, Chuck. This way we can get a full night's rest without sacrificing any fun time after we get to Lanai. We'll watch the rest of the movie and then turn in. Is that okay with you, Sweetie?"

"That's okay with me."

Chuck said, "I guess I had better get back up front. I want to be sure we're not heading north instead of west. If I don't see you before we land at LAX, goodnight and get a good night's rest." With that, he gave Monty a wink and a smile and turned around and returned to the flight deck.

"Joanie, I've sorta lost interest in this movie."

"I have, too."

"Do you want to go back and get ready for bed?"

"I was wondering when you were going to bring that up. I'm ready."

The bedroom on the plane measured twenty feet by almost eleven and a half feet. There was a bathroom at the end of the room and a sofa next to the wall by the bathroom door.

Monty said, "Honey, you go in first, and do what you have to do; then, when you're ready, just crack the door, and let me know, and I'll come do my stuff. I don't have much to do, except use the bathroom, brush my teeth, and put on my pajamas."

Monty was getting nervous as he waited, and in a few minutes, Joan cracked the door and told him she was ready, and he could come in. He walked into the bedroom, and sitting on the sofa was the prettiest sight he had ever laid his eyes on. Joan had changed into a pale aqua, knee-length peignoir set with matching scuffs. She didn't say anything. She didn't have to. The outfit and the expression on her face said enough.

Monty's heart was beating ninety miles an hour as he went into the bathroom to change into his pajamas, and when he came out, Joan patted the sofa so Monty would sit down beside her. They

3

Since neither of them had ever been to bed with

embraced and kissed for a long time and finally got up the nerve to get into the bed. Since neither of them had ever been to bed with anyone else, it took some time to figure out some things, but nature took over and soon they were in the lap of ecstasy.

"I can't believe that was so wonderful, Monty. I'm glad I waited to make love with you. Did you enjoy it?"

"More than anything I've ever experienced. I love you, Joanie."

"I love you, too. Let's just stay here forever, want to?"

"That's tempting, but we had better get some sleep, or else we will be too tired to enjoy all the activities we have planned for tomorrow. If we don't get to sleep, we might have to take a nap tomorrow afternoon."

"Well, if that means we will have to go back to bed, then I think I'm all for it. This was wonderful."

Monty picked up his watch off the bedside table, and it read one-fifteen a.m., Chattanooga time. "We're scheduled to be in Los Angeles in less than an hour. Do you want to try to go to sleep now or wait 'til after we take off from L.A.?"

"You tired me out. I'm ready to go to sleep now."

"Okay. I'll turn off the light."

At seven-thirty, Monty was awakened by a knock on the bedroom door. He got up and cracked the door a few inches and looked into the face of Chuck Jacobs. "Monty, you had better get up if you're going to have time for coffee before you leave to catch your flight to Lanai."

"Okay. Thanks, Chuck."

Monty closed the door and went over to Joan's side of the bed and woke her up with a kiss on the cheek. "Wake up, Sleepyhead. It's time to get up and go explore Paradise."

"I thought we were in Paradise last night. Weren't we?"

"Yeah, I guess we were, but I'll tell you what. Today let's go explore a different kind, then tonight we can go back to the one we experienced last night."

"That sounds wonderful."

When Joan got up and went into the bathroom, Monty walked to the galley in his pajamas. The flight crew was sitting there, having coffee. "Good morning, guys."

"Good morning, Monty. Did you get a good night's rest?"

"Yeah, boy. Did you guys get any sleep?"

"Yeah, these bunks are pretty good beds."

As Monty poured two cups of coffee, he asked, "How do we get to the gate where we catch the commuter to Lanai?"

"I've ordered a shuttle for you. It's supposed to be there at nine o'clock, and it'll take you to the gate where you'll board," Chuck said. "You have your tickets, don't you?"

"Yeah, we have our tickets. We're only going to be in Lanai three days; then we're coming back here, so we'll see you when we get back. We're scheduled to go home Sunday, right?"

"Right."

Monty took the coffee back to the bedroom and gave Joan one of the cups. She took it and commented on how good it was. Monty spent so much time in the galley that Joan finished her shower while he was gone. Before he finished all his coffee, he got his shaving kit and went into the bathroom and shaved and showered. He was so happy, and Joan got a kick out of listening to him try to sing as he took his shower.

Promptly at nine-o'clock, the shuttle arrived and took the couple to the gate where they boarded the commuter flight to Lanai. There they checked into one of the three Four Seasons resorts.

They had read about Lanai and were anxious to get there. The brochures talked about the ease that comes from being so remote, making it an ideal destination for couples who eschew crowded beaches and towering resorts. The island's offerings are concentrated in small areas, either upcountry in the picturesque Lanai City or around the pristine Hulopoe Bay, leaving a couple all the privacy they could wish for—a romantic picnic, a sunset hike or a Jeep ride to a secluded beach. That truly sounded like Paradise to Joan and Monty.

As soon as they got to their room and began unpacking, Monty took his Bible out of his suitcase and told Joan, "Honey, this might seem a strange time to do this, but I promised God that I would try to live for Him and would make our family a Christian family, and I asked His blessings on our marriage. Today is the first full day of our marriage, and I would like to begin it with a Scripture. Sweetie, sit down a minute. I want to read this to you. I'm going to read Ephesians 5: 25-31, then we'll pray, okay?"

"Monty, I'm so proud of you for this."

Monty began reading verse twenty-five: *And you husbands, show the same kind of love to your wives as Christ showed to the church when he died for her, to make her holy and clean, washed by baptism and God's Word; so that he could give her to himself as a glorious church without a single spot or wrinkle or any other blemish, being holy and without a single fault. That is how husbands should treat their wives, loving them as parts of themselves. For since a man and his wife are now one, a man is really doing himself a favor and loving himself when he loves his wife! No one hates his own body, but lovingly cares for it, just as Christ cares for his body, the church, of which we are parts. That the husband and wife are one body is proved by the Scripture which says, "A man must leave his father and mother when he marries, so that he can be perfectly joined to his wife, and the two shall be one.*

Monty closed the Bible and took Joan by the hand. He then bowed his head and thanked God for all his blessings and asked God to please bless their marriage.

When he finished praying, he looked into Joan's eyes and gave her a big kiss. "I love you, Joanie."

"I love you, too."

Monty asked, "How would you like to go on a Hawaiian style picnic? I read that there's a really pretty, secluded beach about three miles from here. We can get the dining room here to fix the food, and we can rent a Jeep to drive there. How about it? It sounds like a lot of fun to me."

"Me too. Let's do it."

It was already lunchtime when they arrived at the beach, so they spread their food and ate just as soon as they got there. When they finished, they cleaned up their mess and then spread a blanket close to the water. Occasionally they would go in to get wet, then come out and lay on the blanket. The afternoon was totally relaxing, and they both hated to leave, but around five o'clock they decided to go back and lie by the pool before they had to get ready for dinner.

They said they were going back to lie by the pool, but both of them had something else in mind. When they arrived back at the resort, Joan went to the room while Monty turned the Jeep in. He then went to their room, and when he opened the door, Joan was lying in bed under a sheet without any clothes on. He could feel his face turning red, but how could he pass up an opportunity like this? He sat down on the edge of the bed and took off his shirt and shorts, then slipped into bed next to Joan. There were no words to describe the feelings of the love they experienced next.

The next two days were equally as great as the first. They slept late on Monday, then had lunch at the resort, and took a late-afternoon hike before returning in time for dinner. On Tuesday, Monty rented a Jeep again, and this time they drove all over the island, enjoying the views and flowers that seemed to be everywhere. Late in the afternoon, they came back by the beach where they went the first day and waded in the surf before returning to the resort for dinner. Each afternoon they made it a point to get back to their bedroom in time to work up an appetite before they ate.

The resort's shuttle took the couple to the little airport on Wednesday morning, where they caught their flight back to Honolulu. Upon arriving at Honolulu International, they caught a limo to their hotel and checked in a little before noon. The flight crew was staying at the same hotel, and Monty gave them a call after he and Joan checked in. There was no answer, so he left a message that he and Joan were back and gave them their room number.

They hadn't projected ahead on what they were going to do, so they decided to have just a lazy day. After lunch, the afternoon consisted of reading brochures, sun-bathing, and napping at one of the pools.

The rest of the week was spent doing what millions of tourists do every year in Hawaii: sight-seeing, swimming, visiting the volcano, and all the other things Paradise offers. Monty was able to get up with Chuck, Pat, and Bob and on Saturday night, they all went to a fantastic luau. It was one of those where they cooked the pig in the ground, had hula dancers, guys dancing with swords, and all the other things they do at a first-class luau. Joan looked gorgeous in her Hawaiian print sundress, and Monty looked as if he had just stepped out of the pages of a *hunk* magazine.

Saturday night was so much fun, they all hated to see it end, but unfortunately, they had to take off the next morning and return home.

CHAPTER TWO

Morning came early. It was hard to get up after the late night before at the luau, but since they all behaved, there were no problems other than trying to get awake.

Chuck and the other guys in the flight crew got to the plane at seven o'clock and started their pre-flight checks. They had ordered food from a catering service to have on the way home, and they had to be there for that, too.

Monty and Joan arrived at seven-thirty, and after putting their things up, they went straight to the coffee maker, where they had coffee and a croissant. At eight o'clock, Chuck came on the speaker and said for them to sit down and fasten their seatbelts because they were getting ready to take off. As they were speeding down the runway, Monty took Joan by the hand. "Well, Sweetie, we're leaving Paradise. Are you sorry?"

"I'm sorry to be leaving Hawaii, but as far as I'm concerned, anywhere I am, as long as I'm with you, is Paradise for me. I've had a wonderful time here, but we're going to have a wonderful time in Chattanooga, too. That will be my Paradise."

Smiling, Monty said, "It's no wonder I love you so much. Anyone with an attitude like that is someone so special, it's unbelievable. I will thank God every day of my life for giving you to me. I'm still hungry. Do you want something else to eat?"

"No, the croissant filled me up, but I think I'll have another cup of coffee. Are you going to eat at the table?"

"Yeah, I think I will. Why don't you come sit with me?" Joan poured both of them a cup and sat down while Monty rifled through the food selection. He finally found a sweet roll and heated it in the microwave before joining her. While they were sitting at the table, Pat James, the co-pilot, came back and sat with them for a couple of minutes. "Are you guys ready to get back to reality?"

Joan said, "In a way I am. This has been nice, but I'm ready to get back and start making a home for my new husband."

"That's really nice, Joan. Monty, it looks like you have a winner here."

"I know I do." He reached over and took Joan's hand and kissed it.

"Monty, our plans are still to land at LAX and re-fuel. We should be there around three o'clock, Los Angeles time, and will be on the ground for about an hour. If all goes well, we should be in Chattanooga around eleven o'clock tonight."

"Thanks, Pat. I think I'll call my Mom when we get to L.A. and let her know when we'll be there. She can either meet us or leave a car at the airport for us."

Pat went back to the flight deck, and Monty poured another cup and sat at the table for a while longer. Joan excused herself, saying she had to go to the bathroom. When she didn't come back for a long time, Monty went back to check on her and found her lying on the bed, sound asleep. He didn't wake her; instead, he went up to the flight deck and sat and talked to the crew.

Whoever calculated the time was very good because they landed at LAX almost exactly when they were supposed to. Taxiing to the area where corporate and private planes parked, they were directed to a spot where a tanker truck drove out and filled the 707 with fuel. Monty had heard that a 707 used about twelve-hundred gallons of fuel per hour, and they had flown about eight hours since they last re-fueled. He was glad he wasn't having to pay for it.

While the plane was taking on fuel, he and Joan went into the building next to the area where they were, and Monty called Thil to tell her when they would be in Chattanooga. She said she would be at the airport to meet them. Joan also called her parents to tell them when she would be home, and they were happy to hear from her.

The time passed fairly quickly between Los Angeles and Chattanooga. As soon as they took off and gained altitude, they went to the galley and got out food for lunch. They took their time eating, and when they were about finished, Monty asked Joan if she would like to watch a John Wayne movie. She said she would, so they looked through the movie selection and took out *McClintock*. The movie lasted about two hours, and soon after it was over, they started the descent to Lovell Field in Chattanooga.

They had had a favorable tailwind most of the way from Los Angeles, so they arrived in Chattanooga about fifteen minutes early. They landed at ten-forty-seven, and not only was Thil there to meet them, but David had come, too. Monty was surprised because David had been going to bed early since having a heart attack. Everybody hugged and kissed and had a great reunion.

When they got in the car, Monty said he was hungry, and Joan said she was, too. It was eleven p.m. and only four hours since they ate lunch, but they were hungry. Monty asked Joan, "How about some Krystals?"

"That sounds wonderful."

"Dad, would you mind stopping and let us get a sack full? We'll take them home and eat them there."

"Okay, Son. Thil, Do you want some?"

"No, thank you. I don't want to eat this late."

On the way home the hamburgers smelled so good, they could hardly wait to get there, and David and Thil wished they had gotten some. As they pulled into the driveway, Thil told Joan and Monty, "I went in your house today and checked your pantry. You needed some things, so I bought a few items that you can cook for breakfast in the morning. You will have to go to the store, but at least, you have food for breakfast."

"Thanks, Mom."

"Thanks, Thil. I appreciate that."

The newlyweds were tired when they got home, and pretty soon after they finished their Krystals, they went to bed and went to sleep. Monty had to get up early and go to work the next morning, but Joan still had another day before she had to go back.

Monty got up at six o'clock and left Joan in bed, sleeping. He fixed coffee, shaved, showered, dressed, read a Scripture and was out of the house by seven o'clock. On the way to the office, he stopped at Hardee's and got a steak biscuit and took it to work with him. He was anxious to see what had been going on since he left. When he got there, Tom was already there, so the two of them went to the break room and talked while they had coffee, and Monty ate his biscuit.

After he finished his biscuit and coffee, he had some time before the staff meeting, so he closed his office door and got on his knees. He prayed, "Heavenly Father, I'm beginning a new phase in my life, and I want to be sure I'm doing what is pleasing in your sight. You were wonderfully kind to my Dad, David, because he was honest and true and faithful to you. Lord, now you have made me the President instead of my Dad, but I'm like a little child who doesn't know his way around. And here I am, not much more than a child, among this large company of experienced and knowledgeable people that make up this great company. Father, please give me an understanding mind, so I can preside over this firm and know the difference in what is the right decision and what is the wrong decision. This is too much responsibility for a person like me to handle by myself, so I'm pleading for your guidance. Father, I ask this in the name of Jesus. Amen."

At nine o'clock Monty and all the department heads had the regular Monday morning staff meeting, and when they were through, Monty went down the hall to Charlie Crawford's office. Charlie said, "Monty, I'm sure glad you're back. If you hadn't been on your honeymoon, I would have called you last week. I've got something to tell you that's really big. It's big enough that we may have to have another plant or two to handle it."

"What in the world are you talking about?" Charlie was extremely excited. Monty had never seen him this excited. "Let's go get a cup of coffee, and you can tell me about it."

They went to the break room, got a Coke and sat down. "Now, what's this big news?" Monty asked.

"Well, last week while I was in Denver, this guy called me. He had tracked me down to talk to me. Monty, this guy is vice-president of the largest athletic shoe company in the world. They're also one of the top sportswear companies, and he wants us to start making their logo goods: t-shirts, sweats, shorts, and socks."

"Are you talking about *Fin*?"

"Yeah, *Fin*. Their company name is All Conference Sports. Monty, this could mean millions in additional volume for us each year. And if we can get into the sock business, that alone would mean several thousand dozen pairs each week at twelve to fifteen dollars per dozen."

"I know our plants are running pretty much to capacity now, so if we get this business, it will probably mean building another one. And if you get into the socks, you might be able to buy a mill down in Fort Payne. I don't know about these things. I just know this could be the biggest thing to happen to Shepherd Apparel since Urey Steen opened up Europe for us twenty-five years ago."

Monty asked, "Do you have this guy's number?"

"Yeah, His name is Wayne Morris, and I told him I would have you call him as soon as you got back."

"Let me have it, and I'll give him a call. Is this a Washington number?"

"Yeah, Seattle. That's where their headquarters are located."

"Charles, if this turns out to be as big as you think it will be, I'll probably have to try and get my Dad involved, since I'm still new at running the company."

"That's a good idea, Monty. You know, I've been here almost twenty-five years, and I've never had anything this large just fall into our lap. I sure hope you get it worked out."

Since Washington was on Pacific time, Monty thought he would wait until after lunch to call. In the meantime, he had Connie come in, and they talked at length about what went on while he was on his honeymoon. After he finished talking to Connie, he reviewed the production reports from last week and was pleased with how well things went.

Before he went to lunch, he called Joan. She answered, "Hello."

"Hey good-looking, miss me?"

"Who is this? Is this an obscene phone call?"

"Yes it is, and I know where you live. I think I'll come to your house and have my way with you. What do you think about that?"

"That sounds good, Bill."

Monty said, "I think Bill can't hold a candle to the Monty man. Do I need to prove it?"

"No, I'll take your word. What did you say your name was?"

"Just call me Stud."

Then on a more serious note, Monty said, "How does it feel to wake up in your own house and realize you're married?"

"It feels wonderful. I called Mama, and she's going to come over after a while. I'm anxious to see her, but I've got to go to the store first. There's nothing here to eat. Anything special you'd like?"

"No. I like what you like, so just buy whatever you want."

"I've got to go, Baby. Thil just came in. I'll talk to you later. Love ya."

"Love you, too. Bye."

Monty walked down to Don's office and invited him to lunch, and he accepted. They went to Oscars and had one of their world-famous hamburgers. Don was interested in the honeymoon, so Monty told him all about Lanai, the luau, the flight, everything. Then he asked Don how things were going for him. Don said, "Okay. I'm trying to learn to tighten my belt some, since I'm having five hundred bucks a week deducted from my check, but I'll make it."

They finished eating and went back to the office. Monty called Wayne Morris in Seattle and had a very interesting conversation. Charles Crawford was right. It could be huge. "Mr. Morris, would you like for me to come to Seattle to discuss these possibilities?"

"Monty, I think I would rather come to Chattanooga. We definitely need to engage in much discussion, but I need to see your facilities, among other things. When would be a good time for you?"

"How about next week?"

"Next week will be fine. Will Tuesday be okay?"

"That will be perfect. How long will you be here?"

"I would like to think we'll be busy for a couple of days. I'll plan to return to Seattle on Thursday."

"Will you be getting into Chattanooga on Monday?"

"Yeah, then I'll come to your place Tuesday morning."

"Great. There's a nice Holiday Inn not too far from here. I'll book a room for you for three nights. If you'll let me know what time your flight will arrive, I'll have someone pick you up."

"Sounds good. I'll be back in touch."

"Nice talking to you, Mr. Morris. I'll look forward to seeing you. Goodbye."

When Monty hung up, he went to Charles Crawford's office and told him about the conversation he just had and said, "You were right. This could be very big. I wanted him to wait until next week before coming, so we would have time to digest all our thoughts and options and be ready to make the proper decisions. I'm going to go see Dad tonight after I get home and pick his brain a little. You'll probably be in on some of the talks, too, so be thinking about different things from a sales standpoint. We'll at least look as if we know what we're doing."

After he left Charlie's office, Monty returned to his own office and tried to concentrate on some of the paperwork stacked up on his desk, but all he could think of was the huge program they might get. He decided to call David to see if he could come and talk to him. He dialed the number and Thil answered. "Hey Mom, How're you doing?"

"Fine. I just left your wife. I went with her to the grocery store. You won't have to worry about something to eat for a while. She nearly bought out the Red Food Store."

"Good. Thanks for going with her. Listen, Mom, do you think

Dad would feel like talking to me for a minute?"

"I think so. Let me get him."

David came to the phone and Monty asked him if he would mind if he came to see him. He had something important to talk to him about, and David told him to come on.

Walking into his parents' house, Monty didn't see anybody, so we went upstairs to the balcony. Thil and David were both stretched out on chaise lounges, Thil got up when she saw Monty. Monty walked over and kissed her and said, "Hi, Mom."

"Hi, Honey. Look, I've got to go get dinner started. You stay up here and talk to your Dad." She excused herself and left the two alone to talk.

David pulled Thil's chaise closer to his and said, "Sit down, Son. What is it you want to talk about?"

"Dad, I know you're familiar with the mega-business being done in the athletic shoe business."

"Yeah, it's unbelievable. Why? Are you wanting to get into the shoe business?"

"No, sir, but the largest athletic shoe supplier in the world wants Shepherd Global to make clothes and socks for them. Dad, the man is coming next week to talk to me about it, and I've never been involved with something this large. As Charlie Crawford said, this is the biggest thing to happen to Shepherd since Urey opened up Europe."

"You said socks. We can't make socks. What are you going to tell him about that?"

"I don't know yet. That's why I wanted to talk to you. I do know this; if we sign on with them, in all likelihood we will have to buy or build an additional plant and maybe a sock mill."

David asked, "Do you have any idea the kind of money you're talking about to do that kind of thing?"

"No, sir, I really don't, but with the kind of volume they're talking about, we can't afford not to do it."

"What about socks? Do you know how to make socks? I don't."

"I don't either, Dad, but there are dozens of sock mills within a seventy-five mile radius of Chattanooga, and I figure we might be able to buy an existing mill. If we build one, there are plenty of experienced workers we can hire. We're talking several thousand dozen pairs of socks per week, year around.

14

"Dad, it's too premature to come up with any concrete decisions. We hardly know anything about it yet. I'm just trying to anticipate. I know these people are probably ten times larger than we are, and they can furnish us with more business than your average apparel manufacturer generates total. I don't want us to jump into anything risky, but I do think we should look at it. I just wanted to get your thoughts."

"Well, I think we should definitely look at it. While you were talking, I had a thought. What if we get into this program, and maybe let Don play a part in it in some capacity?"

Monty didn't say anything. He didn't want to get into that. As far as he was concerned, Don was where he should be: renting the airplane under strict controls.

"Okay, Dad, I won't bother you any longer. I just wanted to get your thoughts on this. Knowing what you know about the costs of building and equipping a plant, what would you say would be the minimum length of time we would have to have a contract in order for a program like this to pay off?"

"That's hard to say without sitting down and doing some figuring, but off the top of my head I'd say at least five years before we would reach the break-even point. What do you think they're thinking?"

"I don't know, but we'll find out next week. Bye, Dad. Love ya."

Monty went home, and when he walked in the door, Joan was in the kitchen. She saw him come in and yelled, "Is that you, Bill?"

"I'll Bill you. Come here and give your hard-working husband a kiss." She ran to him and they embraced and kissed. He asked, "Is that smell what I think it is?"

"If you think it's meatloaf, it is. I thought for our first meal in our house as a married couple, you should have your favorite, so wa-la. Your Mom gave me her recipe."

"Thank you, Sweetheart. I know it'll be good."

After they finished a delicious dinner, Monty helped clean up the kitchen, and the two went into the den and sat down. They each asked about the other's day, and Monty told her a little about the possibility of getting the new contract. They talked about other unimportant things, then Monty dropped a bombshell on Joan.

"Honey, how would you feel about quitting work?"

"Are you serious?"

"I'm as serious as I can be."

"Why do you want me to quit? I know I don't make a lot, but what I do make should help, shouldn't it?"

"Yeah, it would help, but I make enough for both of us; in fact, I make more than enough. Here's what I'm thinking: now that Dad's pretty much retired, I'm going to have to do a whole lot of traveling, and every time I go to Europe or the Mid-East, I'll be gone a week or more. If you're not working and want to, you can go with me on some or all the trips, and we won't have to be apart. It would be like international dating. Whatta you think?"

"How can I refuse such an offer, you silver-tongued devil? When do you want me to quit?"

"Are you sure you're okay with it? I don't want you to quit if you would rather keep working. I just thought we could travel together and not be apart."

"Traveling with you would be a lot more fun than working. I think I'd like to be a lady of leisure."

"Why don't you tell Mr. Tomlinson tomorrow when you go in. You should work out a two week notice, if he wants you to, then you can go to Munich with me when I go in two weeks. We'll have a good time."

"I know we will."

CHAPTER 3

Wayne Morris's plane got in a little after five Monday afternoon, and Monty and Charlie Crawford were there to meet it. Wayne had told Monty what he would be wearing, so it was easy to recognize him when he came through the gate. Charlie went to the baggage claim with him while Monty went to get the car. As soon as they got in the car, Monty headed for the Holiday Inn where Wayne checked in.

"Wayne, what time would you like for us to pick you up for dinner?"

"Monty, if it's all right with you, I think I'll just grab a bite here at the motel and turn in early. It has been a long day, and I'm pretty tired. What time do you want to get started in the morning?"

"I usually get to the office around eight o'clock. Is that okay with you, or would you rather wait 'til a little later?"

"Eight's fine. I'll get a cab and see you in the morning."

"No sir. I'll pick you up—say, seven forty-five. Is that all right?"

"That's fine. See ya in the morning."

Monty arrived at seven forty-five, and Wayne was outside, waiting on him. "Good morning, Wayne."

"Good morning."

"Did you have breakfast?"

"No, I didn't want anything this early. You know, it's only five o'clock where I live."

"Well, if you don't mind, I think I'll stop and get a steak biscuit and take it to the office. We can have coffee there before we start on the tour of our facilities." When Monty pulled up to the drive-thru window at Hardee's, he asked Wayne if he wanted a biscuit, and he decided he did want one. They arrived at the office, and Monty introduced Wayne to Connie. Then they went into Monty's office and had coffee and ate their biscuits while they made small talk.

The Shepherd Global Apparel Group had grown so large, key people in the office were using a golf cart to travel between the office and the different plants. Wayne was impressed when Monty led him to an E-Z-Go and invited him to have a seat. He was also impressed with the cleanliness and general appearance of each plant and the look of efficiency that each one projected. When he found out Shepherd had its own truck line, he was blown away.

After an hour and a half tour, they returned to Monty's office to get down to serious talks. Monty began by asking Wayne to lay out just what his company was looking for. As he talked, Monty could see that if Shepherd were going to do the business Wayne wanted, they could not do it with their existing facilities; a new plant would have to be built.

When he finished talking about the different styles of apparel, Wayne began to talk about socks. Monty said, "Wayne, we can't make socks; we don't own any knitting machines."

"Well you can get some, can't you? It's my understanding that this area is saturated with sock manufacturing. It shouldn't be hard for you to set something up."

"Why don't you just go to Ft. Payne or to one of the sock mills around here and work out something with them?"

"Because if we get lined up with you, we will want to have everything come from only one source."

"How many socks are you looking at?"

"Approximately thirty thousand dozen pairs a week, guaranteed for fifty weeks a year. We will sign a contract for five years' production, with an option to renew for another five years."

"Wayne, will you excuse me for a minute?"

Monty went into the outer office and called David. "Dad, I'm in the middle of talks with this man from Seattle and the numbers he's talking about are staggering. There's no doubt that we would have to build a new sewing plant to handle the volume, and he insists that if we get the apparel, we do the socks, too. That will mean a sock mill also. If I delay giving him an answer today, do you think you would feel like coming in tomorrow and helping me a little?"

"I guess I can. Tell him I'll be in around nine in the morning. Son, when you come home tonight, come over here and let's talk about this. Will you do that?"

"Yes sir. I'll see you around six o'clock."

Monty went back to his office and told Wayne, "Wayne, while I'm President of Shepherd Global, my Dad is the CEO and is far more expert than I am when it comes to large programs like you're proposing. I've only been President for a short time, so I asked him to come in tomorrow morning and give us some input based on his expertise. I hope you don't mind."

"I think that's a good idea, Monty."

"How 'bout some lunch? Has that steak biscuit left you yet?"

"Yeah, I could use something to eat."

Monty took him to The Greystone where they had a nice lunch and had a chance to get better acquainted. They didn't talk business; rather they talked about each other's family and other personal things.

On the way back to the office, Wayne asked, "What do you think the chances are that you Dad will want to do business with us?"

"I think they're good. The main thing he's going to look at is whether or not we can make any money. If we can, then we'll probably do it, but if we can't, I'm sure he'll say 'no.'"

"Monty, I know you aren't and haven't been in the sock business, and I don't think you realize how much money you can make when you make socks. The contract we'll give you will amount to around a million dollars a month, and your profit percentage will be higher than the apparel profit. Your initial cost will be high, but with that kind of volume, it shouldn't take long to recoup your investment and start showing a profit. I hope your Dad will understand that."

"He's very sharp, Wayne. If you explain things to him in terms of investment and profits, he'll understand."

Since they had done about all they could do until David got involved, there wasn't much more to do that afternoon, so Monty took him to the truck line and showed him that part of the Shepherd organization. He wanted Wayne to see it because if Shepherd started making goods for Wayne's company, he would want to ship everything by Shepherd trucks. The sleek tractor trailers with the Staff logo on the sides were very pretty, and Monty could tell Wayne was impressed.

There was still time left in the afternoon, so they headed to Lovell Field. Monty wanted to show off the 707, and Wayne couldn't believe what he was seeing. They got out of the car and boarded the plane, and when Wayne got inside, he was like a little kid. He wanted to see everything. There were still some soft drinks in the refrigerator, so they opened one apiece and sat down to relax for a few minutes. Wayne wanted to know all about their trips to Munich, Tel Aviv, and other places they travel. He thoroughly enjoyed his afternoon with Monty, and was looking forward to the next morning, when David would be at the office to talk to him.

Monty drove him to the Holiday Inn and let him out. "Wayne, I'm sorry to leave you by yourself, but I've got an appointment tonight, and I can't stay and eat with you."

"That's all right, Monty. I've got a lot of paperwork to do before we meet tomorrow, so I'll just grab a bite here at the restaurant and see you in the morning. Seven forty-five again?"

"Yeah. I'll see you then. Goodnight."

Before he went home, Monty went to his Dad's as he was told. He went straight to the balcony where both parents were sitting. He pulled a chair over to where they were and sat down. "Well, Son, did you get everything worked out with Wayne Morris today?"

"Dad, I'm thankful I can still call on you for help. This thing is way over my head. In my opinion, we should sign on with them, but when it comes to adding plants and equipment, I'm lost. Dad, most apparel companies don't do as much total sales as this one. This guy is talking twelve million a year in just socks. Can you believe that? Twelve mil a year in socks? I don't know how much the apparel would amount to, but it would be plenty. And you know something, Dad? Our sales force wouldn't have to be involved in it. We would be strictly a contractor, and our customer would have to worry about sales. Apparently, they don't have any trouble selling their stuff."

"Monty, I've been thinking a lot about this today, and if your guy can satisfy me with contract terms and things like that, I believe we can make it work. I will want to meet with the head of his company, however, just to make sure the authority to execute such a contract comes from the top."

"I called a couple of people I know in the sock business and found that in order to do what these people want done will cost us about eight million dollars in knitting machines alone. That does not count a building, seaming machines, boarders, dye tubs, and all the other things involved. We're looking at twelve to fifteen million dollars just to get started. Now, if twelve million a year is a realistic figure, we can maybe get payback in five years. That's pretty good for that much money. Do you have any questions?"

"No sir. I'm anxious to see how you handle this tomorrow. I hope it will work out,"

"By the way, Monty. If we get this program worked out, I would like to involve Don."

"Dad, I think Don is in the best place for him right now. He's doing a good job leasing the plane."

"I know, but I would like to see him shoulder more responsibility in the company."

"Dad, can we address this later?"

"Sure, son. You act like you don't want to have him move up."

"I've got to go, Dad. I'll see you in the morning. Bye. Love ya."

Monty yelled through the house, "Bye, Mom. Love ya."

After Monty left, David spent quite a while pondering over the attitude he seemed to have about Don. *Something must have happened between those two. Monty has always looked up to his big brother, but now he acts as if he doesn't want him to be a part of this potential new program. I wonder what's gone wrong with their relationship. I need to find out. Maybe I'll talk to Monty about it tomorrow. He is so trusting and naïve about certain things, I just hope Don hasn't pulled another one of his idiotic escapades.*

***

Monty picked Wayne up the next morning, and since they were at least an hour earlier than David would be, he asked Wayne if he would like to have a good, sure 'nuff, southern breakfast. Wayne said he would, so Monty pulled into the Cracker Barrel. Monty ordered the smokehouse breakfast for each of them, and Wayne loved the biscuits and gravy. It took the standard forty-five minutes to finish, so they had to pick up speed and hurry to the office before David got there.

When they reached the office, they both went to the restroom to lose some of the coffee they had drunk, and as they were coming out, David came in.

Monty introduced him to Wayne, and they all went into Monty's office. "Connie, please hold all my calls unless it's an emergency. Thank you."

After spending some time getting acquainted and other small talk, David began to ask Wayne questions. He asked basically the same questions Monty had asked before, and Wayne gave him the same answers. He outlined the types of apparel and the dozens anticipated and the amount of socks and all the other things he had

21

already told Monty. David then asked him, "What is your job title, Wayne?"

"I'm what's known as the Contract Manager. I travel around, finding companies to manufacture goods for All Conference Sports."

"So you're not a part of the management team?"

"No sir. I just find contractors for our company."

"Okay, here's where we stand, Wayne. Monty and I have talked about this and I have talked to others, especially in the sock industry, and we're interested in getting hooked up with All Conference Sports. However, if we are to get into a relationship with you, it's going to cost us a lot of money, around twenty million dollars. Wayne, please don't take this wrong; I mean no disrespect, but before I spend that kind of money, I want to talk to the man at the top. I want his guarantee about the length of the contract, the volume, the costs, everything about it. Again, I'm not disrespecting you; I just need to protect Shepherd Global. Do you think your head man would agree to come to Chattanooga?"

"I'm sure he will. When we finish up, I'll call him."

"Why don't you call him now?"

"Okay. Would you mind if I use the phone in the conference room?"

"That'll be fine." Wayne excused himself and went to call the head of All Conference Sports.

While he was gone, David and Monty talked. "What do you think, Dad?"

"I think this could be a gold mine. Did you talk to him about shipping on our trucks?"

"Yes sir, and he's okay with it."

In a minute, Wayne interrupted them and said, "Mr. Shepherd, would you mind talking to Mr. Brownlee? He would like to speak to you."

"Okay." David went into the conference room and picked up the phone. "Hello. Mr. Brownlee, David Shepherd here. Good morning."

Mr. Brownlee asked David some questions, apparently about why he wanted him to come to Chattanooga. David told him, "Your man Wayne has approached us about doing work for your company, and we are very interested, but if we do what he says you want from us, it will cost a lot of money. Before we spend that kind of money, I want to look you in the eye, shake your hand, and be sure when we sign a contract that we have the authorization from the very top. Otherwise, we're not interested."

Mr. Brownlee talked some more, and then David said, "Tuesday will be good. Are you flying commercial or do you have a plane? Okay. My son Monty will meet your plane Monday afternoon if you'll let him know what time you'll be landing, and I'll look forward to seeing you Tuesday morning. Good bye, Mr. Brownlee. Nice talking to you."

David and Wayne went back to Monty's office, and David said, "Well I guess that's about all we can do until Mr. Brownlee gets here. By the way, Wayne, what's Mr. Brownlee's first name?"

"It's David,"

"David!! I knew I liked him. Are you young men hungry?"

"I am. How about you, Wayne?"

"Yeah, I could eat."

"Monty, have you initiated Wayne into Krystals yet?"

"No, but this would be a good time to do it."

"What are Krystals?"

"The best little hamburgers you ever tasted. It'll probably take about six to fill you up."

"Well, what are we waiting for?"

They all got into Monty's car and headed to the Krystal. Wayne thought Monty was right; the little burgers were about the best thing he had ever eaten.

On the way back to the office, Wayne said, "I think I'll call Mr. Brownlee when we get back to see if he wants me to make him a reservation at the Holiday Inn next week."

David said, "That's a good idea. Tell me, Wayne, what kind of a guy is David Brownlee?"

"He's a great guy. I would say he's about your age, Mr. Shepherd. He was an All-American football player in college and with backing from some alumni, he started All Conference Sports soon after he graduated. They struggled for several years; then all at once a professional football team signed on, and the *Fin* brand caught fire. It has been unbelievably good ever since, and it's still increasing every day. Mr. Brownlee's personality, athletic background, and his concern for others, not to mention the high-quality products, have made All Conference Sports an incredible place to work. I have been with them four years, and I hope to stay until I retire."

"That's good to know. I'm not interested in doing business with someone I can't trust or get along with. Although I'm not as active as I was, Monty will be the one who has to deal with the situation, and I want him to be exposed to good people. By the way, Monty wasn't All- America, but he was All Conference at Tech, so he and your boss should have something in common."

"You were All Conference, Monty? Fantastic! Mr. Brownlee loves to deal with athletes."

When they pulled into the Shepherd parking lot, David said, "I don't think you need me this afternoon, so I won't go in. If I don't go home and take my nap, your Mother will get after me, and I don't want that. Wayne, it was nice meeting you and I hope to see you again. Will you be coming back with your boss next week?"

"I don't know. There's a good chance I will."

"Okay, you guys have a good afternoon. Monty, stop by the house one day this weekend. I want to talk to you about something."

"Okay, Dad. I'll see you."

When they went into the office, Wayne went into the conference room and called his office. He talked to Mr. Brownlee and then came back to Monty's office. "Mr. Brownlee wants me to make hotel reservations for next week, and I will be coming back with him. He said we won't be getting in until late, so we'll catch the hotel's shuttle, and you won't have to meet us."

"All right, but I'll pick you up Tuesday morning. Since Dad probably won't come in until around nine, why don't I pick you up at eight-thirty?"

"That will be fine. Monty, since we can't do much more until Mr. Brownlee gets here and he and your dad talk, I would like to go back to the hotel if you could give me a ride."

"No problem, but would you mind if I have someone take you?"

"Whatever's best for you."

"Connie, call Eddie Randolph and have him come to my office, please."

When Eddie arrived, Monty told him to take Wayne to the Holiday Inn. He and Wayne shook hands and said they would see each other next week.

As soon as Wayne left, Monty called Joan. "Hi, Sweetheart. What's going on?"

"Nothing much. Mr. Tomlinson's gone this afternoon, and I'm

24

bored. I'll be glad when my two-week notice is over. I'm ready to stay home and make a real *love-nest* for you."

"That will be nice. Dad and Wayne are gone, and it looks like we may get that big contract. Wayne and his boss are coming back next week, and maybe we'll know something then."

"That sounds really good."

"Would you like to go out and eat tonight?"

"I sure would."

"Okay, I may leave here a little early. Dad wants to talk to me about something, so I may be over there when you get home."

"Okay, Hunk. I'll see you tonight."

When Monty got home, he went into the kitchen and got a Diet Coke out of the refrigerator and went next door to see his Dad. David was still a little groggy from his nap, but perked up when he saw Monty. "Hey, Big Man."

"Hey, Dad. You said you wanted to talk to me about something."

"I do. Monty, have you and Don been into it about something?"

"No sir. Why?"

"Well, ever since this *Fin* thing came up, you have pretty much cut me off whenever I have mentioned Don, and I thought you two might have a problem. Monty, if this *Fin* program becomes a reality, I would really like to get Don involved in it someway, but every time I mention it, you either cut me off or just ignore what I said. Do you have a problem with him being included?"

"Dad, I do have a problem including him. He's my big brother and you know I love him, and I've looked up to him all my life, but I really don't want him involved with the *Fin* program. All Conference Sports is a first-rate company that operates with the utmost integrity, and Shepherd Global does the same, and as hard as it is to say, I don't think Don has the integrity to work with either company. I think where he is now is the best place for him. He seems to be happy renting the plane, so why stir up something if you don't have to?"

David asked, "Do you know something I don't?"

"Dad, let's just say I would prefer to keep him where he is."

"You know, you're really putting me in an uncomfortable spot, don't you?"

"Why, Dad? Have you said something to Don about this?"

"No, but Don's my son just like you are. Shepherd Apparel has grown into such a gigantic company, it's hard for me to think about my oldest son being relegated to that of a rental agent for an airplane. I realize I've had problems with him in the past and have fired him two or three times, but he's still my son. You're running the company now, Son, and I'm not going to overrule you, but I would really appreciate it if you would give this matter some consideration."

"Dad, once we get the contract, let's see what all is going to be involved, and if I see that Don would fit somewhere, I'll consider him for the job. Will that be okay?"

"That will be okay, Son. Thank you."

"Another thing, Dad. I will want Don to think any job offer is my idea. Just in case he were to pull one of his shenanigans, I don't want him to think he can get by with it because of you."

CHAPTER FOUR

On Tuesday morning Monty went in early so he would have time to stop and get a biscuit before he had to pick up Wayne and Mr. Brownlee. They were going to eat at the hotel. At eight-thirty he arrived at the Holiday Inn, and they were standing out front, waiting for him.

Wayne introduced Monty to Mr. Brownlee, and they headed to the Shepherd campus. On the way, Mr. Brownlee said, "Monty, I understand you played college football."

"Yes sir, I played at Tennessee Tech."

"What position?"

"I played wide receiver."

"I used to clear the way for the likes of you."

"What position did you play, Mr. Brownlee?"

"I played offensive right guard."

"I guess you did clear the way for people like me. Any success I might have had was because of the good offensive line we had. Well, here we are."

Monty parked the car, and they walked into the office where they were greeted by the receptionist. On the way to Monty's office, they passed Connie's desk, and Monty introduced her to Mr. Brownlee. Wayne spoke to her, and they went into Monty's office. Connie poured each of them a cup of coffee, and while they waited for David to arrive, they talked about football and how it was such a large part of the lives of most people in Tennessee.

At nine o'clock, David walked in. "Good morning, gentlemen."

All three responded with "Good morning."

"Dad, I'd like for you to meet David Brownlee. Mr. Brownlee is President and CEO of All Conference Sports, and you know Wayne."

David and Mr. Brownlee shook hands and Mr. Brownlee said, "Hi, David. Please call me David."

Smiling, David Shepherd replied, "I'll call you David if you'll call me David."

"Okay, David."

After a few minutes of small talk, they got down to business.

David Brownlee laid out everything his company wanted to accomplish with Shepherd Global, and every section was covered to the minutest detail. Monty and his Dad asked questions as he explained each part, and by the time they finished, it was lunchtime.

David said, "Before we get into Shepherd's side of this program, why don't we go somewhere and get some lunch?"

"Let's do. I'm sure I've worn you out with my talking."

"Monty, why don't we take these fellows to Tomlinson's? It's quiet there, and we won't have to shout in order to hear each other."

They piled into David's car, since it was larger than Monty's, and drove to Tomlinson's Restaurant where they had a delicious meal. They talked about a little of everything except business. David Brownlee was very interested in Monty and wanted to know all about him. When Monty mentioned that he was active in the Fellowship of Christian Athletes and had spoken at different churches and before several sports teams, David nearly exploded with excitement because he was a past leader of the FCA on the West Coast.

Speaking to Monty's Dad, he said, "David, in my investigation of Shepherd Global, I was told that you operate with character and integrity, but I had no idea how much of those two traits played a part in your organization until now when I heard Monty speak. You know, whenever we decide to get hooked up with a contractor, we look for two things: integrity and know-how. When we get back to the office, if your track record is as good in manufacturing as it is in your character, I will be ready to sign a contract; that is, if you want a contract with us."

"Thanks, David. I think you'll be impressed with our production figures. And yes, we would like a contract with you. As I see it right now, timing may be an issue, but we'll go over that when we get back to the office."

When they finished lunch, they went back to the Shepherd office. Some went to the restroom, while others made phone calls. Monty went over something with Tom Ratcliff, and finally they sat down and resumed their discussions.

David Shepherd took the floor, and he started by giving a brief history of the company. He broke it down into two parts: up until they went international, and from the time they first went international until now. "I tell you our history to bring me to this: while we at Shepherd are always looking to grow our business, we are in a position to reject things that are not advantageous to us. I don't mean to sound too independent; I just want you to understand that a contract between us will have to be as good for us as it is for you.

"From the sound of the program you outlined, we would be foolish to pass it up, but here's where *there might be a lump in the churn.* David, ever since Monty told me about Wayne's call, I have been talking with people, especially people in the sock business, and have come up with some figures.

"First of all, our existing factories are operating at full capacity right now, and there's no way we could sew another stitch in any of them. This means we'll have to build a new apparel plant as well as a new hosiery plant. We know how to build and equip an apparel plant, but a sock factory is a different animal.

"I talked to some very good friends in the sock business, and after describing the kinds of socks you want and the number of dozens, I was told that we would need between two hundred fifty and three hundred knitting machines. The cost of the type machines needed to knit the *Fin* logo is between thirty-five and forty thousand dollars. When you do the math, that comes up to eight million dollars, and that doesn't even count the building and other equipment needed just to get started. I estimate it will cost twelve to fifteen million dollars to build and equip a sock mill.

"A sewing factory won't be quite as expensive, but it will still cost around seven million dollars. Add that to the cost of a sock mill, and you come up with twenty million dollars. Now, these factories would be dedicated to All Conference Sports exclusively, and of course, we would have to recoup our investment and hopefully make a profit. As best I can tell, it will take five years just to get our money back, and that doesn't include any profit. Now, assuming that can be done, I don't see how we could begin any kind of production for at least six months and maybe longer.

"David, we would like to proceed with this, but considering all the things I've outlined, I feel we would have to have a contract for a minimum of seven years. Would that fit into your plans?"

David Brownlee replied, "David, I can see that you've done your homework, and I really want Shepherd Global to join the All Conference family, but I was thinking in terms of a five- year contract. More than likely we would have to renew it for another five years, but I'm not comfortable signing for more than five years to begin with."

"David, I'm sorry to hear that," David Shepherd said. "We would like to partner with you, but if we're going to invest twenty million dollars, we need to turn a profit at some point, and that point will not be until after five years."

"Yeah, but you'll be paying for the factories and equipment, and at the end of five years, you'll have all those assets free and clear," David Brownlee retorted.

"Tell you what we'll do, David; you build and equip both plants, and we'll run them for you and sign a five-year contract."

"That's a good thought, but I'm afraid I'll have to decline. David, what's the best you can do in terms of contract length?"

"Okay, David, here's the deal. We'll build and set up an apparel factory and a sock mill, and we'll sign a six-year contract, if you'll make the contract for six years actual production. In other words, you will sign a contract immediately, allowing us six to nine months of construction and then six years' production."

"You won't settle for five years plus construction time?"

"No, I feel we need at least six years."

"Okay, David. You're a tough cookie, but you've got a deal. We're going back to Seattle when we leave here, and I'll have the contract drawn up and sent *next day air*, so you'll have it next week. Is that all right with you?"

"That's perfect. We'll look forward to working with you folks."

As the meeting was breaking up, Wayne said, "Monty, I'm sorry we didn't get to take Mr. Brownlee to the Krystal. I think he would love those hamburgers."

"Let me make a suggestion," Monty said. "Why don't we pick up three or four sacks full on the way to the airport, and you all can have them for supper on the way home. Three sacks full should fill you two and your pilots up." Smiling, he said, "The new contract is wonderful, but three sacks full of Krystals make the trip truly worthwhile."

They all had a laugh about the comment, and then David Shepherd told the group that he was going home. "I don't know if Monty told you or not, but I'm trying to get well from a heart attack, and my stamina isn't what it used to be. It has been a real pleasure meeting both of you, and I look forward to seeing you again. In the course of our business together, Monty is the one you'll be working with, but I'll try to make an appearance from time to time.

"You fellows have a nice trip home and enjoy your Krystals. I'll see you later," and he left. The other three got into Monty's car, and after stopping at the Krystal, they went to the airport where David Brownlee and Wayne boarded the *Fin* Gulfstream and took off for Seattle.

It was still early, but since the day had been so productive, Monty left the office and went home. He had set aside the whole day for the men from All Conference, but since they finished early, he didn't have time to start another project, and he wanted to get home early to tell Joan about their contract.

She hadn't come in from work when he got there, so he went over to see his Dad for a minute. "What do you think about what happened today, Dad?"

"I think you hit the jackpot. If you play it right and do a good job for those people, I have no doubt that they will stay with you for as long as you want them. Son, you need to find a real expert to run the sock mill for you. If you can find the right man to set the mill up with maximum efficiency, you might be able make payback in four years. That would mean many dollars profit for the rest of the six years. We already know how to make apparel, so that shouldn't be a problem, but you should start looking for a plant manager, one who really knows his stuff. We have a chance to make a lot of money on this thing, and I want us to start out efficiently. Oh, and while you're looking for people, see what you can come up with for Don."

Monty thought, *he's not going to let this thing with Don go. I can't tell him what Don did; that he embezzled almost a half-million dollars from the company. It would kill him if he knew. He and Granddad own the company, but they've entrusted me to run it, and I know Don shouldn't be a part of the Fin contract, so how do I handle it? I've never crossed Dad when it comes to business, but in this case I might have to. Lord, I ask you to help me in this matter. Please give me the answer.*

"Dad, do you still have the blueprints that were used when the other plants were built? If you do, it might help in deciding what we're going to need for the new one. Also, Dad, how would you suggest I go about finding some plans for a sock mill?"

"Yeah, we still have the blueprints from our last two plants. Tell

Tom to find them for you. I'll call a couple people I know in Ft. Payne and will see what I can come up with on some plans for a sock mill."

"Thanks, Dad. I've got to go. I'll see you later. Thanks for your help today. Love you." He stopped by the kitchen and told Thil goodbye as well. "I love you, Mom," and then walked next door to his house to wait on Joan to get home from work.

When Joan came in, they kissed hello, and she went to the bedroom to change clothes. Monty followed her, talking all the way, and before she changed, Monty asked if she wanted to go out to eat. She said she did, so they went to an Italian place and had spaghetti. While they were there, Monty said, "Sweetie, do you remember me telling you about the possibility of our getting a large contract for *Fin*?" Joan said she did. "Well, we got it today, and it's going to be huge; in fact, we're going to have to build two new factories just to do *Fin*. Isn't that something?"

"It sure is."

"You've only got three more days to work, don't you, Sweetie?"

"Yeah, and I can't wait 'til Friday afternoon gets here. I think when next Monday gets here, I'll sleep until noon."

Kidding, Monty said, "Well, I've been counting on you to get up before me every morning and have my breakfast cooked when I get out of bed."

"Yeah, right." Then she said, "If you want me to, I will. I'll do anything you want me to do."

"I know you would. I was just kidding. I hope you do sleep late, but maybe not until noon. Are you still planning to go to Munich with me?"

"Yeah, why?"

"You know, we were supposed to go next week, but this new contract is coming in next week and it'll have to be signed, so the Munich trip is going to have to wait until week after next. Is that okay with you?"

"Anything you say, my prince."

"Listen, I just had an idea. I already know a few words, but why don't we have Mom teach us how to speak German? I'll be going over there about once a month after we get the new contract going, and I hope you'll go with me most of the time. If we could speak and understand what the people say, it would be good. Since you won't

32

be working, you'll have time to learn, if Mom is willing to teach you. I'd like to learn the language, too, but I can get by pretty well without knowing it because our men in Munich are able to speak fairly good English. What do you think?"

"I think it's a great idea. Why don't you ask your Mom?"

***

Wednesday began with Monty and Tom finding the plans for the last plant that was built. David had suggested they use the same general contractor since he was pleased with the way he did before. Monty called him and was able to set up an appointment for two o'clock that afternoon.

Monty and Tom went to lunch together, and they talked so much about the new buildings that they were late getting back to the office; in fact, it was nearly two o'clock. Soon after they returned, Connie buzzed Monty and told him that Bob Martin, the general contractor, was there. Monty told her to have him come in.

"Hi, Mr. Shepherd. I'm Bob Martin."

"Hi, Bob, I'm Monty. Mr. Shepherd's my Dad."

"Okay, Monty. I know your Dad. He's a fine man. Has he retired?"

"Sort of. He had a heart attack several months ago and kicked me up to President, but he still manages to stay in touch enough to keep me straight. Bob, Dad said you built our last two plants and did a good job. We're getting ready to build an additional apparel plant plus a sock mill. I don't know if anything different has to be done for a sock mill or not, but I wanted to talk with you, at least about the apparel plant."

"Wow! You guys just keep growing. I think that's great. Are you looking to build the same thing as the last one? If my memory serves me correct, it had 150,000 square feet."

"That's correct. We want essentially the same thing, but we don't need that much footage. Fifty to seventy-five thousand should be enough. Is it possible to build a building that can be added onto in case more space is needed later?"

"Absolutely. That's no problem at all, and Monty, I have built two fairly large sock plants, and I would be happy to work with you on yours. Do you know how large a building you will need?"

"Not right now. Dad is calling a couple people in Ft. Payne today to pick their brain, so we should know what size we need after he talks to them. I can tell you this; it will have to be big enough to house maybe three hundred knitting machines plus all the other stuff that goes with it."

"Monty, I don't know what your Dad's friends will tell him, but I will guess that you're going to have to have pretty close to that 150,000 square foot mark. If you're going to knit and finish the socks, the dye house alone will take nearly half that amount. Maybe you should plan on duplicating the last plant we built for you to use as your sock mill. From what you're telling me, it's going to be a sizable project, and I hope you will let my company do it for you."

"Bob, if we decide to have you do the new buildings, when could you start?"

"Well, we're finishing up a large job next week and could get started on yours as soon as we're through with that one. Are you in a hurry?"

"Yes. Here's the deal. We came to an agreement on a huge, long-term contract yesterday, and we're to receive it and have it signed by next week. From the day we sign the contract, we have six months to start producing apparel and socks. Every day we don't produce after six months will cost us a lot of money. My question to you is this: can you do that?"

"If we get the go-ahead by the end of next week, we can definitely have your buildings done in six months. Actually, we'll have them finished in less than six months. Monty, it has been my experience that when somebody wants a factory built, it takes longer to get the equipment set up and operating than it does to build the building. I'm sure your Dad's aware of that."

"Bob, how did you price our last two buildings?"

"On a cost plus basis. That works out better for both of us."

"Okay. Let me get up with Dad, and we'll go over everything and get back to you in a few days. We're one hundred percent sure we're getting the contract, but still, we want to wait 'til it's signed before we proceed any further."

After Bob left, Monty walked down to Charles Crawford's office. "Hi, Charlie. I thought I should touch base with you since we didn't include you in any of our talks with the All Conference Sports people. The way it worked out was that we don't have to concern our company with any sales. All the sales will be done by their company, and they will guarantee a steady volume for our plants. Incidentally, we're going to build two new plants: one for apparel and a big one for socks. I'm sure thankful Dad was able to help. He demanded certain things that I didn't even think about, and All Conference seems very happy about everything. They're giving us a six-year contract to begin after the new buildings are built. Pretty good, huh?"

"It's excellent. I'm glad to hear it."

Don's office was next to Charles', and as Monty walked past, Don called to him, "Hey, Little Brother, come in here for a minute."

Monty turned around and went in. "What are you up to, Big Brother?"

"Did I hear you telling Charlie Crawford about a big contract with somebody?"

"Yeah. We're going to start making *Fin*, but we've got to build more plants first. It's a really big deal."

"Were you going to tell me about it? I am part of this family, you know."

"I know, Don. I just haven't had a chance yet, and of course we would tell you, but since you're not directly connected to it, I didn't think to tell you before now."

"Well, tell me about it."

Monty went over the major parts of the contract, and Don asked, "Kid, do you think there might be a spot in there for me?"

"I don't know, Don. We'll have to see. Look, I've got to go. I'll talk to you later."

Troubled by Don's request, Monty thought, *It looks like I may have a problem. Between Don wanting a spot in the new program, and Dad wanting him in it, too, I might not have a choice. Oh well, I've got some time before I have to do anything, so maybe I can think of something. I really don't want him involved with All Conference Sports. There's no telling what he might try to pull.*

As he was passing Connie's desk, she was on the phone, and he heard her say, "Here he is now, Mr. Shepherd. Hold on just a minute." Monty stopped and Connie said, "Monty, it's your Dad."

He went into his office and picked up the phone. "Hi, Dad. What are you up to this afternoon?"

"Hi, Son. Do you have a pen?"

"Yes sir."

"Write this down. *Tom Everett, 205-555-1885*. Son, this is a man who has been in the sock business in Ft. Payne for about twenty years. He recently sold his mill for a huge amount of money, but he's not ready to retire yet because he's still a relatively young man. He knows what it takes to set up and run a large mill, and he's willing to help you if you'll give him a call. He indicated he might be willing to come to work for you if the two of you could hit it off. Call him and see what you think."

"Okay, Dad. Thanks,"

"By the way, have you thought any more about something for Don?"

"Not yet, Dad. I've been really busy." When he hung up the phone, he thought to himself, *Man, he's not going to let me forget it. I guess I'll have to come up with something, but what?*

He called Tom Everett and set up a time for him to come to Chattanooga the next morning.

When Tom got to Monty's office the next morning, one would think they had known each other for years by the way they hit it off. Monty explained the *Fin* deal to him, and right away, Tom knew exactly what would be needed to set up a state-of-the-art hosiery mill. As they progressed further into their talks, Monty asked, "Tom, would you consider coming to work for Shepherd Global as plant superintendent of our new sock factory?"

Tom replied, "Monty, I was hoping on my way up here that you would ask me to come to work."

"Well, don't you live in Ft. Payne? That's a pretty long commute, isn't it?"

"I actually live in Rising Fawn. That's five miles south of Trenton and about twenty-two miles from Chattanooga. Depending on traffic, it usually takes around thirty minutes to get from my house to South Broad Street."

"Will a drive like that be something you would be willing to do every day?"

"Absolutely. It took me nearly that long to get to my mill in Ft. Payne."

"Okay. It's a deal then, but Tom, I don't think we can put you on payroll until we get a little closer to getting our building started, and that might be two or three weeks away. At that point, I'd like to have you come in and help us plan out our equipment needs, when we will need to order them, and a host of other things that we are not familiar with, since we have never been in the sock business."

"Monty, that sounds great. I know I can help you because I've already successfully done all those things, and I know where to go to find just what will be needed to get started."

They stood and Tom shook hands with Monty before telling him goodbye. As he was walking out of the building, Charlie Crawford walked up and said, "I'm going to Oscars and get a hamburger. Wanna go?"

Monty said, "Yeah, I'd like to. Let me see if Tom would like to go with us. Is that all right with you?"

"Yeah, that's fine."

Monty called to Tom before he got into his car, and they all three went to get a burger. While they were eating, Monty briefly told Charlie what they were going to do about making the *Fin* socks, and Charlie said, "It's a shame we can't make socks with the Shepherd Staff on them. I bet they would sell like hotcakes."

Monty asked, "What did you say?"

"I said "We could sell socks with the Staff on them like crazy. With all the customers we have using the Staff sportswear, socks would be a natural."

"Let me think about that."

"Tom, how big a deal would it be to maybe add another line to make a different logo?"

"It wouldn't be a big deal at all. Of course, you would have to have additional knitting machines, but you're probably going to have enough bleaching and drying capacity to take care of the additional dozens. How many additional dozens do you think we're talking about?"

Monty said, "How many do you think, Charlie?"

"Right now, I don't know. I wasn't even thinking about socks before we got here. I was thinking about hamburgers."

"Well, you've opened the door, so you had better start working on some projections when we get back."

Just then the food came, and they all stopped talking and concentrated on the important matter at hand: hamburgers and French fries. When they finished eating, they went back to the Shepherd office, and Tom got into his car and left.

Charlie's offhand remark about making Staff logo socks had

created no minor excitement on the parts of Monty and Charlie. "Charlie, I think your Staff logo idea is a good one, and if we're going to do something like that, now's the time to start planning. We'll break ground on the new building in about a week or ten days, and we'll need to consider everything before we get too far along. How about doing some research on logo socks. I'm sure you know some people who sell that kind of goods, so call whoever you can and pick their brains. I'd like to get into it when we start *Fin*. We need to come up with some realistic projections in order to know how many extra machines we'll have to buy."

Charlie walked down to his office, and Monty went into his and called Joan. "Hi, Sugar. What's up?"

"Not much. Just doing a little cleaning. This is a big house. Did you know that?"

"I know that. Tell you what: to reward you for doing a good cleaning job, why don't I take you out to eat?"

"You're my hero, did you know that? Where are we going?"

"Wherever you want to go. Think about it, and your hero will take you there. I've got to go. I'll see ya later. I love you."

"Love you, too."

CHAPTER FIVE

About nine-thirty the following Wednesday morning Fed-Ex delivered a package from All Conference Sports containing the contracts. Monty wanted David to see them, so he took them to his house for him to examine. David carefully read everything and decided everything was in order. He asked Monty, "Do you want to sign these or do you want me to?"

"Since you're the CEO and own the company, why don't you sign?"

"Okay, I'll do it." Then he borrowed a pen from Monty and signed everywhere he was supposed to. "This should keep everybody busy for a while," he said. "Be sure you mail the *Fin* copies back as soon as possible."

"I will, Dad. This is pretty exciting, isn't it?"

"Yes, it is, and you're the right person to handle this job. Your athletic background makes you a natural when corresponding with a company like All Conference Sports."

****

After a week's delay, Monty left the following Monday for Munich and London, and Joan went with him. This was her first trip, and she was really excited. She hadn't been on the plane since their honeymoon, and she was looking forward to being with Monty for an extended amount of time without having to excuse him for some business thing. He would be hers for the twelve or thirteen hours it would take to fly to Europe.

When Thil found out that Joan was going, she called Daniele, Gerhard's wife, and asked if she would please show her some of the sights of Munich while Monty worked, and she gladly agreed to do it. Daniele had learned to speak pretty good English, so there should not be a huge language barrier.

David had suggested to Monty that he leave Chattanooga around one p.m., and that way, he could get a good night's rest and land in Munich in time to get to the office around ten the next morning. By doing that, he could get in a full day's work, so that's what they did.

The caterers had brought snacks and food for dinner and breakfast, so around seven, somewhere over the Atlantic, they went to the galley and got out food. The entrees were pre-packaged, as were the salads, desserts, and breads, so they both took one of each to the table. Joan poured iced tea, and they sat and had a very enjoyable dinner. Joan thought it was super romantic, and Monty sensed an evening of fun and pleasure ahead.

When they finished eating, Monty asked, "Would you like to see a movie?"

"Yeah, that would be nice."

"What are you in the mood for? Western or romance?"

"I feel romantic. Let's watch something romantic."

"Okay, but we're in a small area up here, and you might not be able to get away from me."

"Sounds interesting."

"Is that a threat or a promise?"

"Which one do you want it to be?"

"A promise."

"Okay, let me see what our library has to offer." Monty looked at the catalog of movies and asked, "How about *Love Story* with Ali MacGraw and Ryan O'Neal?"

"Oh yes. I've seen it once, but I'd like to see it again." With that, Monty thumbed through the movies until he found what he was looking for. He pulled it out, put it in the player, then went back to where Joan was sitting and sat down beside her. As they watched the movie, they held hands and cuddled as much as they dared, concerned that one of the crew might come back from the cockpit.

The movie was over about nine-thirty, Chattanooga time, and after watching *Love Story*, they were both ready for bed, but not necessarily ready to go to sleep. Joan went to the bedroom to get ready for bed, while Monty went to the flight deck to tell the crew goodnight. When he got to the bedroom, Joan was already in bed waiting for him. He undressed and didn't take time to put his clothes up. He just let them fall to the floor and jumped into bed as fast as he could. They locked arms and kissed passionately. After a while they went to sleep and slept like babies until six the next morning.

Monty got up first and went to the galley where one of the crew had already fixed a pot of coffee. Soon Joan came in, smiling, and joined him, and then Chuck Jacobs, the pilot, came back and joined the two. After he had poured his coffee, he sat down and said they would be landing in Munich in about two hours. In a few minutes Joan asked, "Are you boys ready for something to eat?" They both said they were, so she got up and took out three covered trays from the caterer, and after setting them on the table, she sat down, and they all ate their breakfast.

In a little bit, Monty said, "I guess we had better get ready, Sugar. We want to be ready when we land. Gerhard is to be at the airport to meet us, and we have a full day planned. We'll probably drop you off at the apartment to wait on Daniele. Gerhard and I have a lunch date with the buyer at Ludwig Beck, and if we get through working with him in time, we're going to try to see the Funf Hofe buyer later this afternoon."

"I'm anxious to present our new sock program to them, even though I don't have samples. Gerhard doesn't even know about it yet. I think he'll be happy to have socks to sell."

"Okay, boss. I'll be ready."

When they landed at Munich's Flughafen Munchen airport, they were pleasantly surprised; Gerhard and Daniele were both there to meet them. After all the pleasantries, they got into Gerhard's car and headed toward town. "Monty, Daniele dropped her car off at the office, so if it's all right with you and Joan, we'll go to the office, and the girls can get her car and do whatever they want to do."

"That will be fine, Gerhard. I've got some things I want to go over with you before we go for our appointment. We'll have some time to spend at the office before we go, won't we?"

"Yes. We'll have plenty of time. Daniele, this afternoon why don't you take Joan to her apartment in time for her to rest before dinner. Monty and I should be through by four-thirty or five, and I'll bring him home so he can relax a little while. Later, we'll take them to Dallmayr's. Monty, you're in for a treat at Dallmayr's."

"I'm looking forward to it."

When they got to the Shepherd office, the girls didn't go in. They kissed their husbands goodbye and took off in Daniele's car like a couple of teen-aged girls.

Gerhard and Monty went in. Bruno and Marlene were both there, and Monty was especially glad to see Bruno because he wanted to talk to him and Gerhard about the new sock program he was working on. After they sat down in Gerhard's office, Marlene brought each of them a cup of tea, and Monty invited her to stay and hear what he had to say about the socks. He told them about the large contract they had just signed with All Conference Sports and how part of the contract was to produce socks. "At lunch one day, while we were talking about getting into the sock business, Charles Crawford, our North American sales manager came up with the idea of making socks with the *Staff* logo on them. It's a natural for us, because we are having to build a new facility in which to make the *Fin* socks, and we can simply add more machines and set up a separate line for the *Staff*. They're all the same sock; they will just have different logos."

Bruno asked, "Will we be able to sell *Fin*?"

"No. We won't have anything to do with *Fin* sales. We will only be manufacturing the socks for All Conference Sports."

"Fellows and lady, I'm totally convinced that these new items will add a huge amount of sales to our already large *Staff* volume. We hope to be producing and shipping within six months. Now here's what I need for you to do. I want you to talk this up with the rest of your sales staff and have each one talk it up with their customers to try and get an idea of what kind of figures we're looking at. Not having been in the sock business before, we're sort of *flying blind* and everything up to this point is a guess, so if you could help us by doing this, I would appreciate it. Gerhard, I'd like to talk to the accounts we're going to see today and tomorrow to see what kind of interest they have."

"We are tentatively planning to start out making five thousand dozen per week, worldwide, but I think this might be low. I would like to have some input from you within the next two or three weeks, if possible. We have already broken ground on the two new factories and would love to have to increase the size before we get too far along. Our American guys are doing this, and I'm going to London Thursday and will instruct Liam to do it as well. I'll be in Tel Aviv soon and will find out how our guys over there feel about it then."

The Ludwig Beck and Funf Hofe buyers were very receptive to Monty's pitch, and they both assured him they would buy the socks when they become available. Monty asked if they would place advance orders within a month, and they both said "yes."

When they finished at Funf Hofe, Gerhard took Monty back to the apartment. Joan was already there and was asleep on the sofa. Monty tried not to wake her, but she woke up when he tried to tip-toe through the room into the bedroom.

"Hi, gorgeous, did you have a good day?"

"I had a wonderful day. I just love Daniele. Even though she's a lot older than I am, she's a load of fun. She says the restaurant where we're going tonight is so good that she can hardly wait to get there, and that makes me anxious to go, too. How was your day?"

"Great. I told Bruno and Gerhard about the socks and then told the customers we saw, and everybody was excited about them. The two accounts even went so far as to say they will place advance orders when we are ready for them. How good is that?"

"It's probably because you're so good-looking and such a great salesman."

"I'm sure that's it. Look, I need to get a shower and put on some cleaner clothes. Gerhard said they would pick us up at seven o'clock."

Dallmayr turned out to be a complete surprise. It not only has a very expensive restaurant and café, but it owes its culinary reputation to the famous delicatessens Dallmayr and Kafer. It's the oldest gourmet shop in Munich, and a walk through its historical sales rooms just to see what is offered will turn out to be an experience for the senses. There are small bars where one can enjoy the delicacies on sale. This gourmet paradise is an absolute must, and here epicureans meet from all over the world.

Gerhard brought Monty and Joan here to eat at the restaurant, but after touring the shops and eating cheese here and truffles there, and a cup of their world-famous coffee with a pastry/croissant somewhere else, they were too full to eat a meal. They thoroughly enjoyed the experience, and after nibbling until they were stuffed, they decided to go home and loosen their belts.

The next morning Gerhard came to pick up Monty, and they spent the entire day seeing Shepherd accounts and hawking the new, upcoming sock line. They went to Arcade first, then to Karstadt. Karstadt was very impressive. It covered an entire city block. Next, they went to Kaufinger Tor, where they ate lunch after calling on the sportswear buyer. They finished out the day by seeing Oberpollinger, an upscale department store, and finally Galeria Kaufhof.

Both men were tired, and Gerhard took Monty to the apartment. He said he would be back to get him and Joan around seven, and they would go somewhere to eat. Joan wasn't there yet, so Monty stretched out on the bed and took a nap before she returned.

That evening they ate at a small, neighborhood restaurant. Joan and Monty let Gerhard order for them, and they had no idea what they were eating, but both of them really enjoyed it. When they got back to the apartment, Joan and Monty told Daniele goodbye, because they were leaving for London the next morning. Gerhard said he would be there to pick them up at eight o'clock, and they all said good night.

Wheels were up on the 707 at nine-fifteen for their trip to London. This was going to be an abbreviated sales trip. Monty and Liam would only see two accounts this time, but would see more on Monty's next trip. He wanted to go over the sock program with Liam, but he also wanted to see a couple of their larger accounts to get their reactions.

Liam was there to meet the plane when it landed at Heathrow Airport, and he drove the couple to the Airport Hilton where they checked in. Since they were only going to see one customer, Harrods, Monty asked Joan if she would like to go there while he and Liam worked with the buyer, and she said she would. They left the Hilton and went to the Shepherd office before going to Harrods. Anna, Liam's assistant was the only one there, so she and Joan talked while Liam and Monty conducted their business. In a little while, they were ready to go to Harrods, and when they got there, Joan was overwhelmed by its size and the variety of things they sold.

When they finished at Harrods, Liam drove them back to the Hilton, where they ate dinner and spent the night.

The next morning Monty and Liam went to see Fenwick of Bond Street and left Joan at the hotel. They returned to the Hilton around noon to pick her up, and then Liam took them to their plane. They took off a little after one p.m. on their way back to Chattanooga. Considering the time difference and flying time, Chuck estimated they would land at Lovell Field around seven a.m. tomorrow morning. Monty just hoped Joan would feel romantic on the return trip the way she did on the way over because he enjoyed the loving at six miles up.

When the plane leveled off over the Atlantic, Monty sat on a sofa thinking, while Joan read some magazines she had picked up on their trip. What to do with Don was bothering him a lot.

I'm gonna have to come up with something or else Dad's gonna come up with something, himself, and I can't let that happen. Don has worked in just about every department in the company and hasn't done well in any of them. He should be in sales; that's where his personality is best suited, but I can't put him back in there because of his "don't care" attitude. The only thing left is something with Fin and that's really risky. Fin is so tightly controlled, I've heard they actually count their labels, and if they come up short, then a penalty is charged for each label missing. Don could be a disaster there. Maybe he could work in the sock mill. When I get back, I'll talk to Tommy Everett about it and see if he has any suggestions.

Joan interrupted his train of thought by asking, "Honey, would you like to have something to drink?"

"That would be nice. How about a Coke?"

Joan opened and poured both of them one and came back and sat down on the sofa close to him. "You seem preoccupied. What are you thinking about, Big Boy?"

"Nothing much. I was just thinking about all those pretty German girls we saw at Dallmayr's the other night."

"Yeah, right. I must not have been in the same place as you because all I saw was a gang of handsome men that wanted to flirt with me."

"I think they wanted to flirt with you. I'm gonna tell you something, young lady; you had better be on your best behavior after dinner, because the Tennessee Stud is on board, and he's full of testosterone. Once he sets his sights on you, there's no telling what might happen."

"All I can say is, promises, promises." And with that, she turned to him, leaned over and kissed him on the cheek. "You talk a big game. We'll see what the stud does later."

"You asked me what I was thinking about; well, I was thinking about what I'm gonna do with Don. Dad's after me to find something for him after we start the new contract, and so is Don. You know most of the story about Don, and you know I don't think I can trust him, but Dad outranks me, and if I don't find something I can live with, then Dad will find something. I told Don that I wasn't going to tell Dad about what he did, and I haven't, but if they force my hand by insisting that he be given a job that might jeopardize the company in some way or the *Fin* contract, I might have to tell him. It's worrying me, Babe, and I don't know what to do."

"Have you prayed about it?"

"Yeah, but I don't have the answer yet."

"Try not to worry. The answer will come."

"Thanks, Babe. You know, I wouldn't take a hundred dollars for you. Do you know that?"

"I would hope not. I think I'm worth at least five hundred."

They kissed, then sat back and sipped on their Cokes.

The rest of the afternoon passed rather quickly, and when it came time for dinner, the German caterers had outdone themselves. The food was outstanding. After they ate, they watched a Cary Grant movie and then went to bed. The Tennessee Stud turned out to be everything he said he was, and all Joan could do was to succumb to his wishes, and she loved it.

Pretty soon they went to sleep and Joan slept like a log all night, but Monty didn't sleep as well. He couldn't help but think about the Don problem, and it caused him to be restless.

Monty had asked the crew to wake him at five o'clock, but before they could do it he awoke and got up. As usual, someone had made coffee, and he was ready for some. He sat at the table alone and thought about what he was going to do with Don. Finally, he decided he would offer him a job as Tommy Everett's assistant in the sock plant, and if he didn't like that, he could stay where he was. He was tired of worrying about it. *After a while I'll go tell Dad what I've decided. I hope he agrees.*

Around five-thirty, Pat James, the co-pilot, came back to the cabin and sat down. "Monty, we got a call from Chattanooga control a few minutes ago. They said to tell you that your Mother left your car at the airport, and the keys are inside at the desk."

"That's great. I forgot to call and tell anybody when we would get home. Thank you, Pat."

At about six o'clock, Monty excused himself and went to the bedroom to wake Joan up. "Good morning, Sugar Pie. It's time to rise and shine. I'll bet you're smiling this morning. I know I am. Get up; we'll be landing in a little over an hour, and the coffee's hot. I'll be at the table outside the galley."

In a few minutes she came out of the bedroom and looked gorgeous. She walked over to Monty and gave him a kiss on the top of his head before pouring her coffee. Then she sat down, and they enjoyed each other's company until Chuck announced that they were getting ready to land.

CHAPTER SIX

They didn't eat breakfast on the plane, but Joan gathered it all up and asked the crew if they wanted it. None of them did, so she put it in some bags and took it with her. On the way home, they stopped and had a big breakfast at the Cracker Barrel and arrived home between nine thirty and ten o'clock.

After unloading the car and getting everything settled, Monty said, "Honey, I'm going over to Dad's for a few minutes."

"Wait a minute and I'll go with you. I want to see Thil."

They walked next door, and the door was still locked, so Monty knocked. He didn't want to ring the bell, just in case his Dad was still in bed. In a few seconds, Thil opened the door, and when she saw them, she squealed the way she always did when she was excited. She hugged and kissed both of them. "Want some coffee?"

"No thanks. We ate at the Cracker Barrel and had some there, unless Joan wants some."

"No thank you."

"Well, how about some orange juice?"

"That sounds good. Yes ma'am, I'll have a glass if you don't mind."

"I will, too. Thank you."

While Joan and Thil stayed in the kitchen, Monty went to the den to see his Dad. "Good morning, Dad."

"Well, I didn't know you were home. I'm glad to see you. Did you have a good trip?"

"Yes sir. I had a good trip. All the customers I saw seem to be very happy with Shepherd Global, and they all assured me that they would do everything they could to keep showing increases. I don't think I had a chance to tell you about the sock I'm introducing before I left, but it was received unbelievably well."

Monty spent a good deal of time outlining the program to David and when he finished, David backed him one hundred percent. He told Monty, "This reminds me of when I took over from my Dad and decided to take the company international. When I hired Urey Steen, we had unbelievable growth, and we're still growing. I believe this sock program of yours is going to easily match that. Way to go, Son."

"Dad, before I forget it, I've decided to move Don into the sock plant as assistant to Tommy Everett. I don't know if this is a good move or not, but it's the only thing I can think of to get him away from where he is. I would like to keep him where he is, but you seem determined to move him somewhere else. Maybe he'll be happy in the sock mill. I hope so."

"Monty, ever since I first said something to you about finding something for Don, you have either dodged the subject or acted as if you didn't hear me. What's going on between you guys? I'd like to know."

"Dad, I love Don. He's my big brother, but with his background and lackadaisical attitude, I just don't think he needs to be in a position of responsibility. I would really like to not talk about it, but since you outrank me, I'll do what you say. I know things that you don't, and I don't want to violate Don's confidence in me by breaking my word to him. Dad, I'm taking my position as President of Shepherd Global as serious as I know how, and I will appreciate it if you will just trust me. I'm not going to do anything that will hurt Don, but I don't want to do anything that will hurt the company either. Do you understand what I'm trying to say?"

"I understand, Son. I'm sorry if you think I've pressured you. I won't do it again. You're doing a great job, and I'm glad I made you President."

"Thanks, Dad. Did I hear that you and Mom are going to Florida?"

"Yeah, if all goes well, we're going to go down Friday. Do you know if the plane is available?"

"No, but I'll ask Don. I feel sure it is. Dad, even though it's Saturday, I think I'll go to the office for a little while to see what's been going on since I've been gone. I want to go to the building site, too. I can hardly wait to get the new plants up and running, especially the sock mill. Is there anything I can do for you before I go?"

"No thanks. I'm glad you're home, Son. I'll see ya later."

****

When Monty got to the office, he was shocked to find Don there. When Don saw him, he asked, "Hey, Little Brother, what are you doing here? I thought you were in Germany."

48

"I just got back a couple hours ago. Why are you here? I thought working on Saturday was against your principles."

"It is, but there's a company wanting to rent the plane, and I had to come in and do some things beforehand."

"When are they wanting it?"

"I'm not sure. Maybe next weekend."

"Have you talked to Dad?"

"No, why?"

"He and Mom want to go to Florida, Friday. Do you think those people will have the plane then?"

"I don't know. I'll have to try and pin them down on a date."

"Okay, but if it looks like they want it next Friday, you need to call Dad and work out something."

"Okay. I'll take care of it."

"Don, I'm glad you're here because there's something I want to talk to you about. When you finish what you're doing, come up to my office, will you?"

"Yeah. I'm about through. I'll be there in a minute."

In about ten minutes, Don walked into Monty's office. "Okay, Little Brother, what's on your mind?"

Monty told him his thoughts about transferring him to the sock mill, and he asked if he would have a problem working for Tommy Everett. Don asked a lot of questions, and said he wouldn't have a problem working for Tommy, but indicated that he would like to think about it. He said he didn't know if he wanted to be tied down to one place all day, every day. Monty told him, "Well, think about it. You said you wanted something other than what you're doing, and the sock job is the only thing I can come up with right now. Do you have any suggestions for something?"

"Not really. I would just like to get away from where I am now. Let me think about your offer over the weekend and get back to you next week. Can I do that?"

"Sure. Whenever you're ready."

"Monty, you know I've been working here ever since I was in school, and Dad used to tell me I would someday take over the business. Well, I screwed up, and he turned it over to you. Everything that's happened to me has been my fault, and I can't blame Dad for not wanting me in charge of Shepherd Apparel, and I know you deserve to be where you are, but Little Brother, it still hurts. I'll say this: I will always be grateful to you for not telling Dad about what I did with the lease money, and I know that if you weren't my brother, I'd be in prison right now."

"That's what brothers do. Just stay straight and work hard, and everything will work out. I love you, Don."

"Love you, too."

Don left, and Monty stayed at the office for about another hour, then got into the car and drove over to the building sites on the way home. The apparel building was moving right along, but the sock mill was stuck, waiting on all the plumbing to be done in order to bleach and finish the socks. Satisfied with everything, he went home.

The next week, Monday came, then Tuesday, then Wednesday, but no answer from Don. Monty wondered about it, but he didn't want to say anything because he hoped Don would stay where he was instead of moving to the sock plant. Finally, on the following Monday, Tommy called, and said he had a couple guys that he had worked with in Ft. Payne that he would like for Monty to consider hiring, so now a deadline was created for Don's answer.

Monty picked up the phone. "Don, Monty. Have you decided what you want to do about the sock plant job yet? There are two men with a lot of experience in socks that want a job, and I need to know what you're going to do before I make a decision about either of them."

"Monty, I've been thinking about this ever since we talked last week, and I was hoping I would have more time, but since you have to know something, I'll take your offer. Now you know I don't have a clue about how to make socks."

"I know. You'll have to have quite a bit of training, but I think Tommy can teach you a lot before we start manufacturing. I just hope he can teach you enough to be a help to him when we start knitting. I might have to hire the other two as well. This is going to be a big operation; in fact, it will be larger than a lot of the hosiery mills in Ft. Payne."

****

Six months later

Start-up on the new apparel plant was right on time, but the sock mill ran nearly a month behind. Everything was wide open now, and

50

All Conference Sports was pleased with the initial shipments. Normally, on a start-up of this magnitude, there would be a lot of quality problems, but every cutting passed the audits with flying colors; even the socks passed. After the first two truckloads of socks and apparel were received in Seattle, David Brownlee called Monty to tell him how pleased they were with the merchandise, and this pleased Monty greatly.

Something else that pleased Monty was the way Don had applied himself. For the first time in his life, Don was doing everything in his power to be the best he could be. A lot of the credit had to go to Tommy Everett for the way he took Don under his wing and taught him sock manufacturing. Don and Tommy were close to the same age, and they seemed to have a lot in common.

Any time a new plant starts up, there will be problems with the equipment until the technicians can get everything tweaked just right. Every time a tech was called to a machine, Don would go with him and look over his shoulder. Most of the time, the tech would explain to Don what he was doing to the machine, and this was a tremendous help in furthering Don's education in making socks.

One Tuesday evening, Joan and Monty were over at David and Thil's when the door opened, and Don came in with a very attractive lady. Everyone was shocked because he never brought any women around. The only ones he ever had anything to do with were the ones he picked up in some bar, and he didn't want to bring any of them to meet his parents, but maybe this one was different. "Pat, I'd like for you to meet my Mom, Thil, and my Dad, David. The young guy here is my brother, Monty and his wife, Joan. Everybody, this is Pat Marsh."

The whole time he was introducing the others, Thil was thinking about Don calling her *Mom* instead of *Step-Mom* or Thil. Her track-record with him over the last few years made her think, *I wonder what he's up to.*

They all said they were glad to meet her, and David invited them to sit down. Thil said, "Pat, we're happy to have you with us. Are you a Chattanooga girl?"

"No, I actually live in Knoxville, but I work down here during the week. I go home on Friday night and come back on Monday."

"Where do you work?"

"I work for the Ward-McRae Corporation. I'm a designer for them."

"Do you have a family?"

"I have a seventeen-year-old son who stays with my mother while I'm away. I would like to be able to move down here, but Ronnie plays sports and is really active in other things, and I promised I wouldn't make him move and leave his friends until he graduates. That will be another year, and I miss him terribly when I'm away from him, but we both agreed that we could stand it for that long."

"Well, we're glad to have you, and you're welcome here anytime."

"Thank you. It's awfully nice to meet you folks, too. You have a lovely home."

After a few more minutes of unimportant small talk, Don said they had to be going, so they told everyone goodbye and left. After they had gone, Monty said, "What was that all about?"

On the way back to his apartment, Don thought, *I'm glad we went to Dad's. I hope I scored some points with him. I really need to just in case, one day, Monty might decide he wants to tell him what I did. I guess I need to score some points with Monty, too.*

Back at David's house, Monty said, "Dad, I'm going to Tel Aviv next week. Would you and Mom like to go? Joan's going, and we could make it like a family vacation. Of course, I'll be working during the day, but I can be with y'all at night, and we can have a real good time. Mom, I've heard you talk about how nice the beach is there, and I know you'd like to go. How 'bout it Dad?"

"I don't know, Son. Let me think about it. You know, we haven't been back from Florida very long."

"So what, Dad? What else do you have to do? You've worked hard all your life, and it's time you enjoyed yourself. I'm gonna plan on y'all going with us."

"We'll see. I'll let you know."

"Joan, we had better be going. I'm a little tired, and I've got a hard day ahead of me tomorrow. Mom, Dad, I'll see you guys later. I love you."

Thil walked with them to the door. "Mom, do you want to go to Tel Aviv?"

"Oh yes, I'd love to."

"Then use your convincing ways to make Dad say yes. I'll call you tomorrow." Monty and Joan both kissed her, said goodnight, and walked next door to their house.

When they got to their house, Monty said, "Do you know what would be neat?"

"What?"

"You know, our flight crew has to take us to all the places we have to go, but they never get to take their wives. Why don't we invite their wives on the Tel Aviv trip, and we could all have a real good time. Business is good, and we're making a lot of money, and we could pay for their trip. That's one way we could share some of our good fortune."

"Sweetheart, I'm prouder of you every day that we're together. I think that's one of the best and sweetest ideas I've ever heard. I'm sure the wives will love it. Let's do that, even if your Mom and Dad don't go."

"Okay. I'll call the guys tomorrow and set it up."

When Monty called the guys the next morning, they were all thrilled and said they would ask their wives. Two of the wives would have to get off work, but they didn't think that would be a problem. They would call him back later in the day or the next morning. Next, he called Thil to see if she was successful convincing David they should go, and she said she was, so everything was all set. The only drawback was that Monty would be working each day instead of lying on the beach, but that was okay. He would have his family and friends to be with at night. When his Mom said they were going, he bowed his head and said, *Heavenly Father, thank you so much for this, another blessing. You're an awesome God. Thank you.*

The rest of the day, Wednesday, and all day Thursday were very busy days; in fact, Monty didn't get home until almost eight o'clock Thursday night. He spent most of Friday morning outlining plans for Tom's duties the following week, and then he spent Friday afternoon at the sock plant, where he was impressed with the way Don was working out.

If he only knew some of the thoughts Don was hatching out in his devious mind, he wouldn't be so impressed.

He told Tommy that he was going to be in Tel Aviv the following week, but didn't tell Don. Since he wasn't working directly with him, he didn't think it necessary to tell him. After all, when the cat's away, the mice will play, and in this case, the mouse doesn't need to know the cat's away.

When he left Friday afternoon, he was satisfied that everything was running smoothly, and there should be no problems while he's gone. He would be back in his office Saturday morning to get his papers, and everything else he would need for the business part of the trip. There was one thing he forgot to do, and that was to call Chuck Jacobs, his pilot, and have him be sure there would be enough food on board the plane for ten people. They would need food for the London leg, and then food for the trip from London to Tel Aviv. Chuck knew how to do all this; Monty just wanted to remind him, since there were going to be extra people on board.

Instead of leaving on Monday, they left Sunday on this trip. Monty needed to spend as much time as possible working while he was in Israel, plus, this would give his guests an extra day to enjoy the beach and other attractions in Tel Aviv. The plane was equipped with sleeping accommodations for eight, so Monty assigned beds for each person. He gave his Mom and Dad the bedroom, and he, Joan, and the three wives would each sleep in a bunk. The flight crew would, of course, be flying the plane and wouldn't need a bed. The term *bunk* sounds a little rustic, but these bunks were far from that. They were plush beds mounted in their own little room sort of like a roomette on a passenger train.

The London leg took a little over eight hours of flying time, and they checked in the Airport Hilton after they landed at Heathrow Airport. The flight to Ben Gurion Airport in Tel Aviv the next day would take around five hours. Monty asked Chuck if they could leave around eight o'clock the next morning, and Chuck said he would go ahead and file a flight plan.

After a good night's rest, the group left London for Tel Aviv at exactly eight the next morning and landed at Ben Gurion Airport five hours and ten minutes later. They called the hotel where their reservations were, and soon a van arrived to take them to the hotel. All ten couldn't get in, so the van had to make two trips. Monty, Joan, and Monty's parents made the first trip, and the flight crew and their wives made up the second load. It was a beautiful waterfront hotel, and the beach was magnificent. David and Thil had stayed there before, and Thil just loved it. She could hardly wait to get her suit on and get out in the sun. She was in her fifties now, but she still looked like a high-dollar fashion model when she appeared in a swimsuit. David still looked good, too, but his age was beginning to show a little.

Redemption?

While Joan was getting ready to go out on the beach, Monty called Myron Hober to come to the hotel to get him, so they could go to work. Joan liked all the wives of the flight crew, but she was especially drawn to Julia Kanipe, the flight engineers wife. They seemed to have a lot in common, and Julia was very easy to like. David and Thil's room was next door to Monty and Joan's and across the hall from the other three couples. Soon everyone, except Monty, was lying on the beach, enjoying the Mediterranean sun. Joan wished Monty was there, but Thil and Julia being with her helped the loneliness.

Monty got back around five thirty, and the others had returned to their rooms to get ready for dinner. They chose one of the restaurants at the hotel and had the time of their lives before and after dinner. All of them were suffering from jet lag, so they went to their rooms soon after they ate to get a good night's rest.

Joan and Monty talked after they got back to their room and agreed that the week was going to be the perfect vacation for the flight crew and their wives. It was going to be fun for all of them, but especially for the crew and their wives.

Myron was at the hotel early the next morning to pick Monty up, and they spent all day calling on customers. Myron was one heck of a salesman and so was Monty, and between the two of them, the buyers were putty in their hands. They showed some new sportswear styles, and they got some really nice orders, and then Monty talked to them and showed the new *Staff* socks. The socks really bowled them over, and they couldn't wait to place large orders for them.

Shepherd *Staff* was a natural for Israel. Everyone in the country revered King David, who was a shepherd boy, and when David Shepherd first came to Israel with the Shepherd *Staff* products, it seemed that everybody had to have at least one piece. Now with the *Staff* socks, there was no telling how much volume would be created. When they finished work Tuesday, and Myron brought Monty back to the hotel, he came in to speak to David, because David was in charge of Shepherd Global when Urey Steen hired him.

Wednesday was a very profitable day, and Monty decided to only work half a day on Thursday. He wanted to be with the rest of the group for at least that long, and they had to head back home on Friday. Many of the stores in Israel were closed on Friday because of the Sabbath. Actually, it began at sundown on Friday, so Monty didn't really lose that much time.

As a token of their appreciation for the nice vacation, the flight crew and their wives treated David, Thil, Joan, and Monty to dinner at Manta Ray's, a killer seafood restaurant located on the beachfront. It was amazing how ten people, who were strangers to half the group a week ago, got along as well as they did. Everyone seemed to have a ball the entire week, and the last night at Manta Ray's was the icing on the cake.

Monty told Chuck he wanted to leave Tel Aviv for London at nine the next morning. That way, they could get to London around two o'clock and have the rest of the day to do whatever anybody wanted to do because everybody would be on their own. They wouldn't have any food catered until they left London for Chattanooga.

Everyone got up early on Friday, and those who wanted breakfast ate, and the hotel van began its two trips to the airport. Chuck and the other two got to the plane early to check everything out, and when the rest of them got there, all they had to do was board and take off. "Dad, did you have a good time?"

"I sure did. It was very relaxing, and I enjoyed meeting all these people, too. I'm just sorry that you had to work the whole time."

"Well, having you, Mom, Joan, and the rest of the group made my week. I didn't mind working because I'm having such a good time selling the new socks, and getting together with all of you after work just capped off a perfect day, every day. Thanks for coming with us."

After they landed in London, they checked into the Airport Hilton, and everybody split up. Some caught cabs and went to town to shop, and others went sightseeing. Joan and Julia caught a bus and went to the British Museum, Madame Tussauds, and the Tower of London. Monty stayed at the hotel and did paperwork, so he wouldn't have to do it when he got home. When Joan and Julia got back, they were tired, so Monty and Joan thought they would just grab a bite at the hotel and turn in early. Joan called Julia and invited her and Bob to join them, which they did.

After they were seated, Monty asked, "Bob, did you have a good time?"

"Yes sir, I sure did. This is the first time Julia and I have been able to get away together for several years, and I want to thank you for that."

56

"Julia, how about you? Did you have a good time?"

"I really did. Not only did I get to spend a week with my man, I made a new, good friend." As she said that, she reached over and squeezed Joan's hand.

The next day went smoothly. The group took off from London at nine o'clock and made it to Chattanooga in a little over eight hours. With the time difference, they landed at Lovell Field around ten p.m. They all hugged, shook hands, and said what a good time they had, then got into their cars and went home. David and Thil rode with Monty and Joan in Monty's car, and David was worn out when Monty pulled into the driveway. "Good night, Dad. Sleep tight. Good night, Mom. I'm sure glad y'all went with us. I love you."

Monty and Joan went home and went straight to bed. They didn't even unload the car. They just took in what they needed and waited to get the rest the next morning. They were beat.

CHAPTER SEVEN

Monday started out with the regular staff meeting. Ever since the two new plants came on line, Tommy Everett, the sock mill manager, and Fred Harmon, the *Fin* apparel manager, were included in the staff, so the meeting took a little longer than it used to. Monty was pleased with all the departments because on-time attendance was up, and the efficiency ratings had all improved. He jokingly commented, "If you do this well when I'm gone, maybe I should leave more often."

Ed Henry, one of the plant managers, spoke up and said, "If you're planning on leaving again, how about taking me with you?" Everybody laughed.

After lunch, Monty went to the sock mill to meet with Tommy Everett. He wanted to tell him about the nice reception the *Staff* socks received in Tel Aviv, and he was thinking they might need to increase production before long. Tommy told him that that would be no problem. They might have to buy a few more knitting machines and hire a few more people, but increasing production would be fine with him.

"Monty, I want to mention something to you, since you're here. There have been several people come in, since they found out we're making *Fin,* wanting to buy socks. I told them we couldn't sell them any. Was I right?"

"You absolutely were. If All Conference Sports ever found out that we sold some of their socks, they would probably cancel our contract. If some employees should want some, you can let them have irregulars, but no firsts. You just can't believe how strict they are about their brand."

Just then Don walked in. "Hey, Little Brother, whatta you up to?"

"I just came by to make sure you're behaving," he smiled. "What are you up to?"

"Well, I'm working my tail off. You're gonna have to quit selling so many socks, so I can get some rest."

"Get some rest? I'm afraid you're not gonna get any for a long time. I came by to talk to Tommy about maybe increasing production. When I was in Tel Aviv last week, they nearly took the new *Staff* socks away from me."

"You were in Tel Aviv last week? Man! I guess when you're President you've got it made, don't you? I didn't know you were in Tel Aviv."

"Yeah, I left Sunday and got back Saturday. It was a tiring trip, but I think a very profitable one. Are you still seeing that gal you brought to Dad's. What's her name? Pat?"

"Yeah, it's Pat, and yeah, I'm still seeing her. That reminds me; we're going out to eat tonight. Would you and Joan like to go with us?"

"Sounds like fun. Let me check with Joan, and I'll get back to you. Where are you gonna eat?"

"We'll probably go to Fehn's. Their fried chicken is about my favorite."

"Mine, too. As soon as I talk to Joan, I'll call you. I don't know of anything that we have planned."

Joan said they didn't have any plans, and she would like to eat with them, so Monty called Don and said they would meet them at Fehn's at six thirty.

The four of them had a very enjoyable evening. Don and Monty acted like the brothers they were, but not like the way they have been acting towards each other for last few years. They seemed to genuinely enjoy each other's company. Joan tried her best to make Pat feel at ease, but there was something that kept her a little stand-offish. She was friendly enough, but there was just a little hesitancy in her demeanor that wasn't exactly right. It was something only a woman would notice. After topping off an excellent meal with a piece of Fehn's delicious macaroon pie, they got up to leave. Don and Monty argued over the check, and Don wasn't too insistent about paying it, so Monty got it and gladly paid for everybody's dinner.

On the way home, Joan asked, "How did you like Pat?"

"She was okay. Don acts like he's crazy about her, but I don't think she acts the same way. It may just be me. She's nice enough, I guess, but there's something about her I can't put my finger on. How did you like her?"

"I don't know. She's a little distant, but maybe it's because she doesn't know us."

"I'm glad we went. I need to spend more time with Don. Maybe I can help him some way."

For the next couple of weeks, Monty spent more time at the sock mill observing production, but mainly observing Don. Since Don was doing so well with his work ethic and attitude, Monty wanted to move him up a step or two, especially since he had been so hesitant to give him the job in the first place, but he wanted to be sure before he made any decisions. It was unusual for him to be at the sock plant so much, and it looked as if Don could sense something, so he was on his best behavior whenever Monty was there.

If Monty only knew some of the things going through Don's mind, he would step back and wait to see what was going to happen. Don was like the leopard: he couldn't change his spots, and in the meantime, he was getting ready to snow Monty and just about everybody else. He hadn't actually done anything yet, but being the charmer that he was, he came across as Shepherd Global's number one citizen.

One morning, before he went to his office, Monty went by the sock plant and told Don he wanted to talk to him. They went into the office and Monty said, "Big Brother, how do you like making socks?"

"You know, after all the years I've worked in the business, I think I've finally found my niche. I love working over here. Why?"

"Well, I've been watching you without you knowing it, and I've also been talking to Tommy. We both feel you've learned a lot in a short time and can handle some additional duties. Tommy needs some relief from the total responsibility of the *Fin* and *Staff* brands, so effective Monday, you will be put in charge of the Shepherd *Staff* sock line. Tommy Everett will still be general manager, and you will report to him, but you will be on a higher level than where you have been. How does that sound to you?"

"It sounds great. Thank you.

"I've got to get to the office. I just wanted to come by and tell you about your promotion. I know you'll do a good job, and if you need me for anything, call me."

"Thanks, Padna. I'll do a good job for you. Look, Pat and I are going to go grab a bite somewhere tonight. How about you and Joan going with us?"

"I wish we could, but I'm speaking at the Grace Christian Center tonight. Why don't you and Pat come to the service?"

Redemption?

"Thanks, Little Brother, but I think we'll pass. Maybe we can get together another time soon."

"Sure thing. I've gotta go. See ya."

On the way to his office, Monty was feeling good about what he just did. He thought, *Maybe Don just needed somebody to show some faith in him. He has done so many things wrong during his life, he may have just been crying out for attention. If he gets attention without having to do something wrong, it might make a big difference, so I'll pray that he will do well in his new job and build up his self-esteem. I'm still not convinced Pat is the one for him, but I guess that's none of my business.* When he got to his office, he called his Dad. "Hello, Dad. I've been thinking about some things, and I would like to get your advice on some of them. Could I come out after lunch and talk to you for a little while?.... Great. I'll see you around one or one thirty. Bye. Love you."

As soon as he hung up from David, he called Joan. "Hey, good-looking. What's up?"

"Nothing, really. I just finished running the sweeper, and now I'm getting ready to mop the kitchen. What's up with you?"

"Just trying to stay busy. Listen, I'm going over to Dad's to talk about some things after lunch, and I was wondering if you would like to have a good-looking, Mr. America type come eat lunch with you."

"Oh boy, I'd really love that. Who did you have in mind?"

"Well, I've exhausted all the names on my list, so I guess you'll have to be satisfied with me, Mr. Wonderful."

"Okay, Mr. Wonderful, I'll settle for you, but if you want a sandwich you'll have to stop at the store and get some bread."

"All right. I'll see you somewhere around noon."

Monty stopped at the M and J Supermarket and bought a loaf of bread and then went home to have a nice, leisurely lunch with his wife. When they finished, he kissed Joan and said, "I've got to go talk to Dad. I'll see you tonight. I love you."

He walked over to his parents' house and went in. Thil was nowhere to be seen, so he yelled, "Dad, are you home?"

"In here. Come in the den."

Monty went in and sat down next to David and asked how he felt. They made a little small talk, then David asked, "What is it you want to talk to me about?"

"Well Dad, I know that soon after you took over Shepherd, you

61

made it an international company. I understand that you hired Urey Steen, Mom's first husband, and between the two of you, you hit a major home run. Well, that's what I want to do. I've been thinking about all the places in the world where we're not doing business, and I want to see what it will take to go into some of those countries."

"Where are you wanting to go?"

"In the short term, I'd like to think about South America, especially Brazil and Argentina. Right now, Gerhard and his boys aren't going into Italy, and I think that would be a good market. We could set up an office there like the one in London.

"Then there's the Mid-east; of course, we're doing good business in Israel, but nowhere else in the region."

David interrupted, "Son, I think it's too risky to try to go into the other Middle-Eastern countries right now. The political situation is too volatile. I wouldn't try it. Urey was going to try Egypt, but things got so hot, he never followed through with it. Remember, he got blown up on a bus in Israel. I'd continue to work in Israel, but I'd stay out of the rest of the region."

"All right, I'll cross the Mid-east off the list. Now, where was I? Dad, did you ever think about going into Asia?"

"I thought about it, but never really pursued it."

"Well, you know there are a lot of people over there. You've got Japan and South Korea, which are both pretty much westernized, and that would seem to be a good market to me.

"Then there's the biggie: Australia."

David asked, "Why do you say it's the biggie? I think you've been misinformed. The whole country of Australia has less population than the state of California. Why don't you just concentrate on increasing volume there? It would be a whole lot cheaper."

"Dad, that's why I wanted to talk to you. You already know most of the things that I'm just trying to learn. Okay, I'll forget Australia. Finally, what do you think of South America? I think Brazil and Argentina would be especially good markets."

"I agree. They would be good. I had them on my agenda before my heart attack."

"Well, how should I go about finding people to run offices in those places?"

"The markets are good places to start. The New York Market is coming up pretty soon, isn't it?"

"Yes sir, in three weeks."

"Well, when you get there, ask around and look at the market directory. You'll probably be able to come up with some leads. Do the same thing at the Atlanta and Dallas shows, and I'll bet you'll be able to get more leads. That's what I did when I found Urey. I think you're smart to want to expand the business. Why did you decide to do this all of a sudden?"

"It wasn't all of a sudden. I've been thinking about it ever since you made me President. I've always heard that if you stop moving forward, you start moving backwards, and I sure don't want to do that.

"Dad, I've also been thinking about expanding the Shepherd *Staff* lines. The sock line has really taken off, and I want to increase it almost immediately. I know you wanted to get into outerwear, lingerie and other things, and I want to do that, too, so I'm going to start looking into some of them real soon."

"That's good, Son. Just be sure you've got the business to back everything up before you jump into anything. Are you going to include Don in any of your plans?"

"Yes sir. I gave him a promotion just this morning. He loves being in the sock plant, so I'll more than likely leave him there. Listen, I've got to get back. Thanks for your help. I knew I could depend on your wisdom to guide me. I love you, Dad. See ya later."

****

Smokey's Bar and Grill was located about a mile from the Shepherd Global campus, and every afternoon after work Don went there to have a drink. One day, when he was socializing with the regulars and talking about all the *Fin* and *Staff* socks they were making, he noticed a man he hadn't seen before sitting in a booth, by himself, next to the window. As his friends started leaving, the man got up and came over and introduced himself. "Hi, I'm J.D. Massey. I couldn't help but overhear part of your conversation about making *Fin* socks. Could I buy you a drink?"

"I'm Don Shepherd, and, yes ,you can buy me a drink."

"Why don't we sit in my booth where we can talk?"

"Okay, what's on your mind, Mr. Massey?"

"Call me J.D. I'm a wholesale distributor, and when I heard you say you made *Fin* socks, my ears perked up. Would I be able to buy some of them from you?"

"No, I'm afraid not. They won't let us sell any. Everything has to go to them, and they're pretty strict about it."

"Do you ever make an exception? I can use as many as you can make, and I can take them every week. And oh, yeah, I pay either cash or wire transfer, so there's no paper trail, and you get paid before you ship the goods. How good is that?"

"J.D., that sounds awfully tempting, but I don't see how I could do anything like that. What do you pay for 'em, anyway?"

"I've been paying eleven dollars a dozen for first quality."

"It sounds to me like you've been stealing them. You had better stick with whoever you've been buying them from."

"I know you said you couldn't sell me any, but if you could, what do you think you would have to get for them?"

"Fifteen dollars, and you would have to take all the Irregulars at twelve."

"That's too high, but since you can't sell them anyway, I guess it doesn't make any difference. You could have said twenty dollars since you can't sell them."

"I guess that's right; I could have."

"Don, I'm going to be in town 'til Friday. Do you come in here every day?"

"Yeah, I'm here most afternoons. Maybe I'll see you tomorrow. I've got to go. I'll see ya."

"Before you leave, let me mention one more thing. Let's just say that something happened that would enable you to come up with, say, three thousand dozen per week, and I paid you the fifteen dollars a dozen you mentioned. Can you figure in your head how much money that would be? That would be forty-five thousand dollars a week that you could make. Are you making that much now?"

"You know I'm not."

"Well, think it over. I'll be here again tomorrow if you want to talk about it. One more thing; there won't be any risk if you keep your mouth shut."

"I've got to go, J.D. I'll see ya."

"All right, I'll see you. Think about what we talked about."

On his way home, he couldn't think of anything but forty-five thousand dollars a week. *Man, if I could just figure out how to work that deal out, I would be sitting pretty. It's going to take some thought, but I may try to see what I can come up with. I've already been thinking about doing something like this, but now, this is for real. Man, that's a lot of money.*

Pat had started staying with Don, Monday through Thursday, and when he arrived home, he was still in deep thought. She met him at the door with a kiss, but his heart wasn't in it, and she sensed something. When she asked what, he just said he had some things on his mind. "Are you mad at me, Don?"

"Oh, no. I'm not mad at you. Some things have come up at work, and I've got to work them out, that's all."

"Whew! I thought you were upset with me about something."

He grabbed her and kissed her passionately and said, "Does this look like I'm upset with you? I'm sorry my mind was wandering. You've got my undivided attention now. Are we going out to eat or fix something here?"

"Why don't we go out?"

"Okay, it's a deal. Wanna fool around a little first and work up an appetite?"

"No. Let's wait 'til we get back. I didn't eat lunch today, and I'm hungry."

Is The Greystone all right?"

"Perfect."

Don couldn't put his finger on it, but when he and Pat were together, she was totally at ease and very relaxed, but when they went out somewhere, she acted nervous, like she was looking for someone. He had asked her about it, and she assured him she wasn't nervous, that it was just in his head. He told himself that maybe it was his overactive imagination, but he wasn't convinced of it.

They finished their dinner and went back to Don's apartment. Pat said she wanted to get out of her clothes, so she went into the bedroom and put on her gown and robe before coming back into the living room where Don was. They watched a couple of programs on TV and then started smooching. Pretty soon, things started to get out of hand, so they went into the bedroom and didn't come out 'til the next morning.

Don had to be at work before Pat, so he got up early the next morning and left Pat in bed. He shaved, showered, dressed, and had a cup of coffee, then woke Pat up. After giving her a goodbye kiss, he left for work. He could hardly wait until he got to the plant, so he could check out some things he had thought about overnight. He especially wanted to talk to the fellow who programmed the logos into the knitting machines. A thought had popped into his mind, and he wanted to find out how complicated it was to change a knitting machine from one logo to another.

Don was really slick. Some of the things he had done in his life bore that out, such as running numbers when he was still a teenager. The extortion deal he pulled on the illegal whiskey business was a masterpiece, and the fact that he came out alive was a miracle. He was a senior in high school when he pulled that, and before it ended, he and a friend had pocketed over thirty thousand dollars apiece. Then, there was the large embezzlement where he took nearly a half-million dollars from the company. If it weren't for Monty, he would be in jail, but that didn't seem to bother him. He apparently didn't have a conscience. That was attested to by the fact that he stole from his Dad's company, and his Dad was the only person he truly loved.

The opportunity to make thousands of dollars per week intrigued him, so he made up his mind to do the socks if he could figure out the details. The thing he had to figure out was how to do everything without letting anyone else know what he was doing.

At work that day, he asked many questions and took notes. That impressed Tommy because he naturally thought Don was just trying to learn more about making socks. When David and Monty bought the equipment for the sock mill, they bought state-of-the-art knitting machines. They were all high-speed machines with computers, and once the knowledge of how to work the computers was gained, the machine did the rest, as far as knitting different patterns was concerned. That was the information Don was trying to get by asking all the questions.

As the first shift ended, and the second shift started, he went into his office and sat down with his notes and began putting numbers into the calculator. Tommy had to leave early, and that gave Don the opportunity to try an experiment.

In order to knit in a logo on a sock-knitting machine, a five-and-a-quarter inch floppy disk had to be used. Don learned how to change the disks, so after Tommy left, he went to one of the machines knitting the *Fin* logo and removed the disk. He then took it to one of the *Staff* machines and exchanged that logo disk for the *Fin* logo disk. He didn't change the yarn because he only wanted to see if he could do it and how long would it take. If the logo came out all right, then he would change the yarn and time that. The only yarn that would need to be changed was the color yarn for the logo.

The very first time he tried it worked perfectly, so he changed the yarn and ran a few socks. Everything was perfect. He then went back to the beginning and timed himself from exchanging the floppy disks and changing the yarn and turning on the machine. It took right at ten minutes. After he had done that, he put the correct disks back into the two machines he had experimented with and put the machines back online. Then he went back to his office and began figuring again.

The new, high speed machines were designed to produce thirty dozen pairs of socks every eight-hour shift. Don reasoned that if he could work it out to change over twenty machines to run *Fin* six hours a day for five days, he could sell J.D. twenty-two hundred and fifty dozen pairs a week. Multiply that by fifteen dollars and it comes to almost thirty-four thousand dollars a week. It wasn't forty-five thousand, but thirty-four wasn't bad.

There were still many details to work out, but he thought he would go to Smokey's and show J.D. the socks he had made. They still had to agree on a price. "Those look good, Don. Are those some of what your plant is running now?"

"No, these are some I made today while experimenting with our new, computerized machines."

"Well, they look real good. Have you decided to do business with me?"

"I'm still thinking about it. I did some figuring today, and I found that I might can come up with twenty-two hundred and fifty dozen a week if you'll pay fifteen dollars. Otherwise, I'm not interested. What did the ones you've been paying eleven for include?"

"Knitting, bleaching, and boarding,"

"Not packaged?"

"No, we just took them in long fold."

"Would you prefer to get 'em that way?"

"No, I'd prefer to get them banded and packaged."

"That's what my fifteen dollar price includes, if you furnish the bands."

"Really? I can furnish the bands. When can you start?"

"Right now, I'm still not sure that I can start. There are a lot of details that will have to be worked out. You may or may not know that my Dad is CEO, and my brother is President of our company. I'm on pretty thin ice with my brother, and I can't afford to screw up. If I do, it will be really hard on me because of some past deeds. Look, I'm not going to have a drink today. I've got a lot to do, and I'll see you later."

"All right, but I'm going home this weekend, and I don't know when I'll be back. Do you think you might know something before I leave?"

"I don't know. I'll try. Where do you live?"

"Just outside of Little Rock."

"If I work on it tonight, maybe I can get some of the details worked out. If you're going to be here tomorrow, I'll stop by after work, and we'll see where we are."

"Sounds good. I'll see you tomorrow."

J.D. ordered another drink and Don left.

When he arrived home, Pat was already there. She had stopped by the Pizza Hut and picked up a large pepperoni and bacon pizza. Don had some beer in the fridge, and they had a great dinner.

While they were eating, Don said, "Honey, I hate to tell you, but I've got to go back to the plant for a little while. Do you mind? I'll try not to be gone long, but there's something I have to do, and it can't wait. Watch TV for a little while, or take a nap, and I'll be back, and we'll play, okay?"

"All right, if you have to."

Don sat at his desk and began making a list of everything it would take to do the socks he wanted to do. He knew how to exchange the floppy disks, so that was a major thing out of the way; however, he was going to have to get Shepherd's computer guy to make him twenty disks. That was risky because the guy had already made dozens of them, and he might ask someone why he needed to make more. Don would make up something to tell him, and since he was the son and brother of the two top echelon people in the company, he hoped the guy wouldn't take it any farther.

The next thing was boarding, packaging, and shipping, and a place to do all of them. He thought, *I can't do those things here. I'll have to rent a building somewhere and hire people to do them. Man,*

Redemption?

that's going to eat into my profits. I wonder where I can find a building, and if I can find one, where can I get a couple of boarding machines? Then, I've got to think of some way to get the socks from here to the building, and then how to find people to hire without word getting back here. This might just be too much to try. I sure don't want Monty to get wind of any of this, because he told me I would go to jail if I ever got out of line again, and I think he would do it. He's that much of a no-nonsense guy. I guess I'll just tell J.D. that I won't be able to furnish the socks.

He tried to figure every angle, but the building and hiring people were just too much of an obstacle to overcome. He got up, went to his car and headed home where Pat was waiting on him. Soon, they were having their nightly romp in the sack. Socks were the farthest thing from Don's mind.

The next day was Friday and Pat would be going to Knoxville, so Don didn't have to be in any hurry to get home. He went to Smokey's after work and told J.D. that he didn't think he was going to be able to work things out, and they had a couple drinks together. J.D. kept making suggestions, but none of them were anything Don could use to help solve his problem. Finally, he told J.D., "I'll keep trying to figure something out, and if I do, I'll call you. Do you have a card?"

"No, but let me give you my number. Do I have your number?"

They exchanged numbers, shook hands, and J.D. left. Don ordered another drink and sat there for a long time, still trying to come up with a plan.

Smokey's was a place where many mill workers went every afternoon after work to unwind, and those mill workers included several from local hosiery mills. The week after J.D. was there, Don met a couple of guys from one of the sock mills, and they struck up a conversation. During the conversation, one of the guys told the other, "I heard today that Ridgemont's going out of business."

"Really? What happened?"

"I'm not sure. I guess they just didn't have enough business."

"Man! That's a nice little mill, too. I know a guy that works there, and he told me they had just got some new machines."

Don asked, "Do they knit and finish?"

"Yeah, they do it all."

"Are they going bankrupt or just closing up?

69

"I think they're just closing."

Don asked, "Who owns Ridgemont, anyway? Is it a big place?"

"No, it's a small mill, but it's really nice. A fellow by the name of Eddy McGee owns it. He's a real nice guy."

Don found out where Ridgemont was located, and when he left Smokey's he rode by and saw the place. *This could solve my problem. I think I'll try to see Eddy McGee tomorrow.*

The next day he told Tommy he had to do some things and asked if it would be all right if he was gone for a couple hours. Tommy told him he could, so he went to Ridgemont Hosiery to see Eddy McGee. When he got there, he was confronted by a really cute, middle-aged receptionist. He looked her up and down and looked for a wedding ring, which he didn't see, before asking to see Eddy McGee. She buzzed Eddy and said, "There's a Mr. Don Shepherd here to see you."

"Send him back."

She smiled and Don winked, then he went back to Eddy's office. "Hi, Eddy, I'm Don Shepherd."

"Nice to see you, Don. What can I do for you today?"

"Well, I heard yesterday that you may be closing your mill. Is that right?"

"Yes, that's right. Why?"

"Are you familiar with Shepherd Apparel?"

"Of course. Everybody's familiar with Shepherd Apparel."

"Eddy, I don't know if you know it or not, but a few months ago, we signed a huge contract with All Conference Sports to make *Fin* apparel and socks."

"Yes, I heard about it."

"Well, it looks as if we're going to have to have some additional equipment, and when I heard that you have just taken delivery of some new machines, I thought we might could help each other out. Actually, I'm thinking about getting the equipment and sub-contracting some of the production myself. If your equipment is what I need, I might be able to buy it, and that way, I could get what I need and you could get rid of it. How many machines do you have?"

"We have thirty-five knitting machines; ten of them are new high speed Lonatis with computers that can knit in logos. The other twenty-five can be converted to knit logos if you buy kits to change them over. The toe-seamers are also fairly new, and there are three boarding machines that are in good shape."

"How about finishing? Are you set up to finish?"

"Oh, yes. There are dye tubs, dryers, and everything needed to finish whatever we knit."

Don's mind was turning about a hundred miles an hour. "Let me ask you this, Eddy. When you finish up and get ready to shut down, would you consider leasing your mill intact?"

"I don't know. I haven't thought about that."

"Let me ask you something else: are the new Lonatis financed or did you pay for them?"

"They're financed."

"I thought they would be. Tell you what, Eddy, think about it and if you are interested in leasing, give me a call. I don't need the older machines, but I do need the Lonatis and the finishing equipment. If your price it right, I'll take over the payments on the machines and lease the whole mill, including the building. By leasing to me, you can get the monkey off your back, have a nice little income, and I can get what I need without having to get in too deep."

"Okay, Don, I'll think about it. You make some interesting points, especially about the continuing income. I'll try to give you a call tomorrow. Where can I reach you?"

"Just call Shepherd Socks and ask for me. Here's my number. Listen, I'm gonna get outa here and let you get back to work. I'll look forward to hearing from you tomorrow. It was nice talking to you. See ya later."

Don left Eddy's office and on his way out, he stopped and talked to the receptionist for a few minutes. He learned that her name was Liz Patterson and she lived alone. Before he left, he was able to get her phone number, and he promised to call. She acted very receptive to his moves, and he felt that he had just found a honey to fill his weekends when Pat had to go back to Knoxville.

On his way back to the mill, he thought, *What a great day. Not only is it possible that I solved my problems about Fin, but I may have found a new squeeze, too. I must be living right.*

Don was whistling when he walked into the plant, and Tommy said, "It looks like you had a worthwhile trip."

"I did. Today's a good day, isn't it?"

He returned to the *Staff* area, and when he was satisfied they didn't need him for anything, he went into his office and began to do some figuring. He was so excited when he saw the numbers, he wanted to tell somebody, but there was nobody to tell.

If he could lease the Ridgemont mill, by working three shifts, seven days a week, he could get around six thousand dozen pairs of socks a week from the ten Lonati machines. If he bought kits and converted the other twenty-five machines, he could possibly get another forty-seven hundred dozen. That would be more than ten thousand dozen per week, and he didn't know if J.D. could buy that many. *Boy, if he could buy ten thousand dozen a week, that would be a hundred and fifty thousand bucks, but I don't see how he could buy that many. I think I'll call him and tell him what's going on and try to find out how many he will take, so I'll know how to talk to Eddy, in case he's willing to work with me.*

There was no answer when he called J.D., so he left word and hoped it wouldn't be long before he called him back.

CHAPTER EIGHT

Before Monty left his office Friday, Joan called and said, "Hi, Sweetums. I know you're busy, and I won't keep you, but I just had a thought, and I wanted to run it by you. You know, Julia Kanipe and I have become good friends ever since we went to Tel Aviv, and I was wondering what you would think about her going to New York with me. That way, I wouldn't have to be by myself all day, every day while you're working the show."

"I don't mind her going, Honey, but she will have to have her own room and pay for it. I don't want to share our room, just in case you might decide to get romantic one night or two or three. Do you think she would do that?"

"Will Bob not be there? Isn't he part of the crew flying you up there?"

"Yes, but he won't be staying. They'll fly us up Sunday and then come back home."

"Oh well, I'll call her, anyway, and see if she would like to go under those conditions."

"Okay. You work it out. I've got to go. I'm in the middle of some things right now, and I don't have time to talk. I'll see you when I get home. Love you. Bye."

When he got home, Joan had fixed his favorite meal: meatloaf, mashed potatoes, and green beans. After they finished eating and cleaning up, they went into the den and relaxed. Monty kicked off his shoes, leaned back in his recliner and said, "I'm tired. This has been a rough day. How was your day?"

"Fine. I called Julia back and told her what you said, and she said she would like to go to New York and pay for her own room. Then she asked, "What if we ask Amy to go? She and I can share a room and split expenses." I told her I would ask you and get back to her. What do you think?"

"Sweetheart, if they want to go, and you want them to go, it's all right with me."

"Thank you, Sugar. We'll buy out New York while you're working. I hope you don't mind."

"I don't mind, but I hope you don't have a problem carrying

everything while you're hitch-hiking home."

"Well, if it's gonna be like that, I guess I'll just buy a little."

"That sounds better."

The New York show was to begin Monday, so Monty and the others flew up on Sunday afternoon. In addition to Monty and Charles Crawford, the salesmen from the southeastern territories came to Chattanooga and caught a ride on the Shepherd plane.

When Monty and Joan arrived at the airport, not only was the crew and the salesmen there, but Joan's guest, Julia had grown to include Amy Jacobs and Kathy James. "Monty, I didn't know Kathy was coming. Amy must have called her. Is it all right?"

"Yeah, it's okay."

Everyone boarded, and the 707 lifted off at one o'clock for the one hour and forty-six minute flight to New York. They checked in their hotel around four, and Monty and Charlie Crawford began working immediately. Charlie had set up a dinner/sales meeting at the hotel for six-thirty. Both he and Monty were excited about the new line and the introduction of the socks, and they hoped everyone on the sales force would be excited as well.

****

Traffic was brisk on opening day of the market, and all the salesmen were writing nice orders. Monty was anxious to see if he could find some people to talk to about setting up offices in other parts of the world, especially South America. He sat down with the Market Directory and circled some showrooms that he wanted to visit. He found a couple in South America and one in Seoul, South Korea.

He left the Shepherd showroom and went to find the South American vendors. When he got to the first one, he noticed that they were fairly small, and he didn't think they would be able to take on anything like the Shepherd line.

The next showroom was more like it. There was a large, attractive sign that said simply *LARA*. The room was large, well-appointed, and the apparel on display was very nice. Monty told the receptionist who he was and what he wanted, and she directed him to a man named Davi Santos, owner of the company. On his way back to see the man, he thought, *I hope this guy speaks English.*

"Hi, Mr. Santos, my name is Monty Shepherd. May I talk to you for a couple minutes?"

In perfect English, he answered, "Of course. Are you by chance part of Shepherd Global Apparel?"

"Yes, I happen to be the President. Shepherd Global is my family's business."

"I'm glad to meet you, Mr. Shepherd. I've long admired your company, and I've thought from time to time about contacting you to see if there might be some way we could work together."

"That's amazing, Davi. Is it all right if I call you Davi?"

"Yes, of course, Mr. Shepherd."

"Please, call me Monty. Davi, the reason I came here this morning was to talk to you and see if you might have an interest in representing our company in Brazil and other places where you go. Do you go outside Brazil?"

"Oh, yes. Come, let me show you a map."

He led Monty to a large wall map of South America filled with push pins. "Brasilia, the city with the star next to it, is the capital of Brazil and where our office is located. Now, look at the entire map of South America. If you draw a mental line around northern Brazil from east to west until you come to the boundary of Peru on the west, then draw your mental line across the northern boundary of Peru; everything south of that line is our territory; however, I'm seriously contemplating moving out of Peru and Bolivia because of the drug situation. We are still in Argentina, but the economy over there is so bad we're unable to do very much business. We are trying to decide whether or not to continue trying."

"Wow! You cover a big area."

"Yes, we do. The areas we cover have a total population of around 250,000,000 people with more than half that in Brazil. If we discontinue doing business in Bolivia and Peru, it will eliminate around 31,000,000 people, but if you get killed while you're there, 31,000,000 people aren't going to help you."

"I see what you mean. Are the push pins where you have customers?"

"Yes, the cities are. In many of the cities, we have multiple accounts."

"Davi, looking at your showroom, it looks as if you might be able to add Shepherd Apparel to what you have without having any conflicts. This would give you and your sales people a complete, well-rounded arsenal of goods. We have just recently added a line of *Staff* logo socks to our repertoire, and sales have exploded with them. Do you sell socks?"

"No, but I've been thinking about it."

"Do you think you might have an interest in Shepherd Apparel?"

"Yes. I most certainly would."

"Well, if you have time during the show, why don't you come up to our showroom and let my Sales Manager and I show you our line?"

"I will do that. Would four o'clock this afternoon be all right?"

"Yes, that would be fine. I'll see you then."

On the way back up to the Shepherd showroom, Monty thought, *Boy, if this outfit is any good, we'll hit a home run if they come with us. They cover durn near as many people as there are in the United States. I hope we can produce enough to cover what they sell. Dad will have a fit if I ask him to build another plant, after we have just built two new ones, but we'll cross that bridge when we come to it.*

After he reached his showroom, he talked to Charlie Crawford about the visit he had with Davi Santos and asked Charlie if he knew any people that he could ask about the *LARA* sales group. Fortunately, he did, and he picked up the phone and called someone he knew.

Charlie's friend gave Davi and his company a glowing recommendation. The friend gave Charlie another name to call, and when Charlie called him, he received an identical report. This told Monty it would be a no-brainer to hook up with them. While Monty and Charlie were talking, Monty suddenly said, "Uh-Oh, I've got to try to get in touch with Joan. I promised her I would take her and her three friends out to dinner tonight, and if Davi Santos doesn't come until four o'clock, it will probably be too late when he leaves to take them out."

Charlie said, "Maybe he won't be here too long tonight. Maybe he'll want to come back tomorrow."

"I hope you're right." Smiling, he asked, "How would you like to have a date with four pretty married women tonight?"

"No thank you, but I wish you luck."

Monty called his and Joan's room, but didn't get an answer.

At four o'clock on the dot, Davi Santos walked into the Shepherd showroom. Monty saw him come in and met him at the receptionist's desk. "Come in, Davi. Welcome to Shepherd Global Apparel Group's market showroom."

Davi walked around and looked at all the styles being displayed. "Very impressive, Monty."

"Thank you."

"And these are the socks you were talking about?"

"Yes. They're giving us quite a bit of extra business, and they're very easy to sell."

"Monty, I don't mean to rush, but I've seen all I need to see to know that I want to become affiliated with your company. Can we get together sometime tomorrow? I promised my wife that I would eat dinner with her tonight. She would only come to New York with me if I promised to be with her every evening after work, so I have to go."

"We have something in common, Davi. I promised my wife I would have dinner with her, also. Yeah, we can get together tomorrow. I'm anxious to talk to you, because I believe we can help each other. Would nine in the morning work for you?"

"Yes, it would. I'll be here then. Have a nice evening."

"You, too." Davi left and Monty was very excited about the prospects of having Davi join Shepherd.

It was five o'clock and Monty was on the way to the hotel to keep his promise to Joan. This might result in some bedtime pleasure if he played his cards right.

****

Before time for Davi to arrive, Monty wanted to speak to his Dad about what he was trying to do, so he called him. He explained everything to David, and David concurred with everything Monty told him, but before they hung up, David said, "Son, do what you have to do, but in the end, be sure that Shepherd is in control. The various offices should be Shepherd offices like in Munich, London, and Tel Aviv."

"Okay, Dad. I'll be sure to do that. I've got to get to work. You have a great day. I love you, Dad, and tell Mom I love her, too. See you Friday night."

Davi was right on time. At nine o'clock he arrived with a fellow named Lucas Silva, who he introduced as his Sales Manager. Monty called Charlie to come to where they were, and he introduced him to Lucas. He told Charlie to show Lucas the line, while he and Davi went into a small office off the showroom floor.

After a three hour question and answer session, they decided to go to lunch, and then after lunch, another shorter question and answer session. They finished up around two o'clock and had come to an agreement. Shepherd Global would now have offices in Brasilia and all the other countries where *LARA* was located. The arrangement was almost exactly like the original agreement between Shepherd and Urey Steen and his men. Monty only hoped it would be as lucrative.

Before he left, Davi asked, "Monty, would you and your wife do me the honor of having dinner with my wife and me tonight?"

"We would love to." They made arrangements for that evening, and Davi left. *That Davi is really something. I didn't dream he and his wife would pick us up in a cab and take us to wherever we're going to eat. That's what I call "Class". It looks like I picked the right guy to do business with.*

At seven o'clock a Yellow Cab pulled up in front of the hotel, and Monty and Joan got in. "Good evening. Monty. This is my wife, Lara."

Monty answered, "It's very nice to meet you, Lara. I'd like for you to meet my wife Joan. Joan, this is Lara and Davi Santos. If all goes well, Davi's company, *LARA*, and Shepherd Global will be doing a tremendous amount of business together."

As most New York cab rides go, everyone's heart was up in their throat until finally they pulled over in front of a very nice restaurant. They went in and had an excellent dinner and conversation. Joan and Lara became instant friends as did Davi and Monty. Monty told Davi that the first thing he should do was to come to Chattanooga and tour the Shepherd campus and see how they do things. He suggested they ride with them on Shepherd's 707 when they left Friday afternoon, if they didn't mind spending an idle weekend. Davi jumped at the chance, and Lara and Joan were excited to have a chance to spend time together.

The evening drew to a close, and Davi paid with his credit card. They hailed a cab and went back to the hotel, where they said goodnight.

"Monty, I liked them. Lara is really nice. It was sweet of Davi to name his company after her."

"My company is named after you: Shepherd."

"It is, isn't it? I never thought of that. You're so smooth."

"I know. You haven't seen anything yet."

"You're so full of surprises; I can't wait to see what's next."

"Wait 'til we get upstairs, and I'll show you."

"Uh-oh. Something tells me I'm in for it."

"You've got that right."

Excellent was the best way to describe the New York show. Every salesman wrote better business than they did at the last show, and the new socks were a hit. Charlie had kept up with the dollar figures, and he told Monty they were quite a bit ahead of the last show, and that made Monty happy. Monty was also happy about the agreement he had made with *LARA,* and it looked as though they were going to be really busy for the foreseeable future. Since he had successfully made the deal with *LARA*, the only other place he wanted to go for the next year or so was Canada, and he already had some ideas about that.

Monty had told Davi which airport they would be leaving from and exactly where to go to find the Shepherd plane. They planned to take off at seven p.m. Monty and the four women, along with Charlie Crawford and the salesmen, got there early, and the crew and their wives had a nice reunion. A little before seven, Davi and Lara arrived, and after the introductions, they all boarded the sleek 707 for the nearly two-hour flight to Chattanooga.

Monty had called Chuck and told him to have enough food catered for fifteen people for dinner. After they were beginning to level off and not in such a steep climb, Joan and Julia went to the galley and began getting food out. When Amy saw what they were doing, she, too, went to help. Soon, everything was ready, and they all had a nice dinner. Charlie remarked to the three women that they might have a future as flight attendants if they ever fell on hard times. They each smiled and said, "Thank you, kind sir."

After they landed at Lovell Field, they all went their separate ways except for Davi and Lara. They got into Monty's car, and he took them to the Holiday Inn, where he had had Connie make reservations. Monty told Davi he would pick him up at nine the next morning and take him to see some of the Shepherd campus. Joan and the flight crew wives had discussed getting together to take Lara to the Brainerd Tearoom for lunch, so everything was set for Saturday.

Before he left the plane, Monty told Chuck to listen for his call because they would be going to Brazil within the next week or two.

CHAPTER NINE

It wasn't long before the phone rang. "Hello, this is Don."

"Don. J.D. here. Just returning your call."

"Hi, J.D.. I think I may have things worked out, but before I can go any farther, I need to know how many dozens you can take each week. I might can come up with ten thousand. Can you use that many?"

"Don, I can take up to ten thousand. I'm currently buying three thousand from someone else, and I'm talking to another person about two. If you want to sell me five a week, I can use them."

"J.D., if I can furnish all ten thousand dozen, why not buy them from me?"

"It's very simple, Don. I don't want to put all my eggs in one basket. If I bought ten thousand from you, and you got caught, I'd be out of business. This way, if any of you run afoul of the law, I'll still have at least a part of what I need."

"Do you think we might get caught?"

"I hope not. I'm just saying 'what if?'"

"Well, how many do you want me to sell you?"

"I'll take five thousand dozen a week, mixed between crews, quarter socks, and footies. I'll pay the same for all of them."

"We talked before about you furnishing the bands; are you going to do that or do you want to get the socks in long fold?"

"I'll furnish the bands, and you package them. When can you start?"

"First, let me be sure you're going to pay me fifteen dollars a dozen."

"Yeah, I'll pay fifteen."

"I've got to talk to someone tomorrow, and if we can get together on the price of some things, I might be able to start in about a week. I'll have to call you. Will that be all right?"

"One other thing, Don. If we start this, I'll send a truck to pick up the socks once a week. I'll call you the day before to get the number of dozens, and will wire transfer the payment to your bank that day. When the truck comes the next day, you will give them exactly that amount, no more and no less. Is that understood?"

"Loud and clear. I'll call you tomorrow and let you know if I have everything worked out."

"Okay. I hope you can get it done. I'll talk to you later."

When Don hung up the phone, he was floating on cloud nine. He wanted to talk to somebody, but couldn't tell anyone what he was doing. Finally, he picked up the phone and called Ridgemont's number.

"Good afternoon, Ridgemont Hosiery."

"Liz, this is Don Shepherd. How're you doing, Pretty Lady?"

"Fine, thank you. Mr. McGee is not here, Don."

"That's fine. I don't want to talk to him. I want to talk to you."

"Well, all right. What can I do for you?"

"This has been such a fantastic day, I just wanted to share it with someone. I thought about the pretty lady I met earlier today, and thought I would just call and tell her what a great day it is. I also wanted to ask you if you will have dinner with me Friday night?"

"Wow! You come on strong, don't you? I'm flattered that you would want to share your good day with me, and yes, I'll have dinner with you Friday."

"Great. I might be back over there one day this week, and I'll talk to you then, but if I'm not, I'll call you and set up the time and stuff. I hope I'll be back because I'd like to see you again. Eddy and I may do some business together, and he's to call me tomorrow, so I'll know then if I'll be back this week."

"You'll probably be here. Eddy told me that you might lease the mill."

"Well, darlin', I'll let you go. I just wanted to talk to you for a minute. Maybe I'll see you tomorrow."

"Okay, Don. I'll see you."

The business day soon ended, and Don went home, still flying high. Pat would be there in a little bit, and they would go somewhere to eat. Don wanted to tell her about how close he was to consummating the deal with Eddy McGee at Ridgemont Hosiery, but he wasn't sure he should. Even though they were sleeping together nearly every night, what did he really know about her? Nothing, except she was good-looking and great in bed. She always managed to avert any conversation about her family or herself to something completely different. Still, he thought he was falling in love with her.

Don was in such a good mood at dinner, he couldn't help but tell

Pat when she asked why he was acting so giddy. "Why is this deal so different from what you're already doing?"

"Because this is mine and mine only. I stand a chance to make a ton of money, and if all goes well, I may be able to break away from my family's business and be on my own. Besides that, I'll be able to take you to some of those exotic places we see in pictures. How would you like to go to Hawaii or somewhere like that?"

"I don't know. We'll see."

"You sure don't act very interested in going to Paradise. Wouldn't you like to go?"

"I'm interested, but we'll have to see, if that time ever comes. I can't say now whether I could go or not."

"Okay. We'll cross that bridge later. Ready to go home?"

"I'm ready. I want to get out of these clothes and into something more comfortable."

****

Mid-morning the next day, Eddy McGee called. "Good morning, Don. Listen, I've thought a lot about our conversation yesterday, and I would like to talk to you some more. Could you come over here sometime today?"

"Yeah, I can. What time's good for you?"

"Anytime that suits you. This afternoon would probably be better."

"How about right after lunch? Say, one thirty?"

"That will be fine. I'll see you then."

Don thought Liz probably went to lunch at noon and would be back at one, so he arrived at Ridgemont at one o'clock. His deduction was right because she was just getting back when he got there, and that gave him thirty minutes to spend with her before his appointment with Eddy. The more he was around her, the more he liked her; in fact, he thought about calling Pat to tell her he was going to work late, but he decided against that, since she would be staying at his place.

He asked, "Are we still on for tomorrow night?"

"Yes, unless you want to back out."

"Not on your life. I can't wait."

"I'm looking forward to it, too. Where are we going?"

"I've heard there's a good show at the Tivoli. I thought we might go to the Town and Country and have an early dinner and then go to the Tivoli. That is, unless you would rather do something else."

"No, that sounds just fine. I've heard that show is good, too."

"You'll have to tell me where you live."

When she gave him her address, it turned out to be pretty close to where he lived.

"Are you serious? We're almost neighbors." He told her where he lived, and they talked a little about it. While they were talking, Eddy came in, and Don went with him to his office.

"Liz seems to be a nice lady."

"She is. She's been with me for about four years. Her husband died two years ago, and she had a hard time getting over him for the first year, but she's doing fine now."

"Does she have someone in her life now?"

"Not that I know of, but I can tell she's ready for a man. I hope she'll be able to find someone soon."

Don thought, *BINGO!!*

"You said you've thought about our conversation. Have you decided anything?"

"Maybe, but I need more answers first."

"Well, maybe I can answer some of them by asking you some things."

The two asked and answered questions for the better part of two hours, and finally, they came to an agreement. Don would lease Ridgemont as a going business, but would discontinue making socks for their existing customers. He would have the ten Lonatis set up to knit the *Fin* logo socks, and for the time being let the other twenty-five machines sit idle. As far as everyone was concerned, the *Fin* socks were being made for Shepherd Socks, because everybody knew that Shepherd had the contract with All Conference Sports.

Some employees would be retained, but unfortunately some would be laid off. What to do with Liz was now a problem, too. Don wanted her around, but logically, operating ten knitting machines was not enough to warrant having a full-time receptionist. He would need someone to keep track of production, buy yarn and other supplies, do payroll, and a host of other things. Maybe, if she could learn how to do those things, he could keep her. He would ask Eddy if he would stay on long enough to teach her those things.

It was getting late and nearly time for Monty to leave work, and Don wanted to see him before he left, so he left Ridgemont and rushed to the Shepherd office. He parked and literally ran to the front door. "Hi, Connie. Has Monty left yet? If he's still here, I need to see him."

"He's still here. Go on back. I'm sure he'll be glad to see you."

"Hey, Little Brother. What's up?"

"Whatta ya say, Don? What's up with you?"

"I want to ask you something. You know I've been working real hard ever since you put me at Shepherd Socks, and I haven't had any time off. Since I didn't take a vacation, will it be all right if I take off next week? Everything is running smoothly, and I'll talk to Tommy about it tomorrow; I just wanted your okay before I talk to him."

"It's all right with me if it's all right with Tommy. What are you going to do next week?"

"I've got several things I want to do, but mainly, I just need some time off. I may ask Pat if she would like to go somewhere,"

The next day he talked to Tommy, and Tommy said he thought it would be all right for him to take next week off, especially after Don told him Monty said it was all right.

He finished out the day and went home to shower and get ready for his date with Liz. He even shaved and put on a generous dose of Old Spice. Everybody, especially women, liked to smell Old Spice. He was satisfied that he looked good, so he left to pick up Liz, and when she came to the door, WOW!! She looked delicious.

Liz was fifty years old, but looked as if she was thirty-eight or forty. She was tall, maybe five-eight or five-nine, and had a great figure. Her hair was frosted and fairly short. It complimented her beautiful brown eyes and very white, even teeth. She had a C or possibly a D-cup chest and her legs were amazing. It was easy to see that that lady had taken good care of herself. Don couldn't wait to get her out in public and watch the heads turn. She was that nice-looking.

They had a lovely dinner, and the show at the Tivoli met all their expectations. Afterwards, Liz invited Don to her place for a glass of wine. While Don poured the wine, Liz turned on some very easy-listening music, and they sat back, thoroughly enjoying each other. At one point, an especially romantic song came on, and Don stood up, took Liz by the hand, and they danced very closely. When the song ended, and before the next one started, they just stood there with their arms around each other, looking into each other's eyes. Just as the next song began, Don pulled her closer and kissed her. She kissed him back, and he could tell that Eddy was right; she was ready for a man. They kissed a couple more times, then, Liz broke away from him and sat down in a chair. Don followed and sat on the end of the sofa. He asked, "Want another glass of wine?"

"No, thank you. I've had enough. The two glasses I've already had have gone to my head, and I think I've had enough."

Smoothly and tactfully, she let Don know it was time for him to go home. "Don, I've really enjoyed this evening. I've had a wonderful time."

"I have, too. Can we do this again?"

"Yes, we can."

"How about tomorrow night?"

"If you want to. Why don't you come here and I'll cook?"

"That sounds great. What time?"

"How about seven-thirty?"

"Seven-thirty it is. It's going to be hard for me to wait that long to see you again, but I guess I'll have to, won't I?"

"I'm afraid so."

"Okay. I'm gonna take off now. Can I have a goodnight kiss?"

"You sure can," She came over to him, and they tenderly kissed goodnight.

"Good night Liz, I can't wait 'til tomorrow night. See ya."

After he left, for the rest of the night his mind was on Liz. He wished he could turn the clock up twenty-four hours.

He slept 'til eight o'clock Saturday morning and woke up with Liz on his mind. *I think I'll call her and see if she would like to have lunch.*

He dialed her number, and when she answered, her melodic voice sounded like an angel's. "Good morning."

"Good morning, yourself. Did you sleep well?"

"Like a log. How about you?"

"I didn't sleep too well. Somebody named Liz was on my mind all night. I guess if you have to stay awake, that's a good way to do it. What's on your agenda today? I thought we might have lunch."

"I'm sorry, Don, but not today. I have to go to the grocery store this morning, and I promised a friend of mine that I would go shopping with her this afternoon. I wish I could, but we're still on for tonight, aren't we?"

"You bet we are. I can't wait. Is six thirty too early?"

"I'm not sure what time I'll get home. Do you mind if we wait 'til seven thirty? That's the time we said last night."

"That'll be all right; I'm just so anxious to see you. I thought maybe I could move it up an hour. I'll see you then. Oh, what are we having, so I'll know what kind of wine to bring?"

"Italian. Is that all right?"

"My favorite. I'll pick up a bottle of Chianti."

"Okay. I'll see you at seven thirty."

When Don hung up, he could tell Liz wasn't as bowled over with him as he was with her. He would have to work on that.

All day, the only thing he could think about was going to dinner at Liz's. He went to the liquor store and bought a bottle of the best Chianti they had. He started to buy a magnum, but since she cut herself off after two glasses the night before, he decided against it. Chianti sometimes packed a punch, and he was hoping that would happen tonight.

Eddy McGee had given Don a key to the Ridgemont mill, so while he was out, he decided to go by and spend some time alone in the mill visualizing how things would be once he took over. One thing he was going to do, starting Monday, was to switch all of Eddy's knitting on the Lonatis to the other machines, and start setting up the Lonatis to knit *Fin*. He would like to start shipping in two weeks. He remembered he had to call J.D. and make sure the bands would be there in time. If he was going to start shipping in two weeks, the bands would need to be there next week.

When he left Ridgemont, he ran by the Krystal and picked up some hamburgers to take home. He only got four because he didn't want to spoil his dinner, and he thoroughly enjoyed the little burgers. After lunch he turned on the TV and took turns napping and watching a ball game until it was time to start getting ready to go to Liz's.

He made sure not to get to Liz's before seven-thirty because that seemed important to her, and if he had any chance at all of getting lucky, he didn't want to do anything that would upset her. He rang the bell, and when she opened the door, she looked like someone that had just stepped out of a fashion magazine.

"Hi Don. Come in. Dinner's almost ready. Would you like to have a glass of wine while we wait on it?"

"Yes, I would. I brought a bottle to have with our meal, or would you rather have some other and wait on this?"

"There's still some left over from last night. Why don't we finish it before we open the new bottle?"

"Sounds good to me."

Liz got the bottle and glasses, and Don poured. When he had finished pouring both glasses, he raised his glass and said, "Cheers."

They both took a sip and began a conversation while Liz fixed the salad and did other things to get dinner ready.

As soon as Don finished his wine, Liz said dinner was ready. She poured out her remaining wine and held out her glass for Don to fill with the Chianti. He pulled her chair out for her, and they sat down at a beautifully fixed table to a scrumptious looking casserole of baked lasagna.

"Hand me your plate, and I'll give you some lasagna. This bowl is hot."

He did as he was instructed, and the steaming dish looked delicious. When he took the first bite, he thought, *Man, this gal can cook.*

"This is delicious, Liz. I'm certain we couldn't have found anything this good at a restaurant. Thank you for having me over."

"Thank you. You sure know how to flatter a girl, don't you? I'm glad to have you over. I hate to eat by myself, and you probably do, too, so this is good for both of us."

"I like the way you think. I'm glad I found you. Did you know that?"

"Now that you've found me, what are you going to do with me? Are you going to fire me?"

"Fire you? Of course not. Why would you ask such a question?"

"Because I have enough sense to know there's not going to be enough business to need a full-time receptionist after you take over."

"You're right, but there are other things you can do that will be more important to the company than being a receptionist, and I've already thought about that. You're on my 'to do' list Monday, and I hope you'll be agreeable and excited about what I have planned for you, but let's not spoil a very special evening talking about work. Rest assured, your job is safe."

That brief discussion effectively put a damper on an otherwise perfect evening, and Don had to act quickly to revert the mood back to where it was. They finished eating, and instead of sitting at the table talking, Liz got up and began taking dishes and things to the kitchen. She was standing at the sink when Don walked up behind her and put his arms around her. "Is there anything I can say to make you feel better?"

"I'm all right. I just got to thinking about that, and it bothers me. I've had my job for over four years, and I love it, and doing something else scares me."

"Well, don't worry about it. I'm going to take good care of you."

After the kitchen was clean, the couple went into the other room where Liz turned on some good music. They filled their glasses and sat next to each other on the sofa, and after a couple minutes, Don transferred the glass to his left hand and with his right hand, he took Liz's hand in his. They intertwined their fingers and sat silently, listening to the music. Soon, an irresistible song began to play, and Don asked, "Want to dance?"

They stood and with their arms around each other, they began to sway with the music. Their feet were hardly moving; they just swayed, keeping time with the beat. Don could feel Liz relaxing a little, and he gave her a kiss while they were dancing. During the next tune, they kissed again, and then it was almost non-stop kissing. Don went to the sofa and pulled Liz down on top of him, and they continued to kiss. Liz was rubbing her body against his for all it was worth, and he reciprocated.

Just as Don was about ready to pick her up and take her to the bedroom, she suddenly pulled away from him and stood up. "We can't do this."

Startled, Don asked, "Why? I know you want to."

"Because I'm just not ready. This is only our second time to be together, and I hardly even know you. I haven't been with a man since my husband died, and I'm not going to jump into bed with just anybody."

"Okay, okay. I won't press you. Maybe another time."

"Maybe. I'm sorry Don, but right now I can't go to bed with you. If we continue seeing each other, one day I may be ready, but not now. Don't be mad."

"I'm not mad. Just frustrated."

As they were sitting there, cooling off, Don thought to himself, *There's really a big difference between Liz and Pat. I got Pat in bed the first time I saw her, but here I've been with Liz twice, and I'm not even close. This is becoming a challenge, and I'm going to win, no matter how long it takes.*

He asked, "Wanna another glass of Chianti?"

"No, thank you. I've had enough for tonight."

"Look, I think I've upset you enough for one night. I guess I'll take off and see you Monday."

"You don't have to leave. I'm not upset."

"Yes you are. You have things to think about, and I'll let you get to it, so I'll leave you to your thoughts." He lifted her chin and gave her a brief kiss on the lips. "I enjoyed the lasagna, and I really enjoyed the company. I'll see you Monday. Sleep tight."

"Good night, Don. I'm sorry. I hope you're not mad."

"Good night."

CHAPTER TEN

Sunday was a day of rest for the most part. Joan and Monty went to Sunday school and Church, and after they got home, they fixed a sandwich and just laid around and napped most of the afternoon. Joan called Lara at the Holiday Inn, and she and Davi were doing the same thing. She told Joan they were just enjoying the day.

Monty picked Davi up at the hotel Monday morning to begin his Shepherd education. They started out by having coffee in the break room, and then Monty let him sit in on the regular Monday staff meeting. Most of the people at the meeting would be having contact with Davi after *LARA* became an affiliate of Shepherd Global, so it was good that he could meet all of them at one time. Monty especially wanted him to meet Tom Ratcliff and Chip Lowe, since they would be the main people to deal with him other than himself.

Monty had shown him the campus Saturday, but there weren't many people working, and he wanted Davi to see what it looked like when operating at full throttle. Davi was impressed.

After lunch they went to the sales office and saw all the styles in the whole Shepherd line. There were individual pieces, coordinates, groups, and more than anyone could grasp in a day or even two days, but Davi had to learn as much as he could before he left. When he got back to Brasilia, he would have to have all his salesmen in to go over the line, and he would need to know what he was talking about. He and Monty spent all Monday afternoon and the entire day on Tuesday going over all the stuff.

Davi was a quick study when it came to apparel, and both Charlie and Monty felt he was ready to start selling when he got home. It would have been good if he could have stayed a few more days, but he had to leave Wednesday in order to get home in time for a very important meeting on Thursday.

Monty told Charlie to have someone put together a set of samples for every salesman plus two sets for the Brasilia office, and send them out ASAP. While they were winding down their time together, Monty said, "Davi, I just had an idea. I don't know why I didn't think of it before. Why don't I come to your place and meet with your sales people and introduce them to Shepherd. This is the way it should be done, anyway."

"That's a great idea, Monty. I would really like for you to come down. When can you come?"

"How long will it take to get all your people to Brasilia?"

"I'll have my secretary send faxes to everyone Thursday, and we can probably get everyone together by Thursday or Friday of next week."

"How do they feel about working on Saturday?"

"Monty, all my guys are true professionals, and if they need to work on Saturday, they will do it."

"This is what I'm thinking, Davi. If I fly down next Wednesday, and we can start meeting Thursday, we would have Thursday and Friday, and if we need more time, we could go into Saturday. As you can see, the Shepherd line is large and can't be learned in a day. What do you think?"

"I think you have a very good idea. Let's plan on that. I'll tell my people to be in Brasilia on Wednesday, and we'll all meet on Thursday."

Joan had assumed responsibility for entertaining Lara, and they were becoming good friends. The four of them went to dinner together Tuesday night, and Davi said something about Monty coming to Brasilia next week. Lara said, "That's wonderful. Joan, why don't you come with him?"

"I would love to, but you'll have to ask the boss."

Lara said, "Well, boss, what about it?"

Monty and Davi smiled at each other, then Monty kind of shrugged his shoulders and said, "I seem to be outnumbered. What can I say? Of course you can go, Sugar."

Lara said, "That's good. We'll have a wonderful time, Joan."

Monty said, "Davi, I think this will work out really well. You've already met Shepherd.

Now we'll refine your knowledge, and you can pass it on to your people. The trip should be a very profitable one, don't you agree?"

"I definitely do. I'm happy you're coming."

Monty told Davi, "The night is still young and there's someone I would like for you to meet. Davi, my Father, David, is the CEO of our company and the person who really put Shepherd Global Apparel on the map. He's my closest advisor, and I would like for him to meet you. Would you mind if we went by to see him for just a couple minutes?"

Redemption?

"It would be my pleasure, Monty. I have heard of this man. His reputation is known throughout the apparel industry, and it would be my honor to meet him."

"Well, if y'all are ready, let's go. I've got the check, Davi."

Monty borrowed the phone at the restaurant and called his parents' house to make sure David was still up and agreeable to their coming by. He was, so they got into Monty's car and went to see him.

When they got there, Thil came to the door, and Monty introduced her to Lara and Davi. She led them into the den, where David was. He heard them come in and was standing before they came into the room. "Dad, I'd like for you to meet Davi Santos and his wife, Lara. Davi, Lara, this is my Dad, David Shepherd."

Davi said, "Mr. Shepherd, I'm truly honored to meet you. Your name is revered in our industry."

"I'm glad to meet you, too, Davi." Smiling, he said, "I like your name."

Monty interjected, "Dad, Davi owns the *LARA* Company, and they're located in Brazil. They're the one I talked to you about. Davi and I have agreed to start working together, and I'm going down to his place next week to introduce our company and our line to his sales people. We have come to an agreement almost identical to the one between you and Urey Steen, and I feel confident that it will be just as profitable for both companies."

"I believe it will be. When I brought Urey in, Shepherd was just a fairly small company, but thanks to Urey and his group and their aggressive style of doing business, we became a large international organization. We are now a fairly complete company that knows what it's doing, and it should be much easier to be successful in South America. Davi, I'm very proud of my son, and I know he will steer you in the right direction."

"I'm sure he will, sir."

"Dad, we're not going to stay. I just wanted you to meet Davi and Lara. They have an early flight in the morning, and I've got to get them back to the hotel, so they can pack and get some rest."

David said, "Folks, it was a pleasure meeting you. I wish you well in your association with our company, and if all goes well, maybe I can come down to work with you sometime."

"That would be a highlight in my career, Mr. Shepherd. I will

93

look forward to that."

"Okay. Take care. I hope to see you again. Good night, Son. Joan, honey, I'll see you."

They all said good night, and Monty took them to the Holiday Inn.

Davi and Lara's flight was scheduled to leave Lovell Field early the next morning, so Monty let them take the hotel limo to the airport rather than him having to get up and out so early. They said their goodbyes the night before.

****

On Wednesday, Joan had an appointment with her gynecologist, Doctor Robert Miller, and after carefully examining her, he told her the results of his examination. "Mrs. Shepherd, I'm happy to tell you that you're going to be a mommy." After answering some questions asked by the doctor, it was determined that she was a little more than two months pregnant. She was thrilled and couldn't wait to tell Monty. When she left Dr. Miller's office, she didn't go home. Instead, she raced to Shepherd Apparel, and tried to act calm when she told Connie she wanted to see Monty. As luck would have it, Monty was on a conference call, and Connie said he might be on the phone for quite a while.

Finally, after about twenty minutes, Connie told Joan she could go into Monty's office. Still trying to act calm and cool when Monty asked her what she was doing there, she said, "Oh, nothing. I just happened to be in the neighborhood, and thought I would stop in and see what you were doing."

"Honey, I'm really busy, and I don't have much time to talk. Is there anything special that you need?"

"Yes, there is something special that I need. I need for you to tell the mother of your child that you love her."

Total silence. Then, after about eight seconds, Monty said, "You mean we're pregnant?"

"I mean we're pregnant. Whatta ya think?"

"I think it's wonderful. When's it due?"

"Dr. Miller said I'm a little over two months, so in seven months you will be a daddy. I'm going to go ahead and start calling you Daddy Shepherd."

"That's all right with me. Sweetheart, you can't imagine how happy I am right now. I love you so much, and I know you're going to make the world's best mommy."

"You're only saying that because it's true."

"Now, get outa here. I'm busy. How about we celebrate tonight? Let's take our parents out to eat and make the announcement to them, want to?"

"Yeah, let's do. I'll call them when I get home."

They went to the Town and Country, and when Monty announced that he and Joan were happy to be in the presence of four expectant grandparents, it was like when Joan told Monty. Total silence, then Thil let out one of her trademark squeals, and everyone began talking at once. It was a perfect evening, and before they left the restaurant, Monty asked everyone to bow their heads, so he could thank God for their good fortune. After his prayer, Monty picked up the check for everyone, and they all left. Joan and Monty both kissed Joan's parents goodbye, then, with David and Thil, they got into Monty's car and went home.

****

If Monty was going to go to Brazil next Wednesday, he had a lot to do to get ready. Since he had just returned from New York, and Davi had come with him, he hadn't had time to do much of anything except work with Davi. Now, there were only three days left before the weekend, and he wasn't sure how he would get everything done that had to be done. He would have to spend all of Monday and Tuesday getting ready for his meetings with the *LARA* sales people.

He thought, *I'd better call Chuck and tell him we're going to Brazil next week.* He thumbed through the rolodex until he found the number. He picked up the phone and dialed it. "Hello, Chuck, Monty Shepherd here. Listen, can you make a trip next week?"

"Yes sir. Where are we going?"

"I've got to be in Brasilia, Brazil, by next Thursday morning, so we'll have to fly down Wednesday."

"Monty, I'm pretty sure we will have to have a visa to get into the country. Do you have one?"

"No, do you?"

"No, but we can get one from the Consulate in Atlanta."

"How about finding out what we have to do and how long it will take to get one and call me back."

"Okay, I'll make some calls right now."

In about fifteen minutes Chuck called back. He said, "Monty, we have to get the visas from the Brazilian Consulate in Atlanta. Their address is 3500 Lenox Road, NE, Suite 800. The cost is one hundred sixty dollars, and they will only accept a U.S. Postal Money Order. If the application is made by a third party, it costs one hundred eighty dollars, and a letter on your letterhead must accompany the application. Do you have someone you could send down there?"

"I'll have to find somebody. Say, could you find a small plane to rent and fly down there for me?"

"I probably can. Let me look around, and I'll get back to you."

Chuck called back in a few minutes, and told Monty he had found a plane. "Monty, if you can get everything together today, I can go down in the morning. There's a small airport not too far from Lenox Road. I can go in there and take a cab to the Consulate, and unless there's some kind of hold-up, I can be back tomorrow afternoon."

Monty called Connie into his office and told her what they had to do. "Connie, send someone to the Post Office to get five money orders. One for a hundred and sixty dollars and four for a hundred and eighty dollars. Make them all payable to *Consulate of Brazil*. When you get that done, come back in here. I've got to dictate a letter to send with the visa applications."

After a couple hours, all was finished, and Monty told Eddie Randolph to take them to Chuck Jacobs. He told him where to find Chuck at the airport. He thought, *I'm glad I called Chuck when I did. If we hadn't taken care of the visas this week, I might have had to postpone my trip, and there's too much at stake to let a simple oversight put a kink in the works.*

****

Since Don didn't have to work, he wanted to spend all week getting things set up to start knitting the *Fin* socks. J.D. had promised to have the bands to him by Wednesday, and he was counting on them being there. He actually started working Sunday, and when Monday came, he knew pretty much how he wanted things.

When Liz arrived Monday morning, he collared her and took her to the break area, where he had coffee and she, a Coke. He told her he wanted her to learn to do the payroll, learn how to order yarn, pay invoices and a host of other things. He would keep one other lady in the office, but Liz would have the title of Office Manager, with the additional duties, she would get a nice pay raise.

She thanked Don for his confidence in her, and she accepted the new job, but her demeanor indicated that her heart wasn't in it. Don really wanted her to be happy, and he painted a very rosy picture about her future at Ridgemont. He told her all sorts of other positive things, in hopes she would come around and gain some enthusiasm, knowing full-well that most of his promises for future well-being would never materialize. He just wanted to play the game in order to get her in bed.

After his talk with Liz, he told her to go get Ruth Clayton, another office girl, and bring into the break area. When they got there, Liz started to leave, but Don said, "Don't leave yet, Liz. I want you to hear this." Liz and Ruth both sat down, and Don told Ruth about his talk with Liz and asked her to please teach Liz how to do the things she was doing. He told her there would only be the two of them in the office after he laid the others off, and it would be necessary for both of them to know how to do everything in the office.

Ruth agreed to do as Don asked, and when he had finished, she said to Liz, "Come on, Liz. I'm working on payroll this morning, and you can see how I do it." Don was mildly optimistic about Liz staying on with him, and he had a feeling of satisfaction after the two women left the break area.

The rest of the day was devoted to changing the Lonatis over to *Fin* and gearing up the other twenty-five machines to finish out the remainder of Ridgemont's orders. The hardest part of the day was when he had to tell several of the employees that that would be their last week.

All ten machines began their first full day knitting *Fin* on Tuesday, and everything went like clockwork. Each machine produced nearly thirty dozen pairs on the first shift, and that was what Don had projected. Now, if they could just keep it up, he would soon be in the money.

Ironically, Shepherd Truck Line delivered the bands on Tuesday, and Don was glad the driver didn't see him, or there surely would have been questions. Don knew that J.D. knew better than to give the bands to Shepherd Truck Line. They must have interchanged with another line. He would mention it to J.D. to be sure someone else brought future shipments.

J.D. called Thursday to find out how many *Fin* socks would be ready Friday, and Don told him he thought they would have between twenty-five hundred and three thousand dozen. J.D. asked, "Are you confident there will be at least twenty-five hundred?"

"Oh yeah. There should be more than that."

J.D. responded, "Just to be on the safe side, I'm gonna wire money for twenty-five hundred dozen. If you come up with more than five thousand next week, I'll take whatever you have."

"Okay, that sounds good." Don had kept his account at the bank in the Caymans which he opened when he was having plane rental money wired into it, and that was the account he used for the *Fin* money. *Boy!! My first week in business, and I do over thirty-seven thousand dollars. Almost nineteen of that is mine to keep. I'll do twice that next week. Man, life is good.*

Don had one more important thing to do before he went back to Shepherd Socks to work full-time; he had to find someone he could trust to run Ridgemont for him. There were three or four guys working in the plant on each shift, and Don made it a point to hang around where they were working to get an idea of what each one was like. He even stayed over for most of the second shift to watch those guys. Finally, one man stood out more than the others, and he called him aside. His name was Brandon Sterling.

"Brandon, I don't know how much you know about what's going on here, but as you have seen, we are knitting socks with the *Fin* logo on them. My family's company, Shepherd Apparel, has the contract for them, and Ridgemont is acting as a satellite plant, since Shepherd Socks needs the extra production. This has to be a hush-hush operation, because we don't want any of the other sock mills around to know that we are contracting out our work.

"Now, this is why I called you away from what you were doing. I've got to go back to Shepherd Socks next week, and I won't be here except when I come over every afternoon to check on what has gone on during the day. I'm going to need someone to take over and act as plant manager, and I think I would like for you to be that someone. Are you interested?"

"Yes sir. I sure am interested. I've been here for a long time, and

I know how to do it all. You can count on me to do a good job for you."

"I know I can. Look, I know you don't normally work on Saturday, but could you come in for a couple hours in the morning? I need to go over some things with you before I go back to Shepherd Socks. You should be out of here before noon."

"Yes sir. I'll be glad to come in."

Around three o'clock a truck pulled up to the dock, and the driver said he was there to pick up an order. Don got a couple guys, and they loaded the truck with twenty-five hundred dozen *Fin* socks packed in one hundred cases of twenty-five dozen each.

On Saturday morning, Don and Brandon worked on and outlined what and how things were to be done, and by the time Don left, he was satisfied that Brandon would do an excellent job.

With all the changeover and new things taking place, Don had not spent as much time with Pat as usual, and actually hadn't spent much time during the day with Liz. Sometimes he would pretend to have to do something in the office where she was, but he made sure he didn't distract her from her work. He debated with himself about asking her to dinner, but thought he would wait a week or so before asking her out again.

He felt really good about the way things were at Ridgemont and felt very proud of himself for being able to pull off such a coup.

****

Monty and Joan arrived at the airport at eight o'clock Wednesday morning. Chuck Jacobs, their pilot, had told Monty it would take close to nine hours flying time to reach Brasilia, and Monty had told him he would like to get there before dinner. There was only one hour time difference, so that should not be a problem.

Chuck had ordered breakfast and lunch to be catered for the flight, because Monty had told him that he and Joan would not eat before they left. At eight-thirty the big 707 roared down the runway, and they lifted off to a place where none of them had ever been, including the flight crew.

At four fifteen, Brasilia time, they landed at Brasilia International Airport, eight hours and forty-five minutes after they left Chattanooga. Davi had made reservations for all five of them at the

Royal Tulip Brasilia Alvorada Hotel: one room for Monty and Joan and two rooms for the crew. When they arrived at the hotel, they found that Davi had already registered for Monty and Joan and had arranged to pay their bill. Chuck and the other two registered, and Monty gave his credit card to take care of their bill.

Entering their room, there was a vase of beautiful flowers and a note saying Davi and Lara would pick them up at seven thirty. "Look, Monty, it looks like Davi and Lara are going to take us to dinner."

They were in the lobby when Davi came in. After the greetings, Davi led them outside to his car where Lara was waiting. They drove to a nice mansion in the heart of the city that housed a restaurant called Alice. The ambience was exquisite, and the food was wonderful. Alice served French food and vintage wines from France, Argentina, and Chile. Not only was the food good, it was home cooked by Alice Mesquita herself. There was no sign for Alice, but Davi said if you tell your taxi driver, he knows exactly where to go. It was one of the best-rated restaurants in Brasilia, and Monty and Joan could both vouch for the rating.

After a delicious *tartellete de limao;* (lemon tart), Davi said, "Joan, Monty, the company has been wonderful, but I know you must be tired after riding all day, so why don't we take you back to your hotel where you can get some rest? Monty and I have a long, hard day in front of us tomorrow, and you two ladies should rest before a hard day of shopping or whatever you are going to do. Are you ready to go?"

"Yes, we're ready," Monty said. "We have really enjoyed Alice. The food was wonderful."

When they got to their room, Joan said, "Did that wine go to your head?"

"No. Did it go to yours?"

"Yeah, and it's still there. You might have to love me in order to make it go away."

"I can do that, young lady," and they locked arms and locked lips, and Monty picked her up and carried her to the bed where they enjoyed loving each other immensely. In a little while Monty kidded with Joan. "Are you what they call a loose woman?"

"Certainly not. Why would you ask such a question?"

"Well, it's my understanding you've had sex not only in

America, but in London, Munich, Israel, and now, South America. What am I to think?"

She picked up a pillow and hit him with it. "I think 'loose woman.' If I am, then you're the one who made me that way, but you love me, don't you?"

"More than anything else in the world. Now let's get to sleep, Loosey."

She hit him with the pillow again, then laid down beside him, put her arms around him, and in a minute, they were both asleep.

Davi picked Monty up the next morning and drove him to the *LARA* office, where seven nice-looking men were waiting to meet him and hear his presentation. These seven men would be Shepherd's representatives for most of the South American continent after he left, and he wanted to make sure to present the line in such a way that each man could take it and pass his knowledge on to his customers. Davi had laid out his set of samples, and Monty was pleased with the way everything was arranged. It was almost exactly the way he would do it himself.

Five of the seven could speak English, but two of the Spanish speaking men could not. Davi could speak a little Spanish, but he wasn't fluent since Brazil's language was Portuguese, so he chose a man to be interpreter, the one who could speak the best English.

Monty began with the presentation, and it wasn't long before they were well entrenched with styling, construction, fiber content, price, and all that goes with learning a new line of apparel. The presentation lasted for two days, and Friday afternoon, Davi and Monty agreed that everyone would be able to take the new line and sell it to his customers, so Monty called Chuck and told him to get ready to leave Saturday morning and to be sure and get plenty of food catered for breakfast and lunch.

Davi and Lara took them out again Friday night, and this time they went to a place called Porcao. It had a huge picture of a pig on the sign. At Porcao, the customers can eat as much as they want. There is a sign on the table with a stop sign on one side, and a green "go" sign on the other. Once the sign is turned to "go," waiters will come around with plates of food (mostly meat, although there is salad and sushi as well) about as quickly as the customer can eat it. They won't stop until the sign is turned to "stop." The beef and pork are especially delicious there. They all got plenty to eat.

Davi took them back to the hotel after dinner, and the four of them went in and sat in the plush chairs in the lobby. They had all grown fond of each other, and everybody hated to see the week end, but Monty assured Davi he would be back in about a month. Lara said for him to be sure to bring Joan back when he came. In a few minutes, she and Davi stood up to leave. The guys shook hands and hugged the women, then said goodbye. Monty and Joan walked them to the exit, and once again they shook hands and hugged.

The next morning, Monty, Joan, and the crew all went to the airport together. Monty and Joan sat and waited on the plane, while the crew got everything checked out and ready to go. Finally, they were ready to go, and they took off at nine o'clock. They would lose an hour going back, so if it took eight hours and forty-five minutes the way it did coming down, they should be in Chattanooga a little before seven o'clock.

Monty was tired after his trip to the New York Market and the trip to Brazil. On the way home, he asked Joan, "How would you like to go to Florida for a few days? I'm thinking about taking off next week. We could go down to Mom and Dad's place and relax for a couple days."

"I'd love to go. I haven't been there yet, but I hear it's really nice."

"It is nice. What if we asked your Mom and Dad to go?"

"That would be fun. Let's do it. I'll call Mama when we get home. You're a good man; do you know that?"

"I know, just don't you forget it the way you usually do."

"I won't."

"I'll need to go into work Monday, but maybe we can leave Tuesday. I'll go up front and tell Chuck to plan on taking us down. Dad has a car down there, but we'll have to take a cab from the airport to his house."

They landed in Chattanooga at six fifty, and Joan and Monty stopped at a burger joint on the way home and got something to eat.

102

CHAPTER ELEVEN

One of the first things Monty did when he got home was to go over and see his Dad. Joan went with him, and spent time with Thil while David and Monty talked.

"How was your trip to Brazil, Son? Did you get everything done that you went down there for?"

"Yes sir, it was a very good trip. I was able to spend two full days with Davi and his sales force, and Dad, I think they're going to be every bit as good as the European group. All but two of them speak English, and that's good. Dad, I got to thinking on the way home that I may have spread myself too thin. As you know well, it's necessary to spend time with each group at least once a month. That means I'm gonna have to be in Munich and London one week, Tel Aviv a week, and now Brasilia a week. That only leaves me one week a month to be at home and to run the company. I don't think the business can be run in one week a month. Do you have any suggestions?"

"It looks to me like you're going to have to have some help."

"Do you think Charlie Crawford would be good?"

"Charlie would be good, but you need him where he is. How about Tom Ratcliff?"

"Tom? Why do think him?"

"Well, think about it. Tom has been with the company since before you were born. He has worked in every department at one time or the other, and before I promoted him to my assistant, he was in sales and doing a real good job. He doesn't have a family to hold him down, and I bet he would jump at the chance. If you offered it to him, and he took it, I guarantee you he would do a good job.

"Another thought, Son. How about your brother? He might be able to help you."

"No thanks, Dad. Don's where he needs to be. I'll think about Tom. He might just fit the bill. Dad, one reason I came over was to ask if you would mind if Joan and I went to your place in Florida for a few days. I need some time off, and I thought I might ask Joan's parents if they would like to go. I thought we might go down Tuesday and come back Saturday, if it's all right with you. Why

103

don't you and Mom go with us?"

"No thanks. Not right now. We just got back a couple or three weeks ago. Y'all go and have a good time."

Joan and Monty stayed a while longer and visited before going home to unpack.

The more he thought about giving Tom the assistant's job, the better he liked it. He would think and pray about it, and if he felt led to do it, he would talk to Tom after the staff meeting Monday.

Getting home from Brazil on Saturday night made the weekend really short. Joan and Monty went to church Sunday, and that left only a few hours to relax in the afternoon. Monty was really tired, and he was looking forward to going to Florida, but a hectic Monday stood in the way of his leaving.

After a restless night, he got up earlier than usual Monday morning, anxious to talk to Tom Ratcliff about taking over some of his travel. He had mixed emotions about it. So much traveling was a grind and telling on him, but it was also enjoyable. He was able to take Joan with him most of the time, and each trip afforded them the opportunity to enjoy new experiences in different parts of the world. He knew he had to give up at least part of it because he couldn't run the company from halfway around the world.

He stopped at Hardee's and got a biscuit on the way to the office and went to the break room when he got there and ate it with a cup of coffee. Tom came in right after he got there and sat with him while he had his coffee. They talked about Monty's trip to Brazil, and before they knew it, it was time to go to work. As they got up to leave, Monty said, "Tom, there's something I want to talk to you about. Stick around after the meeting this morning, will you?"

"Yeah, I'll stick around."

****

On the other side of the campus, work had started at Shepherd Socks, but Don wasn't there. Tommy Everett was running a little behind in the *Fin* production and didn't have time to look after his job and Don's, too. He was getting pretty aggravated when Don rushed in at eight forty-five. Sarcastically, Tommy said, "Good afternoon, Mr. Shepherd. I trust you had a good night's sleep?"

"I'm sorry I'm so late, Tommy, but there was something I had to do that couldn't wait."

Redemption?

"I'm not gonna ask what it was, but you need to really hop to it. Three people who work the *Fin* line didn't show up this morning, and I'm seriously behind on that crew sock order, so I need for you to be here every minute that you're supposed to be, in order for me to get my job done. You're missing two people on the *Staff* line, too."

"I'm sorry, Tommy."

After his encounter with Tommy, Don went to his area in the plant and began doing what he was supposed to do. At eleven o'clock the receptionist paged him and said he had a call.

He went to his office and picked up the phone. "Hello, Don Shepherd."

"Don, this is Brandon. Listen, the yarn didn't get here. The truck line said they didn't have anything for us, so I called the mill, and they haven't shipped it yet. They said they hope to ship tomorrow, and that means we won't have it 'til Wednesday or Thursday. I was planning on having it today, and without it I may have to shut down three machines. What do you want to do?"

Don's mind was racing, and he said, "Tell you what. I'll borrow some yarn from here. Do you have enough to last you the rest of today?"

"Yeah, we can get by 'til tomorrow."

"Okay. Brandon, have our truck over here at four-thirty this afternoon. Don't let it get here a minute earlier. Have it here at four-thirty, and I'll borrow three cases. That should keep you going 'til ours comes in."

"Okay, Boss, I'll have the truck there at four-thirty."

****

The staff meeting was pretty routine. It began at nine o'clock and lasted until a little past ten. About the only thing that was different was Monty's talk about the addition of the South American sales agency: how big it could become, and how important it could be to Shepherd Apparel. When the meeting adjourned, Tom Ratcliff stayed, and he and Monty went to the break room and got a cup of coffee, and then they went to Monty's office.

"Tom, I want to ask you if you would be interested in traveling some for Shepherd Apparel."

"Travel where, Monty?"

"All over the world. As you know, I've been having to be gone at

105

least two weeks a month, and now, with the South American addition, I'll have to be gone three weeks a month.... unless I can get some help, and that's what I want to talk to you about. I'm supposed to be running this company, but how can I run it if I'm gone three-fourths of the time? I want us to expand into Canada, so that will mean even more travel. I talked to Dad about this Saturday night after we got back, and he suggested I talk to you about helping me with some of it. He said you did a good job in the sales department, and he feels you would be good as our contact man in the overseas offices. What would you think about that?"

"I don't know, Monty. I've never been more than a couple hundred miles from Chattanooga in my whole life. Where are you talking about sending me?"

"As I said, all over the world. As you know, we have offices in London, Munich, Tel Aviv, and now Brazil. I wouldn't expect you to travel to all of them, all the time; I'll still be going some, but I would like to have someone to share it with me, and that's why I'm offering it to you first. Now Tom, you don't have to take it if you don't want to. You're doing a really good job where you are, but I'd like for you to think about it. If you decide to do it, we'll probably give you the title of International Sales Manager. Would you be comfortable with Chip Lowe taking your job?"

"Yeah, Chip's a good man, and he would be the perfect choice."

"You don't have to give me an answer right now. I'll give you 'til next Monday to decide. Joan and I are going to take a few days off beginning tomorrow. We're going to Florida to Dad's place, and we'll be back Sunday, so you can give me your answer a week from today."

"I'll do a lot of thinking this week, Monty. What if I decide not to take the job? Will it hurt me?"

"No. It won't hurt at all. We just thought since you don't a have a family to tie you down, you would jump at a chance like this. No, you won't be penalized if you don't take it. Let me tell you this: if you decide to accept my offer, I'll be going with you at least the first time to each office to introduce you to our people, so it wouldn't be like sending you around the world by yourself. Also, the flight crew knows their way around the places we go, so you would have familiar faces with you on every trip. Think about it, Tom, and we'll talk when I get back. Okay?"

Redemption?

"Okay, I'll think about it. Just a minute, Monty, did you say your Dad suggested you ask me?"

"Yeah, he has a lot of confidence in you. If you want to talk later, I'll be here all day."

Monty finished out the day at the office without any more contact with Tom except for normal, routine matters. Tom was so used to running things while Monty was gone, it was unnecessary to meet and go over plans. Monty knew everything would be handled correctly.

After he left the office, he decided to go by the sock plant to tell Don he was going to be gone for the next week. He noticed a Ridgemont Hosiery truck parked at the loading dock, but didn't pay any attention to it. He went in and looked around, and in a couple of minutes, Don caught up to him. "Hi, Little Brother, what's cooking?"

"Nothing, really. I just wanted to stop by to see how things are going."

"Couldn't be better. I'm still learning, but I've already learned a lot, and I really like the sock business. How are things with you?"

"Good. We just picked up a new sales agency to cover South America, so our business should increase quite a bit pretty soon. I've been gone so much, I'm going to take next week off. We're going down to Mom and Dad's place in Florida. If you need me, that's where I'll be. Well, hold it in the road, Big Brother. I'll see you in a week."

As he left, he noticed the Ridgemont truck again, but still didn't pay that much attention to it because there were always trucks from a variety of places parked around the different plants.

When Monty got home that evening, he and Joan went to David's and Thil's for dinner. Thil had made a big pot of vegetable soup, and that was one of Monty's favorites. They didn't stay long after dinner because they had to get things ready for their trip the next day.

After they got home, Joan's mother called to find out what time they were leaving. "Hey, Mama. Yeah, we're packing now. What?... Oh, Monty said to be at the airport at eight o'clock. Be sure you go to the area where the private planes are parked; you remember where that is, don't you?... We're looking forward to it, too. I'll see you in the morning. Love you. Bye."

Charles and Kathleen were so excited. They arrived at the airport

107

at seven-thirty, ready to go. They had only seen the Shepherd plane one time, and that was at night, the night Joan and Monty got married, and when they saw the sleek 707 glimmering in the early-morning sun, they couldn't believe they were going to get to fly on it. The flight wouldn't be long enough to have a meal, but Chuck had the caterer bring snacks for everybody, and they did that before Joan and Monty arrived.

They got to the plane exactly at eight o'clock, and they took off almost immediately. The flight was to take a little over an hour and a half, and Charles spent much of that time exploring the plane. He was especially taken with the flight deck. Monty introduced him to the flight crew, and he was in *seventh heaven* being able to experience everything.

Before they landed, Monty said, "I forgot to tell you. Dad's having the man who looks after his house and yard pick us up at the airport, so we won't have to get a cab." They landed at nine-fifty-three and rode twenty minutes to David's house, where they unpacked and prepared for a very busy week of lying in the sun and eating seafood.

****

J.D. called Don Tuesday afternoon and scared the bejeebes out of him. "Hey Don, if anybody strange happens to come by your place asking questions, be sure you don't tell them anything. My driver was stopped this morning in California by Customs, and I don't know what's going to happen. The freight-forwarder came to his rescue, and hopefully, they got things worked out, but I'm going to pull back and not send any more goods for a while. You might want to stop your production, too."

"Man, if I have to stop production, I'm dead. I was lucky to be able to get things worked out like I did, and if I have to stop producing, I'll be out of business. Do you know anybody else I might call about buying the socks?"

"There's a guy here in Arkansas that buys some. His name is Tim Williams and his number is 501-555-1885. Give him a call and maybe he can help you."

"Can I say you told me to call him?"

"Yeah, we're friends. Don, I want to start buying again in a couple or three weeks, so I hope you don't commit everything to Timmy."

"I'll try not to, but I can't afford to stop my machines. I have too much at stake. Do you know anybody else in case he doesn't want to buy from me?"

"I know a couple guys, but try Timmy first. He'll probably need some."

"Okay, thanks. Call me when you need more goods, and maybe we can do something."

"Okay, Don. I'll see you."

Don called Tim Williams and told him what he wanted and that J.D. Massey had given him his number. They talked for a long time while Tim tried to feel Don out, and finally, satisfied with Don's answers, he agreed to buy socks from him, but he only wanted three thousand dozen per week. Don was hoping he would take the whole five thousand, but that's all he wanted. The arrangement was identical to the one he had with J.D., except for the shipping. Instead of Tim sending a truck to pick up the socks, Don had to ship them across town to Tim's warehouse by truck line, prepaid. The freight would be included with the following week's payment.

Don's stomach was in a knot as he hung up the phone. The day was nearly over, so he called Brandon and told him he wouldn't be coming to Ridgemont. Instead, he went home and sat alone, thinking. He wished Pat wasn't coming tonight; she would want to fool around, and he wasn't in the mood for company.

Don was still sitting in his recliner when Pat arrived an hour or so later, and he barely acknowledged her presence. She stood just inside the door, waiting for him to rush to her and throw his arms around her, but he didn't even get out of his chair. She came over to him, sat in his lap and said, "What's wrong, Baby? Aren't you glad to see Patty? Have you missed me?"

"Yeah, I've missed you," Don said half-heartedly.

Pat kissed him, but he didn't kiss her back. "What's wrong, Baby?"

"Nothing, I've just got a lot on my mind. I'll be all right. Just leave me alone."

"Well, excuuuse me. I'll leave you alone." With that, she got up and went to the door and started out.

"Where you going?"

"I'm going somewhere to get a drink. Maybe I can find somebody who's in a better mood. I may come back, and I may not. Good bye." And she slammed the door.

Don knew she would be back because her clothes were in the closet and chest of drawers, but right then, he didn't much care, one way or the other. He cared for Pat and had gotten used to her being there during the week every week, but he didn't know if he loved her. Sometimes he thought he did, and sometimes he thought he didn't. That was one of the times when he didn't. For some reason, Liz popped into his mind, and he wanted to see her. He picked up the phone and dialed her number.

"Hello, Liz, Don. What are ya doing?"

"I'm just sitting here reading the paper. What are you doing?"

"Sitting here wishing I had somebody to talk to. Could I come over?"

"Of course. Just don't look at this house; it's a mess."

"Okay, I'll be there in ten minutes. Bye."

When Don rang the doorbell, Liz answered almost immediately. She looked so good standing there. She had changed into a pair of jeans and a baggy sweater. Don put his arms around her and almost gave her a bear hug. They stood there with their arms around each other for a long time, and in a couple of minutes Don said, "Thanks for letting me come over. I really need to be with someone tonight, and I couldn't think of anyone I would rather be with than you."

"What's wrong?"

"Oh, just business problems, nothing serious. I'm just kind of down today, and some things came up that I wasn't expecting, so I came over to cry on your shoulder. I'll be fine in the morning. Being with you helps a lot."

"I'm glad. Can I get you something?"

"No, thanks. I'm not going to stay long."

"You're welcome to stay as long as you want to. I fixed a banana pudding when I got home, and it's real good. Could I get you a bowl?"

"Okay. That's my favorite dessert. Thank you."

Liz brought him a generous helping, and he said, "Boy, you're some kind of cook. This is delicious. You and this pudding are just what I need tonight."

"I'm glad to be of help. Do you want to tell me what has gone wrong? It might help to talk about it."

He looked at her while he thought, *I'd sure like to tell her, but I can't let anybody know about the Fin sock deal. I'm pretty sure I can trust her, but you never know about people. She could get mad at me for something and shoot her mouth off. I'd better not.*

The thoughts went through his mind in about two seconds; then he said, "Darlin', I appreciate it, but it's something I can't talk about. I'll be okay now that I've been able to come and be with you. Thank you, anyway."

"Well, the offer will stay open. If you get home, and decide you want to talk, call me or come back over, and we'll talk as long as you want to."

"You're sweet. I appreciate that. Look, I'm not going to interfere with your evening any longer. I'm going to run, and if I get over to Ridgemont tomorrow, I'll see you then. Thank you so much for letting me come over. Can I get a good night kiss?"

She walked over to him, and they kissed. He wasn't expecting much more than a polite, quick kiss, but instead, Liz really planted one on him. Don was changing his mind about leaving because the way Liz was breathing and pressing and grinding against him, he thought she was wanting more than just a kiss. Then all of a sudden, she pulled back and said, "You had better go," and wouldn't let him kiss her again.

Wow!! This gal can drive you crazy, he thought. "I'll see you. Thanks again," and he walked out the door and went home, still excited from the encounter.

When he got home, Pat still hadn't come back, so he left a light on and went to bed Sometime during the night she came in and slipped into bed beside him, but he was sleeping so soundly he didn't open his eyes to look at the clock. He knew it was late, though.

When they got up the next morning, they went about their routines of having coffee and getting ready to go to work. Not one word was said about the night before.

Shortly after Don arrived at work, J.D. called. "Don, did you and Tim Williams get anything worked out?"

"Yeah, he wants three a week."

"Well, my problem turned out not to be a problem, so I'm ready to resume our regular schedule. Can you do it with what you're going to do with Tim?"

"I can do it, but it might take a week or so to get additional machines cranked up. Remember, I told you we could turn out around ten thousand dozen a week. Yours and Tim's will be eight, so if you need more than five, I can do it." He thought, *Man, eight thousand dozen a week. That's sixty thousand dollars a week profit. Way to go, Don.*

"I'll let you know, but right now, five thousand is all I'm prepared to take."

"Okay, we'll crank 'em out. See ya."

Don immediately picked up the phone and called Liz. "Good morning. Just wanted to let you know that everything has been worked out, and I'm not depressed any more. Thank you for letting me cry on your shoulder last night. I'll know where to come next time I need a shoulder. And, listen, that goodnight kiss. Wow!! You're something else, gal. I thought about that kiss for a long, long time. I hope we can do that again real soon."

"Maybe we can. I'm glad you got your problem worked out."

"Look, I've got to go. About three people are hollering for me, so I'd better see what they want. I might be over there late this afternoon. I hope you're still there when I come. Bye."

When things settled down a little, Don called Brandon and told him to start installing the conversion kits on enough machines to knit thirty-five hundred dozen pairs a week. He said not to wait until they were all ready. When he got one set up, start knitting, and do that for each one until they were all changed over.

CHAPTER TWELVE

Monty, Joan and Joan's parents returned to Chattanooga Sunday afternoon. They had left both cars at the airport, so there was no problem having a ride home. Joan's parents couldn't thank Monty enough for taking them to Florida, and Monty told them he would try to take them to one of the foreign countries he goes to when he could. They all hugged, said goodbye, and went home. On their way home, Charles and Kathleen talked about what a good man Monty was, and how thankful they were to have him for a son-in-law.

On Monday morning, Monty attended the staff meeting as usual. Then he and Tom Ratcliff got together in Monty's office. "Have you thought about what we talked about, Tom?"

"Yes I have; in fact, that's about all I have thought about since we talked last Monday."

"Well, what did you decide?"

I haven't made a decision yet. I wanted to talk to you first. Monty, I'm really a home-body, and I love being in Chattanooga. If I understood you correctly, if I take this job, I will have to be gone as much as three out of four weeks and sometimes four out of four. I don't know if I could be gone that much. Even if we split it up, I'd have to be gone about half the time. I've been with Shepherd ever since I was in college, and I love this company, but, Monty, I just don't know. I'd like to ask you this: would you consider letting me go on a trip with you to see how it is and how I like it?"

"I think we could do that. I have to go to Munich and London next week. Would you like to go with me on that one?"

"Yes, I'd love to."

"Okay, we'll let you get your feet wet on a European trip. We'll be leaving Monday morning, and we'll be back Friday night. Is that all right with you?"

"Yes, that's fine. You'll have to tell me what I need to take."

"No problem. I can do that. Oh, just so you'll know, Joan goes with me on most of my trips, and she'll probably go on this one, okay?"

"That's fine."

When Connie returned from the post office with the mail, she sorted through it and immediately took a large brown envelope to

Monty that was postmarked Brasilia, Brazil. He opened it and couldn't believe how many orders there were from Davi. *If this is what they're going to do every week, we're going to have to think about a new plant. I can't believe they sold this much their first week. Wow! Move over, Gerhard; you've got some friendly competition.*

Monty and Charlie Crawford went to lunch together, and Monty told him about the envelope he received with a stack of orders in it. Charlie, not wishing to feel slighted, reminded him of all the orders they received from the United States salesmen over the past month. Monty realized he might have offended Charlie, so he made sure he sang the praises of Charlie's men, too.

"Charlie, do you think we're ready to go into Canada?"

"I think we are; in fact, I wondered why you went to South America before you went to Canada."

"I went there first because of the population. Brazil alone, has over five times as many people as the entire country of Canada. All of South America has ten times the population, so that was a no-brainer. Even California has seven million more people than all of Canada, but I think we need to go up there. Do you have time to set up an agency up there, or do you want me to handle it?"

"Monty, I've really got my hands full right now, but I'll see if I can find time. It would be better if you could do it, and then let me look after it after it's set up, but I'll do whatever you want me to."

"Okay, I'll do it, but I want you to get on the phone and get me some names. I want the names of the top apparel sales agencies and their management teams. I'm going to Europe next week, and when I get back, I would like to see if we can get something started with our northern neighbors."

"I'll see who I can find for you."

"Good. If you're through eating, we need to go. I've got to go to the sock plant this afternoon after I finish everything else I have to do."

Later that afternoon, Monty went to the sock plant to see how things were running. Once again, there was a Ridgemont Hosiery truck parked at the loading dock, and while he wasn't concerned about it, it did create a question in his mind. He vaguely remembered seeing one of their trucks over there before, and he wondered why they were there, since Shepherd didn't do business with Ridgemont.

He went in and found that Tommy wasn't there. The receptionist said he was sick with a cold, so he left early to go home and doctor up. Monty then went to see Don and caught up with him in the yarn storage area, talking to the driver of the Ridgemont truck. They had just loaded three cases of yarn onto the truck, and the driver was getting ready to leave. Monty couldn't hear what they were saying, but he heard enough to know that something was not right.

"Why did you load yarn on that Ridgemont truck?" he asked after the truck left.

"Oh, they called earlier and said their shipment didn't get in this morning, and they asked if we would loan them some until theirs came in, and I thought it would be all right, so I told them to come get a couple cases."

"I thought Ridgemont went out of business."

"I did, too, but apparently they didn't."

"Well, we want to help people out, but be careful with how you handle letting yarn get out of here because our profit to cost ratio is pretty close, and we don't want to lose money because we were careless with raw materials. Okay?"

Don breathed a sigh of relief and said, "Okay, Little Brother, I'll watch it."

The two of them walked through the whole plant, and Monty was satisfied everything was running the way it should, so he told Don goodbye and left to go home. The minute he was out of sight, Don got in his car and went to Ridgemont. He had to see Brandon about some things, but his main purpose was to see Liz, if she were still there.

He found her in the office going over some invoices that she was about to pay. Pulling up a chair, he sat down across from her and asked, "How're you doing today? You sure look pretty."

"I'm fine, and thank you for the nice compliment. What brings you over here?"

"I have to see Brandon, but I mainly wanted to see you." They talked for a few minutes, and then he went out to see Brandon. He told him not to send a truck to Shepherd Socks anymore unless it was after five o'clock, and then, not unless he talked to him first.

After he finished with Brandon, he went back to the office, and Liz was getting ready to leave for the day. He asked, "You want to go someplace for a drink?"

"No thank you, Don. I've got to go home. Maybe another time."

"Well, how about dinner Friday?"

"Maybe, I'll let you know."

Liz was so stand-offish, it bothered him because he really did like her, and he didn't want her to get to where she didn't want to be around him.

"Can I call you tomorrow and maybe just talk?"

"You're my boss, Don. You can do anything you want to do."

"I don't mean as a boss. I mean as a friend. I like you, and I thought you liked me, too. Why are you acting so distant?"

"Don, can I be frank with you?"

"Of course you can."

"Do you remember coming to my house last Tuesday night, depressed and wanting to cry on my shoulder?"

"Yes, and you were a great help."

"Well, I knew we weren't going together or anything like that, but I thought there might be a chance that we could, by the way you talked and acted toward me, and I began to have feelings for you. Even when our emotions were starting to get out of control, and I nearly pushed you out the door, I hated to see you leave. Then, you called Wednesday, very happy, saying your problems had been worked out, and since it was a workday, I didn't expect to see you that night."

She continued, "A friend of mine invited me to go eat with her Wednesday night, and while we were eating, you and some woman came in and were seated with your back to me. Although I couldn't see your face, I could see hers, and she looked as if she could eat you up. You held hands across the table. I could see there was something special between you. Then I got to thinking: why do you only ask me out on weekends? You asked her out on a week-night; why not ask me out on a weeknight? I don't know the answer, but what I do know is that I'm not going to be someone who takes the leftovers. If you have someone you see on a regular basis, fine; you and I have no ties. Just don't come looking for my company because your other squeeze is not available."

Don, taken aback, said, "Wow. You're something else. Do you know that? You're wrong about most of the things you said. It's true that I've been seeing someone else, but it's not serious. You know how it is to be lonely. Well, I'm lonely, too, and the lady is lonely, so we found each other and met a need that each of us had, but there's nothing serious about our relationship. As far as the weeknight and weekend thing you talked about; that's ridiculous. I seldom go out during the week. I work hard every day, and most nights I grab a quick bite and go to bed early. Now, I want you to go home and think about what I said. I like you, and I want to be a part of your life. I'm going to call you tomorrow, not as your boss, but as someone who cares for you and loves to be with you."

"Okay, I'll talk to you tomorrow." She picked up her purse and started out, and as she passed Don, she didn't look up, but said, "Bye."

Don gave her time to get to her car; then he left. On the way home he thought, *Women- you can't live with 'em, and you can't live without 'em, and I'm mixed up with a couple of doozies. Liz was pretty smart to figure out the weekday and weekend deal because that's exactly what I tried to do. Now, what do I do? I like them both. Liz knows about Pat, but Pat doesn't know about Liz. Liz doesn't want me going out with Pat, and I wonder what Pat would think if she knew about Liz. This is a mess.*

Maybe I should encourage Pat to find a motel when she's down here. Her company will pay for it, and that would ease things up for me. The only thing is, I can sleep with her every night, and I haven't been able to get to first base with Liz, but Liz has more class, and that's probably why I haven't been able to get anywhere with her. That's it—that's why I haven't gotten anywhere with her; it just takes more time with classy women. Pat might not have as much class as Liz, but boy, is she great! I'm gonna have to put some thought into this situation. He arrived home just as his thought process ended. He went into his apartment, opened a beer and sat on the deck, waiting for Pat to come home.

The whole time he was waiting for Pat, his mind was on Liz. He looked at his watch and knew it would be fifteen or twenty minutes before Pat arrived, so he picked up the phone and dialed a number. On the other end, a voice answered, "Hello."

"Liz, hi. I just wanted to see if you're all right. I worried all the way home about the way you were feeling. Are you okay?"

"I'm all right. Thank you for asking."

"Is that all you've got to say?"

"What else do you want me to say?"

"Well, I thought you could say something like, 'Hello, Don, I'm glad you called. It's really nice talking to you.' Something like that."

"Okay. Hello, Don, I'm glad you called. It's really nice talking to you. How's that?"

"Never mind. I'll talk to you tomorrow. Good night."

He slammed the phone down, and it was only a few minutes until Pat came in. He offered her a beer, and they sat around, talking about each other's day. The beers they were drinking made them think they would like to have pizza, so they called Dominos and had a large pepperoni and bacon delivered. While they were waiting on the pizza, Pat went into the bedroom and changed out of her nice clothes into a pair of jeans and a sweatshirt. She then went back out on the deck and sat on Don's lap, and they smooched a little until the doorbell rang. The man was there with the pizza, so they got up and Don went to the door. They opened the pizza and sat down to eat, while Pat opened each of them another beer.

****

At noon Monday, Monty called Tom's office and said it was time to leave for the airport. Joan was to meet them there, and they would take off at one o'clock. They would have lunch on the plane. Tom appeared to be excited, but a little nervous at the same time.

The plane lifted off at one ten p.m., and since Joan and Monty had been making so many trips, it was old hat to them, but not to Tom. It was a completely new adventure for him. Not only had he never been to a foreign country, he had never flown before, and everything that took place was amazing to him. When Monty asked him if he would like to watch a John Wayne movie, he was flabbergasted. "Watch a movie on an airplane?" he asked, and he could hardly believe it, and when Joan made a pot of coffee, it nearly blew his mind.

"How do you like this traveling," Monty asked.

"I like it. I guess I didn't realize it would be so exciting."

Everything was pretty routine the rest of the day, and after dinner, Monty showed him where he would sleep. When they got ready to go to bed, Monty told him, I'll get you up at six, Tom, because we will reach Munich around eight o'clock, and we want to have time for coffee and breakfast before we land."

"We're going to eat breakfast on the plane, too?"

"Yep. You do eat breakfast, don't you?"

"Yeah, boy."

Right on time, Chuck landed the plane at Flughafen Munchen airport at eight a.m., and good old, dependable Gerhard was there to meet them. Tom had met Gerhard when he came to Chattanooga, so he knew him slightly, but Monty re-introduced them. After the re-introduction, they went straight to the office where Daniele was waiting for Joan. She knew the routine: have Joan home around four-thirty to rest, and Monty would be there around that time, also. Everything was basically the same as the other times except this time Tom was with them. Monty, wanting to show Tom a good time, asked Gerhard if they could go to Dallmayr's since it was such a neat place, and, of course, Gerhard said they could.

After they said their goodbyes to Joan and Daniele, they went into the office. The first person they saw was Marlene, and Monty introduced her to Tom. If ever sparks flew at an introduction, it was then. Tom and Marlene couldn't take their eyes off each other for what seemed like forever. Monty brought him back down to earth when he said, "Tom, I want you to meet Bruno Meyer. Bruno is the Manager of European Operations."

"Just to bring you up to date: when Shepherd Apparel went global, Urey Steen was the Vice President of Global Operations—you remember Urey—well, when Urey was alive, Gerhard was the Manager of European Operations. Then, when Urey died, Dad gave his job to Gerhard and gave Gerhard's job to Bruno. Marlene has been here the whole time, and she has been working on her English, as has Bruno." Tom and Marlene looked at each other and smiled.

The day was a busy one, and Tom was getting initiated into doing business internationally. Around four thirty, they went back to the office and prepared to call it a day, when Gerhard called Monty aside and said, "Monty, what would you think about inviting Marlene to go to Dallmayr's with us tonight? She isn't married and seems to like Tom, and it might help Tom not feel so out of place if he had an escort of his own."

"I think that's a great idea. Let's do it. Do you want to ask her, or do you want me to?"

"You ask her."

Monty walked over to her desk and said, "Marlene, We're going to Dallmayr's tonight and would like for you to go with us. Would you like to go?"

"Yes sir. I would like very much to go."

"Great. Why don't you meet us there at seven o'clock?"

"I'll be there, and thank you for inviting me."

When they were getting ready to go to Dallmmayr's, Joan couldn't help but notice that Tom was spending a really long time getting ready, and she remarked to Monty, "It looks like our boy is primping to go on a hot date, doesn't it?"

"Yeah. I wish you could have seen their faces when I introduced them. They looked like a couple of kids watching a fireworks display. I'm sure Tom's anxious to see Marlene tonight. I hope things go well for them."

As usual, the experience at Dallmayr's was outstanding, and Tom was blown away by it. Marlene had only been there once before, so it was great for her, also. After the waiter brought the check, and everyone was ready to leave, Marlene asked, "Would you like for me to show you a little bit of Munich, Tom?"

"Why yes, I'd like that."

Marlene told Monty she knew where their apartment was, and she would bring Tom home later, so she and Tom left in one direction and the others in another.

After Joan and Monty got back to their apartment, Monty said, "Honey, there's something wrong with this picture. Here we are, the young couple, staying in, and getting ready for bed, while a couple our parents' age is out on a date. That picture is backwards."

"Well, I hope they're having a good time."

Monty and Joan left the door unlocked and turned in around ten thirty. Because they were afraid Tom would come in at the wrong time, they went right to sleep. Later Joan heard him trying to be quiet as he came in, and she looked at her watch. It was after midnight. She smiled and turned over and went back to sleep with her arms around Monty.

The next day Bruno went with them as they called on some of their better accounts, and Monty could easily see why he had been so successful as a salesman. He was super smooth, and he would have an order written before the buyer even knew what happened. It was a good day, and they returned to the office around four o'clock. Monty had some things to go over with them, and it had to be done that day because they were going to London the next morning.

When they finished and were getting ready to leave, Tom went over to Marlene's desk to say goodbye, and Monty said, "Marlene, did you show Tom everything there is to see in Munich last night?"

"No sir. We didn't have time, but if he would like to see more, I can show him. What about it, Tom?"

"Sure, I'd like that."

"Unless you have to go with Monty, why don't you stay here with me, and I will take you home later?"

Tom asked, "Is that all right with you, Monty?"

"Sure. We'll leave a light on and the door unlocked. Have fun." Gerhard and Monty said bye and walked out of the office, smiling.

Daniele and Gerhard came back to the apartment with Monty and Joan after dinner and visited for a couple hours. A good portion of the conversation was about Tom and Marlene. Monty told the others about how Tom had come to work at Shepherd Apparel while in college and how much David thought of him. He told them about Tom's wife dying a few years ago, how lonely he was and how happy he was that Tom had warmed up to Marlene the way he had.

Gerhard then told about how Marlene was divorced from a husband who had abused her and cheated on her. She had been divorced for about ten years, and they had never seen her act interested in any man until Tom arrived. They had tried to fix her up with dates several times, but she just wasn't interested. They wondered what was going to happen if Tom continued to come to Munich, and Monty wondered the same thing.

At eleven o'clock, Daniele said they had to go, so they got up, hugged and kissed and left.

Monty and Joan went to bed, and like the night before, they left a light on and the door unlocked. Joan heard Tom when he came in, and when she looked at the watch, it was after two o'clock. Again she smiled and went back to sleep.

Gerhard was at the apartment at eight o'clock to pick them up and take them to the airport. They were all kidding Tom about being out so late, and he was being a good sport about it. After Gerhard dropped them off at the airport, Monty remembered something he needed to tell Gerhard and Bruno, so before they took off, he called the office, and Bruno answered.

this is Monty. Why are you answering the phone?...

old Bruno why he called.

up, he told Tom with a smile, "Tom, it looks like

we're going to have to dock your wages."

"Why's that?"

"Because when I called the office just now, Bruno answered and said Marlene had overslept and wasn't in yet. Since Bruno is having to act as receptionist because she couldn't make it in, I think you need to pay for his extra duties, don't you?"

Tom answered with a big grin. "Whatever you say, Boss, but I'll tell you this. It was worth it." They all laughed and kidded around before boarding the plane.

The trip to London was uneventful, and Tom hit it off pretty well with Liam McAlister. The day was a busy one, and then they left the next morning for Chattanooga. They landed at Lovell Field a little after ten p.m., and everyone was tired. There were no long, drawn-out goodbyes; rather everyone said, "I'll see you Monday," and left to go home.

Monty had tried to get a feel for how Tom liked to travel while they were flying back home, but Tom was pretty noncommittal, and Monty didn't push it. He would press for an answer next week when they went back to work.

CHAPTER THIRTEEN

Joan and Monty were tired after the long trip to Munich and London, and they slept late Saturday morning. Normally Monty went to the office on Saturday, but he decided to stay home and rest since the next week was going to be a fairly easy one, and he could catch up anything that needed to be caught up.

On the other hand, Tom didn't stay home. He was at the office bright and early Saturday morning, looking through things around Connie's desk, trying to find an email address for the London office. Finally, when he was unable to find it, he called Connie and asked her for it. She gave it to him, and he sat down at the computer with the intention of sending an email to Marlene. Two things were working against him: it was Saturday and Marlene wasn't at work, and he had no idea how to send an email. After trying for about an hour, disappointed, he decided to wait 'til Monday and get Connie to help him.

He walked back to the break room, got a Coke out of the machine and sat down alone to think things through. *Sure wish I could have gotten hold of Marlene. Monty's going to want to know something Monday about what I want to do, and I can't give him an answer 'til I get in touch with her. If I can see her two or three days a month, I may take the job, but if I can't, I probably won't. That was a fun trip, though, and the airplane—wow! It's probably not fair making my decision on one trip and having Marlene be part of it, but if I have to go over there every month, I sure would like to see her when I go. I wonder what it's like to go to Israel and South America. Shoot, I might just become a world-traveler.*

I wonder what the fare is between here and Munich. Sometime if Monty would let Marlene come over here on the company plane and spend a few days, I could buy her a ticket to go back. You know, that's a pretty good idea. I think I'll see if I can get that worked out.

Spending time thinking about Marlene and what a good time they had last week gave Tom a feeling of euphoria and made him determined to see her again. He left the break room and went to his car to go home. On the way, he thought, *there must be ten thousand single women in Chattanooga, and I have to get hung-up on one five thousand miles away. Idiot.*

****

Monty thought he wanted to stay home all day, but after a while he got restless and wanted to do something. Joan suggested they go out to the new Northgate Mall and look around. Since they slept late, they didn't have breakfast, so they were hungry when they got there. They explored the eating places in the mall and after getting something from this vendor and something else from two or three other vendors, they were stuffed. Joan wanted to look in some of the stores, and Monty patiently waited for her. He sat on one of the benches provided for husbands waiting on their wives and saw several people he knew. Talking with some of them helped pass the time until Joan was ready.

The light was blinking on the answering machine when they arrived. When they listened to the message, it was from Thil, saying to call as soon as they could. Instead, Monty went next door and his Mom met him at the door. "Monty, honey, Grandpa Jesse passed away this morning."

"You're kidding."

"No, I'm not. Essie called and said she woke him up about eight o'clock, and he seemed to be fine. He drank some juice and coffee, then went in the bathroom to shower and shave. When he got dressed, she said he came back to the den and sat down in his leather chair while she fixed his breakfast. When he didn't come when she called him, she went in the den, and he was sitting there dead. I'm sorry, Sweetheart."

"Where's Dad?"

"He's in the den, and he's taking it pretty hard."

"Mom, would you call Joan and tell her to come over here, please?"

"Okay, I'll call her."

The only thing David or Thil had done was call the funeral home to go after Jesse's body. They were waiting for Monty to go with them to make the necessary arrangements. After Joan got there, they decided they would go to the funeral home in about thirty minutes. Monty and Joan had to do some things to get ready, and Thil did, too. David said, "Monty, before we leave, how about calling Tom Ratcliff and telling him about Dad. Dad loved him and would want him to know."

"Okay, Dad. Did you call Don yet?"

"Yeah, Thil called him."

The mood was somber as they picked out the casket and made the funeral arrangements, but they all realized Jesse had lived a long, full life, and remained healthy until the Lord took him. There were no regrets and relatively little sadness because they knew Jesse was a Christian, and they knew where his soul was. Losing a parent is always hard, but those assurances of heaven made their losing him easier. David realized this and soon was doing okay.

Monty wasn't concerned about Jesse's eternal well-being; he knew it was secure. He was taking Jesse's death so hard because of his own personal loss. The two were extremely close. Ever since Monty had played little league sports and all the way through college, Jesse had hardly ever missed a game or any other activity in which Monty was involved. He even went to practice when he could, so his death was particularly tough on Monty.

Visitation at the funeral home was set for the hours of four p.m. to nine p.m. on Sunday, the day before the funeral. Jesse was very well-known and well-liked by everyone, so many, many people came by to pay their respects. Liz Patterson and Ruth Clayton came to pay their respects to Don and stayed for thirty to forty-five minutes. As they were walking out of the funeral home, Pat Marsh was coming in. Ruth and Pat gave each other a courtesy "Hello," but Liz recognized her and didn't speak. Pat only stayed for a few minutes, then left.

When Tom Ratcliff came in, David asked him to be one of the pallbearers, and it touched Tom so much, he broke down in tears.

Since Monty and Tom were both absent, the Monday morning staff meeting was conducted by Chip Lowe and nothing remarkable was experienced.

The celebration of Jesse's life was set for two p.m. Monday, with burial in Chattanooga Memorial Park in White Oak. His grave-site was on top of a hill overlooking the duck pond, and David thought he would have liked that spot.

After the burial, the whole family went back to the funeral home to pick up some vases of flowers that they wanted to take home instead of having them taken to the cemetery. They had left the door open to the house, and when they got home, people had brought several casseroles and other kinds of food and put them on the counter in the kitchen at David's. Others brought food after they got home, so there was no chance anyone would get hungry for a long time. Thil divided it up, and when Monty and Joan went home, they took much of it with them.

Don stayed and ate with David and Thil, then went home. On his way, he had something on his mind. *I wonder how Pat knew about the visitation on Sunday. She's not supposed to be down here 'til Monday, but she showed up Sunday, and where did she spend Sunday night? That's a poser.*

When he got home, he changed out of his good clothes into something more comfortable. He was sad about Grandpa Jesse, but he didn't let it get him down. He reasoned that death was just part of life, and it would happen to everybody at some point. He assumed that Pat would be there in a little while, so he opened a beer and sat on the patio to wait for her.

In a little while she arrived and said she was starving. Don was still full from eating at David's and didn't want anything to eat, so they decided to go to Shoney's, where Pat ordered a full meal and Don just had coffee. While they were at Shoney's, Don questioned her about how she knew about Grandpa Jesse's death on Sunday morning.

"A woman I work with saw it in the paper and called me. She knows about you and me, and she thought I would want to know. As soon as she called, I got ready and came down to be with you."

"But you weren't with me but ten minutes. Why did you leave so soon, and where did you stay Sunday night?"

"Well, I didn't want to be a burden on you, so I thought it would be best if I left. I spent the night at Nancy's."

"Who?"

"Nancy. Nancy Hall, the girl who called me."

"Why didn't you come here?"

"I told you. I didn't want to be a burden on you. Now, let's drop it, okay?"

Don said, "Okay," but judging from her attitude, he smelled something fishy.

After they got back to his apartment, they watched TV and went to bed early. After the day's happenings, Don wasn't in the mood for anything else. Pat had other plans, but she couldn't budge Don, so she finally went to sleep, too.

The next morning, as soon as it reached eight o'clock, Don picked up the phone and dialed a number. "Good morning. Ward-McRae Corporation, how may I help you?"

"May I speak to Nancy Hall, please?"

"One moment, please."

After about thirty seconds the operator came back on the line and said, "Sir. There's no one here named Nancy Hall. Could it be another name?"

"No. No, thank you. I was told she worked there. Thank you, anyway."

When he hung up, he thought, *I knew something was wrong with Pat's story. We don't actually have any commitment to each other, so I wonder why she lied to me. I wonder why she came all the way down here, supposedly to see me, and then didn't stay with me more than about ten minutes. How did she know Grandpa Jesse had died? Maybe she stayed with another guy Sunday night. I hope not, but she's not tied to me. I wonder what's going on. I may just start concentrating my efforts on Liz if this is the way Pat's going to do.*"

He wanted to talk to Liz, so before he went back out in the plant, he called Ridgemont, and Liz answered. "Hey, good-looking, how are you?"

"I'm fine. How are you?"

"I'm okay. I just wanted to call and thank you for coming to the funeral home Sunday. It meant a lot to me."

"Well, it was the least I could do. How is your family doing?"

"They're doing okay. Look, could I come over and buy your lunch after a while?"

"I guess. Where do you want to go?"

"Do you like Tomlinson's?"

"Yes."

"Let's go to Tomlinson's. I'll see you at noon. "

He was excited about getting to see Liz, but he was still a little down about the lies Pat had told him. When he got back to work in the plant, his thoughts of Pat pretty much left him, and he concentrated on the job at hand until it came time to leave and go pick Liz up for lunch.

Tomlinson's was always busy at lunch, but they managed to find a table toward the back, next to a window, where they could talk. Monty was intent on getting on the good side of Liz, so he played the part of *Mr. Congeniality* perfectly, and it seemed to work. To prove to her that her idea about the weekend, weekday thing was incorrect, he asked her to go out Wednesday night, and she said she would. He wasn't sure what he would tell Pat, but he would work on that when he got home after work.

They had a very nice lunch and had to leave before they wanted to, but Don said, "Honey, I need to get you back and get back myself. Tommy has been on my case about being gone too much, so I guess I had better try to keep him happy. I may come to Ridgemont after I leave Shepherd this afternoon, and if you're still there, I'll see you then."

"Okay, I'll look for you. I'll probably still be there."

"Great."

Don dropped Liz off at Ridgemont Hosiery, then headed to Shepherd Socks. His time with Liz put him in an excellent mood, and he could hardly wait to see her again after work. He worked really hard to make sure everything would be in shape for him to leave without any delay and was actually whistling while he worked, but his parade was about to be rained on.

At three o'clock, he was paged over the intercom and told to answer line one. When he picked up, Pat was on the other end. "Hey, big boy. Are you busy?"

"I'm busier than a one-legged man at a fanny-kicking. What's up?"

"I'm getting off early today; in fact, I'm getting ready to leave now. I thought I would come by there and pick you up, and we could go eat before you went home. Would you like to do that?"

Trying unsuccessfully to think of a reason not to, he was forced to say, "Yeah, that sounds good. What time will you be here? I doubt if I can leave before five."

"That's fine. I've got some errands to run, and that will work out just right. I'll see you at five, and if you're not ready when I get there, I'll just come in and wait."

"Okay. I've got to go. I'll see you around five. Bye."

Disappointed, he called Liz. "Hey, Pretty Lady, I've got some bad news. I just found out I'm not going to be able to come over there this afternoon, and I wanted to call and let you know."

"That's too bad. Maybe you can come tomorrow."

"Maybe. I'll try. I'll see you."

After he hung up from Liz, he realized that that would be a good time to check out something he had been wondering about, so he dialed the number of the Ward-McRae Corporation. "Good afternoon, Ward-McRae Corporation. How may I help you?"

"May I speak to Pat Marsh, please?"

"One moment, please."

The operator came back on and said, "Sir, there's no one here by that name. We have a Charles Marsh. Could he help you?"

"Thank you, no." And he hung up.

Now what? Boy, that sucks. She lied to me about Nancy Hall and now this. I know she cares for me, but what's the deal? Something's going on, and I need to find out what it is. I'll just play it cool for a couple days while I check on some things, then I may confront her about the lies. I hate to miss sleeping with her every night, but I can't continue to be with someone I can't trust. What's going to happen when I confront her? I wish I hadn't told her about my Fin sock deal. She could cause big trouble if I make her mad. That's what I get for trusting her. I'll just bide my time for a while.

Pat got to the plant a little before five and waited in the car for Don to come out. They had dinner at Cracker Barrel, and while they were eating, Don told Pat that he would be working late Wednesday night. After they finished eating, they went to the apartment for their usual romp in the hay.

Everything was so rushed at Shepherd Socks Wednesday that Don didn't have time to go to Ridgemont, but he did manage to call after lunch. He talked to Liz, and while he was talking to her, he reconfirmed their date for later, just in case he couldn't call or get by that afternoon. She acted very friendly, and Don thought she was actually looking forward to going out with him. He told her he would pick her up at seven, and they would go to the Town and Country if that was all right with her. They talked for a little while longer, and then Don had her transfer him to Brandon.

Dinner, the atmosphere, and the soft music played by the pianist made the evening almost perfect for Don and Liz. They ate slowly and sat and talked for a long time after they finished. Liz invited Don to her place for coffee when they left, and of course, he said yes. She brewed the coffee when they got there, and they chatted while they drank it. As before, Liz put on some very easy listening music, and when a romantic mood song came on, Don got up, took Liz by the hand, and they danced, rather they stood there swaying to the music. They began kissing, and soon their emotions were starting to get out of hand, and just like before, Liz pulled away, and said, "Don, I can't. I know you don't understand, but I'm just not ready. I'm sorry. I might be ready soon, but not tonight. Please don't be mad at me."

"I'm not mad at you, but you're right; I don't understand. I guess I'll go now. I had a real good time tonight. We'll do it again sometime."

Liz grabbed him and gave him an unbelievable kiss. "Remember this 'til next time, okay?"

"Wow! I'll do that. Good night."

Don got home around eleven o'clock, and when he went in, Pat wasn't there. He went into the bedroom, undressed, and got into bed. At twelve thirty Pat came in, went to the bedroom, undressed, and got into bed next to Don. He still had Liz on his mind and wasn't in the mood for anything except going to sleep, and Pat didn't push for anything either, so they both went to sleep.

****

Two days after Jesse's funeral, Tom, Connie, and the other Shepherd office employees went back to work. Tom wanted to learn how to email Marlene, so he got Connie to write down the address and everything he needed to do it. He also told Connie to please call him the next time she or Monty called the Munich office because he would like to talk to Marlene.

When he got the address and other information, he went to his office and emailed Marlene. He knew emails went through almost instantly, so he waited around the office for at least an hour for an answer, but no answer came, and he was so disappointed. Finally, he said to himself, *Dummy, it's eleven o'clock in Munich. She's not even there. Maybe she'll answer in the morning. I sure do want to talk to her. Oh well, I'll come in early in the morning, and maybe there will be an answer. Monty's going to ask me what I'm going to do when he gets in in the morning, and I'll have to tell him something.*

Sure enough, when Tom got to his office at six a.m., there was a reply to his email to Marlene. He had told her how much he enjoyed being with her last week, and he had to make a decision on taking the traveling job. He wanted to know if she was receptive to seeing him each time he came to Munich, and if he could arrange for her to come to Chattanooga, would she come.

Her reply said she missed him since he left, and she would love to see him anytime he was in Munich. She was thrilled that he asked her to come to Chattanooga, and if it could be worked out, she would definitely like to come.

Tom sent another email, this time getting a little more personal. He confided that he didn't have a girlfriend, and he wished she lived closer because he thought they could hit it off. He told her several other personal and rather romantic things and hit *send*.

In about thirty minutes he received an answer, and Marlene obviously felt the same way he did. He replied to her and told her that based on her answers and feelings toward him, he was going to accept Monty's job offer. He also told her he would be talking to her on the phone whenever Connie had to call them for something.

Monty came in around eight o'clock and immediately went to the break room to get a cup of coffee to go with his steak biscuit. Tom walked in and sat down with him. "Hi, Tom. It's been a busy nine days, hasn't it?"

"It sure has. It seems like a month since I've been in the office."

"Yeah, me too. Have you thought about the traveling job we talked about?"

"I have, and I think I want to try it. I enjoyed the trip to London and Munich, and I look forward to going to the other offices."

Jokingly, Monty said, "Great, but I've got to tell you; there's not a Marlene in any of the other offices."

Tom's face turned red, and he said, Well, I guess one Marlene will have to be enough."

"Listen, Tom, I've got to go to Toronto Monday. Charlie found a guy up there who might make us a good partner for Canada, and I'd like for you to go with me. If it works out with this guy, and we can set up a good, working relationship, then you need to know what we do when we set up an agency. We'll go up Monday morning and come back Monday night."

"In the meantime, we need to find someone to take Chip's place since he will be taking yours. Any ideas?"

"Does it have to be a man, Monty?"

"No, why?"

"I just wondered because there is a woman in plant two that

would be perfect for the job; in fact, she would be good as my replacement. Her name is Jeanette Cox. Do you know her?"

"I probably do; I just can't place her right now. If you think she's the right person, we need to talk to her. How about calling Chip to come to my office, and when we finish with him, call Jeanette in, and let's see if she would like to move up in the company."

"Okay. Are you ready now?"

"Yeah, go ahead and call Chip."

The meetings went well, and Chip and Jeanette were promoted. Tom spent the rest of the week working with Chip, teaching him the things he might not know about Tom's job, and Jeanette followed them around, picking up what she could until Chip could teach her later.

CHAPTER FOURTEEN

A popular Broadway play had been booked for the Tivoli Theater for a long time, and David and Thil bought four tickets. They invited Joan and Monty to go with them Saturday night, and the four of them made it a fun night. They ate at Fehn's and then went downtown to the theater. They arrived early, and there was a pretty long line waiting to get in. While they were waiting, Joan nudged Monty, and, turning her back to David and Thil, said, "Is that gal in the orange outfit who I think it is?"

"Where?"

"Right there; behind that man in the plaid sport coat. Isn't that Pat, Don's friend?"

"It sure looks like her. I believe it is."

In a minute Joan said, "Monty, I think she's wearing a wedding ring. Can you see it?"

"I can't see it, but the guy with her has one on. Yeah, I can see hers now. I wonder what happened between her and Don."

"I don't know. It hasn't been long since I saw them together. Has Don not said anything to you?"

"No. Don never talks to me unless he wants me to do something for him."

"I sure am curious about this. Aren't you curious?"

"Yeah, it's strange, all right. If I see Don next week, I might ask him if he is still seeing her."

The line got shorter, and soon they were able to get inside and find their seats. The show was great, and they thoroughly enjoyed it. Afterwards, when they were on their way home, Monty asked if anyone would like to go to the Cracker Barrel for coffee and chocolate cobbler. Surprisingly, David said he would, so they capped off a very nice evening with a delicious sweet treat.

The 707 lifted off from Lovell Field at eight fifteen Monday morning on its way to Toronto. Chuck said it should take about two and a half hours flying time. Toronto's time zone was the same as Chattanooga's, so they should get there around ten forty-five. Monty told Chuck to be ready to leave to go back at four o'clock.

He and Tom got a cab to a place called Rep North. The head of

Rep North was a fellow named John Christian, and he was highly recommended to Charlie Crawford. Monty was impressed when he talked to him by phone, and he hoped they could get together by opening a Shepherd office in Toronto.

John and Monty had an instant rapport. One would think they had grown up together instead of just meeting, and John was agreeable to the way Monty wanted to set up their working relationship. Monty told him he wanted him to come to Chattanooga as soon as possible to see the entire Shepherd line, visit the campus, and learn how they do things. He and Tom and Charlie Crawford would either come back with him or come up within a week to meet with him and all his sales people to teach them the line. Their visit would depend on how fast John could get everything set up with all the reps. Things went so smoothly they finished up a little after two and went back to the airport. Chuck was able to change the time on their flight plan, and they took off at three o'clock instead of four.

On the way back to Chattanooga, the three guys sat around the table just outside the galley, had a Coke and discussed the day's happenings and the future of Shepherd Global in Canada. They all agreed it looked bright. Then Monty looked at Charlie and said, "Charlie, you said if I would set it up, you would look after it. Well, it looks like I'm getting it set up. Are you ready?"

"I'm ready," Charlie said.

Since they would be home in time for dinner, Monty figured he and Joan would eat out because she wasn't expecting him until late, and she wouldn't have anything fixed. He asked Tom and Charlie to eat with them, and Tom was happy to do it, but Charlie said he would just go on home and eat with his wife. Monty called Joan as soon as they landed, and she came right on to the airport and picked them up. They went to The Greystone and had a scrumptious meal. Joan took the guys back to the airport when they finished dinner. Tom got his car and left for home, and Monty got his and followed Joan home.

The next morning Tom and Monty went to Charlie's office and began planning for the opening of the Shepherd office in Toronto. John Christian had told them there were six sales reps besides himself that made up the Rep North organization, so Monty told Charlie to have seven sets of samples put together, and they would take them when they went back for their organizational meeting.

Redemption?

Monty excused himself and went to his office to get something out of his briefcase and then went to Connie's desk. He handed her a business card and told her to place a call to John Christian at the number on the card, then he returned to Charlie's office. In a minute, Charlie's phone rang, and Monty said, "That's probably for me," so he answered it himself.

"Good morning, John. How are you doing?"

"Fine. Listen, it was great having you fellows here yesterday. I talked to some of my men after you left, and everyone's anxious to hook up with you."

"That's why I'm calling, John. Have you had time to think about a date when Charlie and Tom and I can come up and meet with your guys?"

"Monty, next week would be good for us if that would work for you; say, Wednesday?"

Monty covered the phone with his hand and asked his guys if Wednesday would work for them, and they said it would, so he put the receiver back to his ear. "Wednesday's good. How about ten o'clock Wednesday morning? And John, it will take us at least two days to go over the entire line, so why don't we count on working with your people until the end of the day, Thursday at the earliest, and more than likely until lunch, Friday. I'm going to have my plane pick us up after lunch, Friday. How does that sound?"

"Sounds great, Monty. What about samples?"

"If you can have a truck meet us at the airport, we'll bring them with us. John, a pick-up won't hold them, so you need to send a bigger truck, okay? Also, John, if we're to be at your office by ten, we won't have time to help your man load the truck, so I guess you had better send enough help to do the job. I don't think my flight crew would appreciate having to load a truck after flying a thousand miles. Will that be a problem?"

"No problem. What time will you land?"

"I'll tell the pilot to be there by nine o'clock."

Monty hung up, and he and the other two returned to their planning session. Since Tom hadn't done anything like this before, he sat and observed, because even though he had been involved in the manufacture of everything and knew the fiber content and construction of the entire line, he didn't know the ins and outs of merchandising it. That session was a valuable time for him because

135

he would have to know all those things when he started going to the different sales offices on his own. He was very charismatic and would have no problem working with people; he just had to learn the sales aspect of it.

In a few minutes, Connie paged him over the intercom. "Tom Ratcliff, please come to the front office. Tom Ratcliff, please come to the front office."

Tom excused himself and walked up the hall to Connie's desk. Connie was holding the phone in her hand, and she said, "Tom, Marlene Bauer wants to talk to you. Where do you want to take it?"

"I'll take it in my office. Give me a minute to get back there." He rushed back to his office and picked up the phone. "Hello, Marlene. How are you doing?"

In her broken English she said, "Hello, Tom. I'm fine. Gerhard had to call Connie, and I told him I wanted to talk to you when he finished with her. How are you?"

"I'm fine. It sure is good to talk to you. Did I tell you when I emailed you that I'm taking the traveling job?"

"Yes, you told me. When will you be back to Munich?"

"I hope to come back in two or three weeks. Monty has set up an office in South America, and I'll have to go down there, and I'll have to go to Tel Aviv sometime, but he hasn't given me a schedule yet. I hope I can come see you before I have to go to both those places. I miss seeing you."

"I miss seeing you, too. I wish you lived in Munich."

"I wish you lived in Chattanooga; then we could see each other all the time."

"That would be nice. Tom, I've got to hang up now. Gerhard is giving me a look. Maybe we can talk again soon. Bruno might call Monty."

"Okay, I hate for you to hang up, but I know you have to. I'll tell Connie to let me talk to you whenever a call is made in either direction. I sure do miss you. I'll talk to you soon. Bye."

Tom had only seen Marlene a couple times for a few hours each time, but his feelings for her and her feelings for him were as strong as if they had been sweethearts for a long time. Tom had hardly even looked at a woman since his wife died, and the rush he got whenever he saw or talked to Marlene really took him by surprise. After he hung up, the realization that she had made the move to talk to him gave him a feeling of total exhilaration. Then, when he thought about her saying she missed him, he really felt good. He went back to Charlie's office where the planning session was still going on. While he tried to absorb what was being said, his mind was on Marlene.

The planning session continued for most of the day, and when it was over, Monty went to Tom's office and sat down. "What are you thinking so far, Tom?"

"I'm thinking that this job is sure going to be different than the one I've been doing, but I think I'm going to really like it. You know, I was in the sales department when your Dad promoted me, but I never went out to see customers or other salesmen; I stayed in and worked the telephone, and there is a big difference in that and what I've seen so far."

Still exhilarated, he said, "Monty, remember when Connie paged me earlier?"

"Yeah, why?"

"It was Marlene Bauer. Gerhard had to call Connie for something, and she asked Connie to let her talk to me, and Monty, she said she missed me. And do you know what? I miss her, too. I probably shouldn't tell you this, but I sure do like her. I'm sorry, Monty, that's not why you came in here. I'm just so excited about her. Let's get to why you came. I'm sorry."

"Sounds to me like the love bug bit somebody."

"I don't know about that, but I sure do like her. Enough about my going on; let's get back to business."

Monty said, "Okay, but first, let me say this. Tom, you've been a loyal part of this company since before I was even born, and you never ask for any favors, but I'm going to do you a favor. Since Marlene is so important to you right now, you have my permission to call her every day if you want to. You don't have to talk for thirty minutes, but five or six minutes may be enough if you talk every day. Is that all right with you?"

"Monty, that's wonderful. Thank you so much."

With that, Monty got back to business. "Tom, as you are well aware, we're going to start doing business in Canada. The reason I'm here is to tell you that you probably won't have to go up there very much. Charlie's going to take care of that office. You will go with us next week to meet Rep North's sales staff and learn how we set up new offices, and you might have to go up there from time to time, but that won't be one of your regular stops. Any questions?"

"No questions."

"Okay. It's been a long day. Let's go home."

Wednesday morning, Monty went to the office first; then he went to the sock plant. All Conference Sports had indicated they wanted Shepherd Socks to increase production on the *Fin* socks, and Monty wanted to talk to Tommy Everett about it. When he got there, he and Tommy went into the break room for a Coke, and while they were there, Don came in. "Hey, Little Brother, what brings you over here?"

Kidding, Monty said, "I just came to check on you and see if you're behaving."

He looked at Tommy and smiled. "When you work for Tommy Everett, you don't have any other choice."

"That's good. I'm glad somebody has finally been able to get you under control."

Don got some nabs out of the machine, and as he opened the pack and was walking toward the door, he said, "I've got to go. I'll see you."

Monty replied, "I'll see you before I go." Then he and Tommy resumed their conversation. After they had everything worked out on the increased production, Tommy confronted Monty with a fairly serious problem. "Monty, you know when we built this plant, everything that was put in was state of the art and with the latest in computerized inventory control."

"Yeah, I know, and it cost us a bundle to get it."

"Well, we have a problem with our yarn inventory."

"What kind of problem?"

"We're way short of what we're supposed to have. The computer shows we're supposed to have about fifteen to eighteen cases more than we have, and I don't know how that can be. We have manually counted the stock twice, and it comes up the same each time. I have gone over our procedures with the girls, and everything seems to have been done the way it should be, but we're still short."

"Fifteen to eighteen cases—that's a lot of money. Do you have any idea where it might be?"

"No sir. I can't figure it out."

Monty then asked, "Tommy, have you told anybody that we're short this much yarn?"

"No. Beth, the inventory control clerk knows we've been looking for it, but she doesn't know any details."

"Well, let's keep this under our hats. Tell you what: take another inventory today and adjust the computer figures to show that as the correct inventory, but show what it's supposed to be somewhere else. Today is Wednesday. Next Wednesday take another inventory, and check everything again. Without telling anybody but Beth, you keep all the requisitions for yarn, yourself, then let's see where the figures fall. I've got to go to Canada next Wednesday, and I'll be gone until Friday, but I want you to call me Thursday and tell me what you've found. As you know, we have to commit to the yarn mill months ahead of time in order to get the best price, and with this kind of shortage, we're going to be hurting. This is serious."

As he was leaving Tommy and heading to Don's area, he remembered seeing the Ridgemont Truck when it came over to borrow yarn, so he asked Don about it. "Do you remember that day when I was over here, and a Ridgemont Truck was parked outside, and you said they were picking up some yarn that you told them they could borrow?"

"Yeah, I remember it."

"Did they ever pay it back?"

"I don't know. I think so."

"Well, after I leave, call them and ask if they did. If they haven't repaid it, tell them we need it back right away. Is that the only time they borrowed some?"

Don lied. "I don't know. It's the only time I loaned them any. Is something wrong?"

"No, I just want to keep a close track on our inventory. We committed to buy two million pounds of yarn, and that might not be enough to carry us through the season, so we can't afford to loan yarn to anybody else, unless they pay us back immediately."

"By the way, we haven't seen you out at Dad's for a long time. Where have you been keeping yourself?"

"I've been putting in a lot of hours, and most evenings I go home, grab a quick bite and rest."

"Are you still seeing Pat?"

"Yeah, for the time being. She still comes over just about every night, but I don't know how much longer I'm gonna stay in the relationship. I'm thinking about looking around to see what other fish are in the sea, but until I do, maybe we can get together with you and Joan sometime."

"That would be good. Look, I've got to run. I have a meeting right after lunch, and I have some things to do beforehand, so I'll see ya later."

After Monty left, Don thought about the yarn that Monty saw the Ridgemont Truck picking up, and he became concerned because he had had the truck come over five or six times, and he knew Monty was no dummy. Each case was huge, holding approximately one hundred large spools of yarn. Don knew how much each case cost because he was buying yarn for his knitting at Ridgemont, and it was very expensive. He was just trying to use Shepherd Socks' yarn without having to pay for it, but now that Monty was questioning it, he could foresee a problem.

He picked up the phone and called Ridgemont Hosiery. Liz answered, "Ridgemont Hosiery."

"Hey, Pretty Lady, how are you?"

"I'm fine. How are you?"

"I miss seeing you, but other than that, I'm fine. If Brandon's around, I need to speak to him, please."

"Okay, just one minute."

There was a pause then a voice said, "This is Brandon."

"Brandon, this is Don. Listen, when are you going to order yarn again?"

"I've got to order today or tomorrow, why?"

"Shepherd Socks is wondering about the yarn we borrowed from them, and they want it back. Add fifteen cases to your order and when it comes in, put it in a separate area until I tell you what to do with it."

"Okay, Boss, I'll take care of it."

"Good, I'm going to try to come over there this afternoon. I'll see you then. Bye."

After he hung up, but before he left his office, he thought, *I'm gonna pay that yarn back. I'm making too much money to have to resort to stealing a little yarn.*

For the last several weeks, Don had been able to put more than seventy thousand dollars a week into his bank account in the Caymans. That amount was his after the costs of the counterfeit *Fin* socks were paid. So far, he had accumulated almost four hundred thousand dollars, and wanted to have two to three million within a year. His plan was to leave Shepherd Global and move to one of the islands when he reached that goal, so he had to be careful not to let anything like a few cases of yarn stand in his way. Deep down, he had secret thoughts of Liz moving with him, but that was really a long shot.

Later that day he was able to get away and go over to Ridgemont. As always, he stopped by Liz's desk and talked to her for a while, then went into the plant to see Brandon. The machines were *purring like kittens,* and the sound was music to Don's ears. Every time he saw a sock drop off a machine, he visualized money. He only stayed back there a few minutes because his real reason for coming was to see Liz.

When he got back to her desk, she seemed genuinely glad to see him. It was close to her quitting time, so he didn't keep her long, but he did keep her long enough to ask her out for the next night. "Don, I'd like to go out tomorrow night, but Belk's is having a big, one-day sale, and I was planning on going because they are going to have some shoes on sale that I have been wanting for a long time. Can we make it another night?"

"We can, but why don't I go with you to Belk's? We can go there and anywhere else you want to go. I just want to be with you. Can I go with you?"

"You can if you want to, but I can't imagine a man wanting to go shopping."

"Well, I do. When do you want to go?"

"Why don't you meet me at Belk's at five thirty? You can go to the shoe department, and I'll be there."

"Okay. It's a date."

She got her things together, and as she was leaving, Don walked to the parking lot with her. They stood and chatted for a minute, then both got into their cars and left.

On his way home, Don thought, *I'm going be on my best behavior tomorrow night. Liz isn't like Pat; she has morals, and I'm going to have to pretend I've got some myself, even though I've pretty much forsaken my upbringing. I've already found out she's not going to just jump in the sack with me; she wants something to go with it. I'm not sure what, but I'm going to try to find out. I'll tell Pat tonight that I won't be coming home tomorrow night. I wonder what she's going to say about that.*

He waited until after they had been to bed to tell Pat he wouldn't be home Thursday night, and she didn't like it one bit. She asked several questions, and he lied, saying he would be working late, maybe all night.

She kept on, and Don finally said, "Look, Pat, we're not married, and we don't have any commitment to each other. I don't like your controlling attitude, and it makes me wonder if maybe we shouldn't go our separate ways. I like having you here, and I really like going to bed with you, but that's all there is. We don't associate with other people, and when I suggest we do something with other people, you either don't want to or have some excuse not to. What do you think?"

"I'm sorry, Don. I don't mean to act controlling. I want to be with you every night the way we have been. I won't question you anymore."

"I've been thinking about this for quite a while, and let's see what you think. Why don't we start seeing each other about two or three nights a week? Your company pays for your room anyway, and this way we can still see each other whenever we want to without having to make any explanations when we can't. What do you think about that?"

"I don't like it. I want to be with you every night."

"Well, let's try it my way for a while and see how it works out. You might decide you don't even want to come over at all, once you try it. Since I won't be here tomorrow night, and you won't be here Friday, let's start the new program next week. Since we'll both be without any loving over the weekend, why don't you come over Monday night, and we'll see where to go from there?"

"I don't even want to talk about it. I'm going to bed. Good night." She stormed out of the room, went into the bedroom, got her gown and robe and went into the spare bedroom and slammed the door behind her.

Don took a shower, watched TV for a little while and then went to bed. At twelve thirty he was awakened by Pat slipping into bed with him. She put her arms around him and said she wasn't sleepy and wanted to do other things, and they didn't get to sleep until nearly two o'clock.

Don got up the next morning and left Pat in bed. He showered again, got dressed, and left for work. On the way to the plant he had a feeling of freedom, such as he hadn't felt for a long time. He suddenly came to the realization that he had given up a lot of important things in his life for the sake of sleeping with a woman whose companionship was a lie. The first thing he did when he reached his office was to call Liz. He only talked for a minute; he just wanted to hear her voice. He confirmed that he would see her at Belk's that afternoon and hung up.

****

All went well for the next two weeks. The guys set up the Shepherd office in Toronto, and John Christian rode back to Chattanooga with them the same way Davi Santos did when they set up the Brasilia office. John spent two days with Monty and Charlie, then returned to Toronto. Orders were already beginning to come in, and Charlie was thrilled about the quick start. He was looking forward to developing a large and profitable branch for Shepherd Global.

Tom was talking to Marlene every day, and they seemed to be getting closer with each phone call.

Monty told him they were going to Brasilia the next week, and then they would go back to Munich the week after that. Tom couldn't wait to tell Marlene.

When he called her the next day and told her, she shouted with excitement. He had no idea what she was saying, but he could tell she was happy. After she calmed down, she asked, "Where will you stay when you come here?"

"I guess I'll stay with Monty at his apartment. Why?"

"I would like for you to stay with me."

"I don't know, Honey. I don't think Monty would approve of that, but we'll see. If he comes with me, I'll probably have to stay with him, but if he doesn't, maybe I can stay with you. After this next trip, he probably won't come with me anymore so there won't be any problem. At least, we'll get to be together every day that I'm there. Just be thankful for that."

"I am. I just want you to be with me all the time."

"Marlene, I don't know if I can call you when I'm in South America. I'll just have to see."

"I hope you can."

"Me too. Listen, we're going to have to hang up. I'll call you tomorrow. Think good thoughts about me, all right?"

"All right, my Sweet. I'll dream of you tonight. I can't wait for you to get here."

After they hung up, Tom had his usual feeling of euphoria while he brushed up on facts and figures about the new Brasilia office. He wanted to appear reasonably knowledgeable when he got there next week. While he was doing that, Monty came into his office. "Tom, I nearly forgot that you have to have a visa in order to get into South America. Chuck has flown somewhere for some people that leased the plane and can't go get it, so I guess you'll have to make a quick trip to Atlanta in the morning. Will that be a problem? You can take the company car."

"No problem. You'll have to tell me where to go and what to do."

"I'll do that. You'll have to wait until after the post office opens because the Consulate won't accept anything but a postal money order. I've got the address, and Chuck says it's not hard to find. You should be able to get down there and back by a little after lunch, and you can take off the rest of the day when you get back."

****

When Monty and Tom got to Brasilia and met with Davi, Monty effectively stayed in the background and let Tom take the lead. Monty's first trip there was to set up the office, and the entire time was spent on familiarizing Davi and the *LARA* sales people with the very large Shepherd line, so this trip was mainly to call on customers and potential customers. The stores they were to see were already *LARA* customers, but had not seen any Shepherd merchandise, except for what the *LARA* salesmen had shown them.

Using Davi as his translator, Tom let Davi make the initial salutations and introductions, then, acting like an old pro, he made the presentations as if he had been doing it for years. Not only was Davi impressed, but Monty was both impressed and surprised at the way he was so smooth. He knew after the first sales call that he had made the right decision giving him the job.

Patio Brasil was considered Brasilia's leading modern mall,

being home to in excess of two hundred different stores, and the entire first day was spent opening new accounts there.

The next day, they spent the day at Conjunto Nacioinal, the oldest shopping mall in Brasilia. Again, Tom bowled Davi and Monty over with his knowledge of the line and his smooth presentations.

Thursday morning was spent seeing customers, but the afternoon was spent in the office going over forecasts and projections. Monty explained to Davi that Tom would be coming back more than he would because of the demands on his time running the large Shepherd company, but he felt confident that Tom could do a good job. Davi was pleased and agreed that Tom would do a good job, and he would be welcome anytime.

Thursday night, Davi and Lara took the pair out to dinner, and it was a huge treat for Tom.

When Joan was down there with Monty, Davi and Lara took them to a great restaurant called Alice. Alice is located in a beautiful mansion and serves exquisite French food and wine as well as wines from Argentina, Chile and other fine wine locations. Tom, being just a plain old unsophisticated Tennessee boy, had never eaten French food, but when he tried it, he liked it. Monty didn't have the heart to trick him into eating escargot, but he thought about it. It was a wonderful evening, but it ended too soon. Monty said they had better go, so they could get some rest before having to get up and head back to Chattanooga the next morning.

On the long flight, Monty and Tom had plenty of time to talk. "Tom, I have to admit I was pleasantly surprised with the way you handled yourself with the people we called on. You showed you knew what you were talking about, and your presentations were flawless. That tells me that I won't have any worries about whether you can do the job when you travel to the international offices, and I'm thankful for that. At this point, I don't think it will be necessary for me to come back to Brasilia with you. You can do the job better than I can.

"I think Joan and I will go to Munich with you next week, but that will be our last regularly scheduled trip there. I may go back with you from time to time, but you don't need me anymore. My reason for going with you next week is to see if we can set something up down in Italy. Right now, we're not doing any business there, and we need to be.

"Tel Aviv is another matter. I'll be going with you when you go there for the next couple times, at least. You won't need me to hold your hand when you work Israel, but I think it's time we started thinking about maybe going to a couple other Mid-East countries, such as Egypt and Jordan. Years ago, my Dad and Urey Steen were going to open up those countries, but the Six Day War came and then Urey got killed, so the plans were scrapped. If you work Israel, and I work the other places, we can hit them with both barrels, or it could be that you will work the other places, and I'll work Israel. It won't matter as long as we get the business. Besides, Tel Aviv is a great vacation spot, and Joan loves to go there."

"I'm anxious to see Tel Aviv. I've heard it's beautiful."

"It is, and the best part is, everybody loves Shepherd Apparel. You're gonna have a ball calling on customers over there."

"Monty, are we going to leave Sunday or Monday for Munich?"

"When do you want to leave? We can leave anytime you want to. If we leave Sunday, you can see Marlene earlier. You want to leave then?"

Blushing, Tom said, "That would be great."

"Tell you what," Monty said, "it might be too late for you to call her when we get home this afternoon, but you can call her whenever you want to and tell her to meet us at the airport around nine o'clock Monday morning. Does that sound all right?"

"It sounds perfect. You probably can't tell, Monty, but I'm anxious to see her. I have her home phone number. I'll call her this afternoon if you don't mind."

"I don't mind."

Chuck sat the plane down at Lovell Field a little after five o'clock Friday afternoon, and as soon as they all got checked through customs, Tom and Monty walked outside where Joan was waiting. Monty gave her a big hello kiss, and Tom spoke to her as he hurried to his car. He went straight to the Shepherd office and got on the phone. It was midnight in Munich, but he didn't care, and he knew Marlene wouldn't. It rang several times; then a sleepy voice on the other end said, "Hallo."

"Marlene, it's Tom. How are you?"

"Tom, it's so good to hear your voice. How are you?"

"I'm fine. We just got back from South America where we had a real good trip."

"I wish you were here, Tom. I miss you so much."

"Well Schatzi—did I say that right? I miss you, too. Listen, the reason I'm calling so late is to tell you we'll be in Munich Monday morning. Monty wanted me to tell you to meet our plane at nine o'clock. Gerhard knows we're coming, but Monty wants you to call him or Daniele and tell whichever one you talk to that Joan is coming with us. We'll be there until Wednesday afternoon, then we'll go to London."

"Will you stay with me?"

"I don't know, honey. We'll have to see. I'll let you know when I get there."

Tom considered the call a business call, so after they finished talking about her meeting the plane and their schedule, he talked to Marlene another five or six minutes. Finally, he said, Schatzi, we need to hang up now. I probably won't call you tomorrow, but I'll see you Monday morning. Have a good night, and I'll see you real soon."

"I won't sleep tonight for thinking of you."

"I'll be thinking of you, too, but you need to get some sleep."

"All right, I'll try. Good night, my sweet."

"Good night."

147

Chapter Fifteen

The flight to Munich was uneventful, just a routine flight except for the filet mignon that Chuck had caterers bring in for them. After dinner they watched a movie, and all three turned in early. When they landed the next morning, Marlene was there to meet them instead of Gerhard. She shook hands with Joan and Monty first, then shook hands with Tom and held on a little longer. Tom gave her a polite kiss on the cheek, then they all went to her car.

Tom sat in front with Marlene while Monty and Joan sat in the back. As they were leaving the airport, Marlene said that Gerhard had told her to bring them to the office because Daniele would be there to pick Joan up.

Arriving at the office, they all went into where Bruno, Gerhard, and Daniele were waiting. After the greetings, Joan went to the restroom; then she and Daniele left for a busy day of doing no-telling what. Gerhard, Bruno, and Monty went into Bruno's office, leaving Tom with Marlene at her desk. In a couple of minutes, Monty stuck his head out the door and told Tom to come in with them while they went over the day's plans. After about half an hour, Bruno, Monty, and Tom left for their first call. Gerhard didn't go. He was planning a trip to Romania later in the week, so he stayed behind to work on his plans, and they didn't need him to go with them, anyway.

They arrived back at the office a little after four, and they had no sooner walked in until the phone rang. Marlene answered and held the phone out to Monty and said, "Monty, Connie wants to talk to you."

"I'll take it in Bruno's office."

He picked up the phone and said, "Hi, Connie. Your timing is perfect. We have just this minute walked into the office. What's up?"

"Monty, did you forget Wayne Morris was coming today?"

"No, I didn't forget it. I didn't know he was coming. What does he want?"

"I don't know. He acted a little funny when I told him you were out of the country and wouldn't be back until late Friday afternoon. He said he would wait around and see you Saturday morning after you get back, and then he left. He said he was going to the sock plant, and would be there if anybody needed him."

"Connie, see if you can get in touch with him and tell him to call me. I'll wait here an hour. It's four-fifteen here, and I don't want to keep these people here after five if I can avoid it, so try to find him right now."

After they hung up, Monty was both puzzled and concerned. *Why would Wayne go to Chattanooga unannounced? That doesn't make sense. I haven't heard of anything going wrong. I wonder what's going on.*

Thirty minutes later, the phone rang, and it was Connie. "Monty, here's Wayne."

"Wayne, what are you doing in Chattanooga this week? I wasn't expecting you."

"Hi, Monty. I didn't know I was coming until David Brownlee called me Saturday and told me to come down here. It seems there is a problem, and I need to talk to you about it,"

"What kind of problem?"

"I don't want to talk about it on the phone. I need to sit down with you as soon as possible. I'll tell you this: the problem is not with your quality. The quality of the socks is excellent. I hate I caught you when you're out of the country, but I'll wait and see you when you get back."

"Tell you what, Wayne. We're supposed to go to London from here, but I'm going to cancel that leg of the trip. I'm committed to be in Munich through Wednesday, but if I cancel London, I can be in Chattanooga by early afternoon on Thursday. Will that help?"

"That would be great, Monty. I'll look forward to seeing you then."

"Are you sure you can't tell me what's wrong?"

"Not over the phone. I'll tell you Thursday. See you then." There was a click and then the dial tone.

When he hung up, Tom motioned for him to come to him, and when he did, Tom said, "Monty, Marlene has asked me to stay at her place tonight. Would you have a problem if I did?"

"Tom, that's up to you. You're a grown man."

"Well, I was afraid you would think bad of me if I did, and I don't want that to happen."

"Well, you know how I feel about things like that, but I'm not one to force my beliefs on anyone else. If you feel okay about it and your conscience is clear, then do it, and I'll see you in the morning. Do y'all want to eat with us tonight?"

"Thanks, Monty, but I think Marlene wants me to eat with her, if that's okay with you."

"That's fine. Y'all have a good evening."

They all parted ways except for Gerhard and Monty. Monty didn't have a ride, so Gerhard took him home. When they got to the apartment, Daniele was there, and they decided they would all have an early dinner. That way Gerhard and Daniele wouldn't have to do so much driving; going home and then coming all the way back to pick up Joan and Monty. This suited Monty better, anyway, because Wayne's call was bearing on his mind, and he didn't think he would be very good company if he had to spend an entire evening with other people.

They got home from the restaurant between seven thirty and eight o'clock and immediately changed into their pajamas. Joan dozed on the sofa while Monty watched TV as he tried to understand what the people were saying. As they were getting ready to go to bed around eleven o'clock, there was a knock on the door that startled them. Looking at each other, Joan said, "I wonder who that could be at this hour."

"I don't know, but I'll get it."

When he opened the door, Tom was standing there, holding his suitcase, smiling. "Hi, Monty. Do you have an extra bed?"

"Tom, come in. What happened? Did you and Marlene have a fight?"

"No, no, everything's all right between us. I just got to thinking about something you said, and I decided the right thing to do was to come here and spend the night. We're going to see each other again tomorrow night, so if it's all right with you, I'll spend the night here."

"You bet it's all right. Come in. We were just getting ready to go to bed, but you can stay up as long as you want to. You know where your bed is, so just make yourself at home. I'm really glad you came, Tom. I'll see you in the morning."

When Monty went to bed, he felt good about Tom deciding not to stay with Marlene, and when Tom went to bed, he wondered what he missed by not staying with her.

The next morning, Gerhard was there to pick them up. Daniele

150

would pick Joan up later, so she stayed at the apartment to wait for her. When they got to the office, Marlene had made a pot of tea, and she poured each one a cup. Monty talked with Bruno and Gerhard while Tom stayed at Marlene's desk and talked to her.

Detecting a little sarcasm when she asked, "Did you get a good night's sleep with Monty last night?" he didn't answer for a minute; he just stared at her, then said, "I thought you understood why I didn't stay with you. Monty is my boss, and incidentally, he's your boss, too, and he has strong feelings about people sleeping together when they're not married, and I didn't want him holding something like that against either one of us. When I come back, I'll probably be by myself, and we can do what we want to then. You act like you're mad because I stayed with him and Joan, and if you are, I'm sorry."

"I'm not mad. I'm disappointed. I've been looking so forward to your coming to Munich, and then I don't get to see you very much. Are you going to stay with Monty again tonight?"

"I guess so, but we'll have a long time together before I have to go. I'll tell him to leave the door unlocked, so I can get in no matter what time I get there. We'll have plenty of time to be together tonight, okay?"

"All right. I'm sorry. I guess I thought it would be different when you came, but do what you feel you have to do."

"Let's do this: I'll go with you when we leave here this afternoon, and we can go somewhere and have an early dinner. Then we can go back to your place and spend a romantic evening together before I have to leave. I won't have any certain time to leave. We'll have plenty of time together, and we can talk about your coming to America, too. It'll be a good time."

"All right."

Monty and Bruno came out and said they were ready to go, so Tom told Marlene goodbye, and the three of them left. Again Gerhard stayed at the office preparing for his trip to Romania. He would fly to Bucharest early Wednesday morning and return late Friday night.

Once again the three got back to the office around four o'clock, and by the time they finished wrapping up their day's activities, it was time to leave for the day. Bruno said goodbye and left, then Marlene and Tom left, but before they did, Monty gave Tom a key to the apartment; then he and Gerhard locked up and went to Monty's apartment.

Tom and Marlene spent a very romantic evening together. They talked and smooched, and smooched and talked until after midnight. Marlene then drove him to the apartment, and by the time she got back home, it was almost two o'clock. She hoped she would be able to get up at the right time the next morning and go to work. Sleep wouldn't come easy, though, because Tom had told her he wanted her to go home with him the next time he came to Munich, and she was very excited about it. She was going to start applying for the necessary papers the next day, so she would be ready when he came back.

Gerhard picked Monty and Tom up at the regular time and drove them to the office. He went in with them and talked to Monty for a few minutes, then left for the airport to catch his plane for Bucharest, Romania. As far as the workday went, it was a repeat of the day before except for calling on different customers. The evening was the same, also, except Marlene and Tom went to eat with Monty, Joan, and Bruno and Kirsten Meyer. As soon as they ate, Tom and Marlene excused themselves and went to Marlene's.

Monty had called Chuck earlier and told him to be ready to take off at eight o'clock Thursday morning, and since Gerhard was out of town, Bruno offered to pick them up and take them to the airport. Monty told him he didn't have to since they would have to leave the apartment around seven-fifteen, but Bruno insisted. They broke up about an hour after they finished dinner and Monty thanked them for the ride. Joan and Kirsten had gotten along really well, and they hoped to be able to get together again. Bruno had been studying English, and Kirsten was trying to learn it as well. They both did an adequate job of carrying on a conversation, and it would only get better as they studied the language more.

At eight a.m. sharp, the big 707 roared down the runway, then Chuck raised its nose, and the plane left the ground and aimed toward the sky like an eagle being lifted by invisible updrafts. The three passengers didn't even take time to have coffee before they left the apartment, and they were all starving. One of the crew had made a pot of coffee before they took off, and just as soon as they reached altitude and could unfasten their seatbelts, they all made a beeline to the galley for coffee and breakfast.

After they had finished eating and were having another cup of coffee, Monty left the table and sat on one of the sofas and appeared to be in deep thought. Joan asked, "Is something wrong, Darling?"

"No, nothing's wrong. I just have some business things on my mind, but nothing's wrong."

In a couple hours, Tom walked by, and Monty said, "Tom, sit down a minute, will you?"

"Sure, what's on your mind?"

"Have you seen or heard of any problems, especially at the sock plant?"

"No, I haven't heard anything. Why?"

Monty told him about Wayne Morris's coming, and that was the reason they were going home a day early. "He assured me it wasn't a quality problem and said the quality was excellent. It was something else, but wouldn't tell me over the phone. I can't figure it out, but it must be something serious to bring him all the way from the west coast. I'm going to meet with him this afternoon, just as soon as we get home. I can't imagine what it is."

"It's going to be interesting to see."

The plane landed a little before one, and since Monty and Joan had driven only one car to the airport, "Monty had Joan drive him to the office. They had eaten on the plane an hour earlier. Due to the six-hour time difference, they had dinner for lunch.

Monty walked into the large reception area, and the receptionist told him Wayne was in the break room waiting for him. He went to his office to put his briefcase down, and then went to the break room to see Wayne.

"Hi, Wayne. How you doing?"

"Good, Monty. It's good to see you."

"Okay, Wayne, let's cut to the chase. Why are you here?"

"Monty, can we go to your office where it's more private?"

"Sure, come on."

As soon as they got to Monty's office and sat down, Monty said, "Okay, shoot. What's the problem?"

"Monty, it looks as if we've got a major sock counterfeiting problem."

"What do you mean?"

"Last week, down in San Diego, Customs agents found a truck loaded with *Fin* socks that were not part of our inventory. The shipper was a fictitious company, but the shipment originated in Chattanooga, and Shepherd Socks is our only source in Chattanooga.

David Brownlee is very upset about it because he had put his complete trust in you and your company, and now this happens."

"Wayne, have you said anything to anybody since you've been here?"

"No, I wanted to wait and talk to you."

"Excuse me a minute, Wayne." Monty picked up the phone and buzzed Connie. "Connie, call Tommy Everett at the sock plant and tell him to come to my office right now. Thank you."

While they were waiting for Tommy, they continued to talk about the truckload of counterfeit *Fin* socks. "Wayne, I don't know what's going on, but I'm sure going to try and get to the bottom of it. I don't believe those socks came from here. Do you think David Brownlee thinks they did? Do you know the name of the truck line that was carrying the socks?"

"Scoggins Truck Line. Do you know them?"

"No, not really. I've seen their trucks on the road, but I don't know anything about them. I think they're out of middle Tennessee, somewhere."

In a couple minutes, Monty's phone rang, and Peggy, the receptionist said, "Monty, Tommy Everett is here."

"Tell him to come in."

Tommy knocked as he opened the door and said, "Did you want to see me, Monty?"

"Yeah, I did. Tommy, tell Wayne how we ship the *Fin* socks."

"Well, a Shepherd Truck Line truck stays backed up to our dock all the time, and as we complete enough socks to fill up a pallet, we load the pallet on the truck, and when the truck gets full, we dispatch it to All Conference Sports. Then, another truck is backed up to the dock in its place, and we start all over again."

"Do you ever ship on any other truck line?"

"No, sir. You told me to ship everything on Shepherd trucks."

"Wayne, how about telling Tommy what we've been talking about?"

Wayne filled Tommy in on the story of the customs agents' intercepting the truckload of *Fin* socks, and Tommy asked the same thing Monty did. "What was the name of the truck line that was carrying the socks?"

"Scoggins. Do you know them?"

"No, but I've seen their trucks around."

Monty then asked, "Well, Wayne, what do we do now?"

"I don't know if we do anything. The customs people are all over this case, and I'm sure they'll come up with the guilty ones before they let go."

"You never did answer my question: does David Brownlee think we did this?"

"Monty, I honestly don't know. I know he doesn't want to think you did, but there's the truckload of socks from Chattanooga. Monty, this is a big deal, and your entire contract with our company is in serious jeopardy."

"Wayne, I don't think you think we did that, and I hope you'll give us the benefit of the doubt and stick with us until we can find out who did it."

"You're right, Monty. I don't believe you or Shepherd Apparel are guilty, and I'll do my best to keep your contract intact. I don't think David will do anything, at least, until the Customs Department completes their investigation. In the meantime, why don't you do some investigating on your own and see what you can come up with?"

"Thanks, Wayne. I'm gonna do just that."

Monty told Tommy he could go back to the sock plant, and he and Wayne stayed in Monty's office talking until after five.

"Wayne, I'd ask you to dinner, but I've had a really long day, and I'm beat. Flying ten hours, and the stress of worrying about a serious business problem has taken its toll on me today. I apologize."

"No problem, Monty. The stress of this problem has been traumatic for me as well, and I would just like to grab a bite at the hotel and relax until bedtime. Maybe we can have breakfast in the morning. Want to?"

"Yeah. Why don't I pick you up at seven-thirty, and we'll go to the Cracker Barrel. If you haven't been there, you're in for a treat."

"Okay, sounds like a plan. I'll see you in the morning. Monty, for what it's worth, I feel much better after talking to you and Tommy, and we're going to get this thing worked out."

"Thanks, Wayne. I'll see ya."

When Tommy got back to the sock plant, everyone on the first shift had already gone, so he sat in his office for a long time, thinking, and trying to figure out who could have done such a thing. He had heard of things like that happening, and he had known some people who did that kind of thing in the past, but he couldn't figure out who in Chattanooga would be able to pull it off. He knew he needed to help solve the problem because if All Conference pulled their contract, he could very well be out of a job. He locked his desk and walked out to his car, still thinking, and he decided that he would enlist the help of Don Shepherd the next morning, even though Don didn't have anything to do with *Fin* production.

CHAPTER SIXTEEN

Friday began just like every other day, except it seemed as if a cloud were hanging over Monty and Tommy, and soon it would be hanging over Don.

Tommy got the *Fin* line started as did Don with the *Staff* line. When break time came, Tommy told Don to get his snack and come into his office and eat it or drink his drink or whatever he was going to have. When he came in, Tommy said, "Sit down. We need your help with something. Yesterday, Monty called me to his office, and when I got there, Wayne Morris was sitting there. Remember he's been here all week?"

"Yeah, did you find out why?"

"I did. When I sat down, Monty told me that we have a big problem, and then, he had Wayne tell me what it was. It seems that U.S. Customs intercepted a truck in San Diego, California, that was carrying a load of counterfeit *Fin* socks. The shipping manifest showed it was shipped by a fictitious company, but the scary part of it was that it showed the shipment originated in Chattanooga."

Don could feel the blood draining from his face, and he just hoped Tommy didn't notice any changes in his demeanor.

"You and I need to help Monty find out who shipped those socks because if we don't, there's a real good chance that All Conference Sports will cancel their contract with Shepherd Apparel, and that would be a shame. Are you familiar with a truck line named Scoggins?"

"I don't know them, but I've seen a lot of their trucks around. Why?"

"That's the line that was carrying the *funny* socks. Monty said he thought they were based somewhere in middle Tennessee. Listen, Monty and I are going to try and root out this counterfeiter to save our contract, and I hope you'll help us."

"Of course I will. Just tell me what you want me to do."

"Okay. I'll keep you posted on what's going on, and we'll probably be calling on you. You can get back to whatever you were doing. I just wanted to tell you about this and ask for your help."

Don couldn't wait to get to his office, so he could call J.D.

Massey. When J.D. answered, Don told him everything Tommy had told him, and when he asked if it were his shipment, J.D. said it wasn't. Maybe it was Tim Williams'.

He hung up and called Tim, and Tim said it was indeed his shipment that Customs intercepted. The Scoggins Truck Line didn't know where the socks were made because they picked them up at his warehouse and not a mill.

Don asked, "Do you think they'll find out who made them?"

"I don't know. I'm not going to tell them, but they're smart. They have ways to find out things. Needless to say, don't send me any more socks until this is straightened out. Did they get any of J.D.'s stuff?"

"I just talked to him, and he said they didn't."

"Well, watch yourself. You know he had a problem awhile back, and even though his freight-forwarder got it worked out, I'm sure they've got him on their short list. If I were you, I'd think seriously about shutting down for a while."

"Man, I would hate to do that, but if it comes to it, I guess I'll have to. I'll let you go, Tim. How about keeping me posted on what's happening. Will you do that?"

"I'll try, but they may have my phones bugged; in fact, they might be listening to us talk right now."

That thought scared the bejeebes out of Don, and he told Tim good bye and hung up.

He leaned back in his chair and thought, *What if Tim's phone was bugged, and they heard me talking on a Shepherd Socks phone? That would be a disaster. Maybe I should shut down for a while until things cool off. Customs is only one part of the problem; Monty and Shepherd Apparel is scarier than they are. If I get caught up in this, it will kill Dad. I've got almost eight hundred thousand dollars in the bank, so I can afford it, I guess. If I can just hang on for another three weeks, I can hit the million dollar mark. I sure would like to say I've got a million dollars in the bank. No, that's wrong; without Tim's business, I can't make my normal seventy thousand a week, so it will take longer. This is going to take some careful thought.*

His train of thought was interrupted by Tommy's calling him to come to the boarding machine line to fix something.

As usual, Monty went into the office Saturday morning, and after getting coffee in the break room, he went into his office and closed the door. He took a sip of coffee, then got on one knee and said, "Heavenly Father, thank you for this day and all the blessings you've given me. Father, I'm bringing this *Fin* problem to you, and I ask that you help me solve it. Lord, you know I had no part in making and shipping the counterfeit socks, so please work it out for me. A lot of people are depending on this company for their livelihood, and it wouldn't be fair to them or to us to have to suffer for something we didn't do, so, Heavenly Father, I'm turning it over to you to handle, and I'm going to try not to worry about it. Thank you for taking care of this for me, Lord, and I'm making this prayer in the name of Jesus. Amen."

The rest of the weekend was calm, and nobody outside the business would ever know that there was a major problem that had to be solved. Monty confided in Joan, but he wouldn't dare tell his Dad.

Monty had learned a long time ago that if you turned your problems over to God, you wouldn't have to worry about the outcome because the all-knowing God would handle things the way they should be handled, so he relaxed with Joan and had a wonderful weekend.

Don, on the other hand, was a wreck. A recurring vision in his mind was that of him peering out from behind bars, looking out at his Dad and brother. He called Delta to see about a flight to the Cayman Islands, but temporarily dismissed the thought. He even thought about suicide if he was caught, and again, dismissed the thought.

Then his thoughts were of Liz. *How could I have been so selfish as to let her work at a place where she could be caught up in something like the Fin counterfeiting without any concern for her well-being? Don, you're a real ass. She has quite a bit of experience in the sock business, so maybe I can get Tommy to put her on at Shepherd Socks. She trusts me, and I've got to do right by her. I think I'll see if she would like to go somewhere tonight. Maybe I should tell her what's going on, so she'll be prepared if anything happens.*

He got into the car and drove to Smokey's. Usually on Saturdays there aren't very many people there, but he thought that just maybe, there would be a few guys there that had heard the scuttlebutt about the *Fin* socks. He went in, took a seat at the bar, and ordered a Coors Light. He hung around and had a second beer, but there weren't any people there who he thought would know anything, so he got in the car and went home.

When he got inside, he went to the bathroom and lost the beer he had drunk at Smokey's, and then he called Liz. "Hey, Pretty Lady, how are you today?"

"Hi, Don. I'm fine, thank you."

"Listen, I need some company. How about you?"

"Yes, I could use some, too."

"Would you like to go to dinner tonight?"

"Yes, that would be nice."

"Great. Is seven o'clock okay?"

"Yes, that's fine. I'll be ready. Where are we going?"

"Is The Greystone okay with you?"

"Yeah, I like The Greystone."

"Good, I'll see you at seven."

All the stress was beginning to get to Don. He went to the fridge and got a beer, then went into the living room and sat down in his recliner. He turned on a ball game and watched it for a few minutes, and before long he was snoring. He slept until a little after five, then got up, showered, and got ready to go after Liz.

The parking lot was nearly full when they got to the restaurant. Saturday night was always busy at good restaurants, and The Greystone was a good restaurant. It didn't take reservations, and there was always a line waiting to get a table. The hostess said there would be a fifteen to twenty minute wait and gave Don a buzzer to hold onto. When a table was available, the buzzer buzzed, and they were seated. Before they ordered, Don told the waitress to bring each of them a glass of wine. They sipped their wine as they perused the menu, and in a few minutes the waitress took their order. The excellent service was only exceeded by the outstanding meal they had. After they finished eating, they ordered coffee, and while they were drinking their coffee, Don got an unbelievable shock.

Their table was next to one of the main aisles, and in a few minutes, Don looked up, and walking up the aisle with a man was none other than Pat. They saw each other at the same time, and Don said, "Hi," but Pat ignored the salutation and sat down at a nearby table with the man. She was seated sideways, with her left side toward Don, with Liz's back to her, and all Don had to do was look past Liz to see her. He tried to concentrate on Liz, but it was hard not to look past her to Pat. Once she picked up her water with her left hand, and Don was sure he saw a ring on her finger.

In a few minutes, Liz said she needed to be excused, and when she got up, Don had a clear view of Pat's table. He paid particular attention to her left hand, and he definitely saw the ring, a wedding ring. Then he focused in on her escort's left hand, and there it was, a wedding band.

What's going on here? She's not married. And who's the dude with her? She's supposed to be in Knoxville. Why's she here? Apparently this is another one of her lies. If she comes over Monday, we're going to have to have a long talk.

While he was in thought, Liz returned, and before she could sit down, Don asked if she were ready to leave, and she said she was, so Don left the money in the folder to pay the bill, and they left.

"You wanna come to my place?" Liz asked.

"Yeah, if you don't mind. I need to talk to you."

Gallantly, Don took the key from Liz and opened the front door to her house. When they got inside, Liz asked Don if he wanted anything, and he asked if she had any brandy. She happened to have some blackberry brandy, and she poured each of them a glass.

As they were sipping their brandy, Liz asked, "Are you ready to tell me what you wanted to talk to me about?"

"Not really, but I feel like I have to."

"Is it that bad?"

"It could be. Liz, Honey, as you're well aware, we're making *Fin* socks exclusively at Ridgemont, and we've been shipping ten-thousand dozen pairs per week to two individuals."

"Yes, I know. Is there a problem?"

"Ever since I first came to Ridgemont and talked to Eddy, I was there under false pretenses, and I used the Shepherd name to reinforce my story. Honey, we're making *Fin* socks all right, but we're not sub-contracting for Shepherd Socks, and we're not making them for All Conference Sports, the company that owns *Fin*. Every sock we make is illegal, and if we get caught, bad things can happen. One of the people we have been making the socks for has just been caught, and I don't know what's going to happen. We're in the clear unless he gives us up to the Customs people, and I don't believe he'll do that. We'll just have to wait and see. You know, I can't feel guilty about what we've been doing because all the socks are going to Japan. It's not like we're stealing business from American companies, but the law's the law.

161

"I didn't want to tell you all this, but I'm so crazy about you, I don't want anything to cause you to lose your job. Now here's what I would like to propose, and I want you to think carefully about it: Since that fellow was caught, we won't be doing socks for him any longer, and that cuts our volume down substantially, and naturally there won't be as much office work either. You can stay at Ridgemont as long as you want to, and as long as we have business, but we don't know how long that will be, so I'm suggesting you let me get you a job at Shepherd Socks where you'll have good job security. What do you think?"

"Don, I'm floored. I never would have thought you would do something like that. I don't know what to say. I guess I should have figured that something was not right by the way you and Brandon were so secretive about things, but something like this? I never would have dreamed it. Of course I need job security, and I might want you to see about a job for me at Shepherd Socks, but I need to think about it first. . . You want a refill on your brandy?"

"Yes, please. . . You think about what I told you, and let me know what you want to do. I don't think there's any rush, but I just wanted to make you aware of what's going on. I don't have to tell you that this cannot be mentioned to anyone, especially not to Ruth. I wanted to tell you this because of the feelings I have for you. This is good brandy."

He patted the cushion on the sofa beside him, inviting Liz to come sit next to him, and when she did, he said, "I'm sorry, but it's all going to work out."

"I sure hope so."

They sat silently for a couple of minutes, just sipping their brandy and listening to the good music Liz had turned on. Don didn't know what to expect after what he had just told her, but he decided to try to kiss her, and when he did, she responded enthusiastically. One kiss led to two, and then to non-stop smooching. In a minute, Liz whispered, "Wanna go to the bedroom?"

That took Don completely by surprise, and he was very embarrassed. "You're not going to believe this, but I don't think I can."

In a louder voice, she said, "Are you kidding? I thought this was what you've been wanting ever since we first met."

"It was. . .it is. . . I want to, but I'm afraid I can't. I would have killed to go to bed with you, but it looks as if the circumstances of the last two days have effected more than just my mind, and I'm very embarrassed. Maybe next time, okay?"

Aggravated, she pulled away from him and said, "We'll hafta see." She got up and returned to the chair where she sat before Don invited her to sit next to him on the sofa.

Don said, "I guess I had better be going. I enjoyed being with you tonight, and I hope you'll go out with me again. We'll talk about the Shepherd Socks possibility more next week, okay?"

Still disappointed, she said pointedly, "Okay. I enjoyed the dinner. Goodnight."

Don left, wanting to kick himself. *That's the first time anything like that has ever happened to me, and it had to happen with her. I absolutely cannot believe it. First, there was Tim's arrest, then seeing Pat, and now, not able to pull the trigger with Liz. I might as well quit.*

****

Monday morning rolled around, and Don didn't know what to expect. He went to work, and everything seemed to be normal. When he found time, he called Ridgemont and talked to Liz before he asked to speak to Brandon. While he and Liz were talking, she told him that she thought about it over the weekend, and she would like for him to see if she could come to work at Shepherd Socks. He told her he would see what he could do, then she transferred him to Brandon. He told Brandon to shut down Tim's line and take the conversion kits off those machines, but keep the Lonatis running.

After he hung up, he found Tommy and told him about Liz and how knowledgeable she was when it came to running an office in a sock mill. Tommy said to have her come see him. They would more than likely be able to put her to work, so Don called her back, and she said she would be over right after lunch.

After work, Don went to Smokey's to see who he could see, and there were several sock guys there that afternoon. The buzz was mostly about Customs arresting somebody from Chattanooga who was hustling *Fin* socks. Someone said the socks were shipped from a warehouse in Chattanooga, but a mill in Fort Payne was the one making them. Word was that Signal Mountain Socks was the culprit.

Don listened to every word being said, but he heard nothing that would implicate him or Ridgemont, and that made him feel much better.

When he got home, he was very surprised to see Pat waiting on him. "Well, hello,

Mrs .... what is your last name?"

"My last name is Marsh, just like I told you."

"Is it Miss or Mrs?"

"Mrs."

"Why have you been lying to me, Pat?"

"I shouldn't have. I know that, but I needed you, and I was afraid if you knew I was married, you wouldn't have anything to do with me. You wouldn't, would you?"

"I don't know, but I could probably handle your being married easier than I can handle your lying to me. I've known for a long time that you were lying, but I didn't know you were married until Saturday night. How about filling in the blanks for me."

"All right, I'll be straight with you. First of all, I am married to a man named Charles Marsh, and we live in Chattanooga, not Knoxville. I don't have any children, and I don't work anywhere. Charles is an executive with Ward-McRae Corporation, and he travels all the time. He is only home on weekends, and therein lies my problem. My libido is such that I need to be with a man every day and not just on the weekends. When I found you and saw that you had no ties to anyone, I latched onto you, and together we made life bearable for each other. I hate that I lied to you, but I felt I was safer with just one man than with a different one every night, and I have grown to almost love you. I hope you won't make me stop coming over."

"I don't know what to do. I'll let you come over some, but you can't stay here overnight, every night any more. I have found a lady I'm interested in, and I want to be free to see her whenever she will see me. Right now, it's a couple of times a week, with zero overnight stays, but I'm definitely interested in her. Now that everything's out on the table and there doesn't have to be any more lies, I think we can be together on the nights I'm free if you want to try that, but you've got to understand that I'm not going to bed with you if you go out and sleep with just anybody on the nights I'm not available. I certainly don't want to get AIDS, and that's what will happen, otherwise. What do you think?"

"I'll agree to that, but I hate I can't stay with you every night. Can I stay tonight?"

"You can stay tonight, but you'll have to call me tomorrow to find out about tomorrow night, okay?"

"Okay."

"What are we going to do for dinner?"

"Let's order pizza, want to?"

"That sounds good," Don said, and he picked up the phone and called Dominos.

CHAPTER SEVENTEEN

Shepherd Global Apparel Group was doing an unbelievable amount of business, since Monty added offices in South America and Canada. Charlie Crawford's American sales force was selling more than ever, and under Monty's leadership, it looked as if there was no ceiling. They just kept growing, and with increased volume, increased profits followed.

Monty had been speaking at a few churches ever since he got out of college, and the demands for his appearances were increasing dramatically. People just couldn't believe the words and wisdom coming out of the mouth of one so young. He wanted to make more appearances, but getting to the different places was a real problem. He flew to some of them, but many of the smaller airports couldn't handle the 707; beside, it was leased much of the time when he wasn't using it for Shepherd business.

One day, as he was mulling over the problem, an idea popped into his head. *Why not buy a smaller airplane? Charlie can use it when he travels, and we can all use it when we need to. I think I'll make some calls tomorrow.*

He remembered that his Dad had dealt with a broker named Ted Mosier, so he thought he would call and see if he was still in business. Luckily, he was, and Monty asked to speak to him.

When Ted answered, Monty said, "Hello, Mr. Mosier, this is Monty Shepherd with Shepherd Apparel Group in Chattanooga."

"Monty, hello. Are you David's son?"

"Yes sir, I am."

"Great. What can I do for you this morning?"

"I think I might want to buy an airplane."

"What are you looking for, Monty?"

"I really don't know. I'm hoping you can help me decide." Then, Monty told him what he wanted to do with the plane, and Ted made a couple of suggestions.

"Monty, since you want it to be able to fly to the Northwest and to Canada, I suggest you think about a Gulfstream IV. It has a range of around three thousand miles, and it can cruise up to forty-eight thousand feet where the air is thin and fuel economy is at its maximum. We have several listed, and most of them are in the U.S."

"Do you have some kind of catalog showing photos of the airplanes and pictures of interiors? If you do, I'd like to see them. Could you come by my office?"

"I sure can. When do you want to see me?"

"The sooner, the better."

"How about right after lunch today?"

"Wow! That's sooner all right. Yeah, this afternoon will be great. Say one thirty?"

"One thirty it is. I'll see you then. Oh, Monty, you said you're David's son; how is David?"

"He's fine. He retired and turned the company over to me, but he retained the CEO title. He did that so he could straighten me out from time to time."

"I'm sure that doesn't keep him very busy. Okay, Monty, I'll see you in a little while. Goodbye."

When Ted spread the Gulfstream photos out on Monty's desk, it was like a kid looking at a collection of fancy electric trains. They were magnificent and so were the prices. "Some of these cost more than our 707," Monty said.

"You're right, but they're the ultimate aircraft. They can land at small town airports, or they're at home at Atlanta's Hartsfield Airport. There's nothing about these planes that don't spell success. Monty, this nineteen eighty seven model is the one I suggest you consider, and here's a picture of its interior. Nice, huh?"

"Very nice. Where is it?"

"It's in Maryland, and if you would like to see it, we can fly you up there tomorrow."

"Can I ride in it?"

"If you feel like you are interested in buying it, we can arrange a ride. Can you leave at nine in the morning? If you can, we can go up, see it, and be back here by around three or four o'clock."

"I'd like to. I'd like to take my wife if you don't mind."

"That's fine. Meet me at the airport around eight thirty, and we'll plan to take off at nine. Monty, it's been a pleasure meeting you, and I look forward to seeing you and Mrs. Shepherd in the morning."

"Okay, I'll see you then."

As soon as Ted was gone, Monty called Joan. "Hey, Sweet Lady, wanna fly away with me tomorrow?"

"I'll fly anywhere with you, my love."

"Good, I didn't know if you would go or if I would have to get another woman."

"Nope. You're stuck with me."

"Good, I like being stuck with you. We're going to fly up to Maryland in the morning to look at an airplane, and I thought you would like to go. That's all I wanted. I'll see you after a while. Love you. Bye."

When they met Ted the next morning at the airport, he led them to the plane they were taking to Maryland. Monty didn't know until after they took off that they were flying a Gulfstream IV almost identical to the one they were going to see. The one they were in was three years newer than the one they were going to see, but they were basically the same. Joan said, "Monty, I like this. Why don't you buy this one?"

"Because it's too expensive. You will probably like the one we're going to look at just as well."

The eighty-seven had fourteen seats that consisted of four lounge chairs separated by two tables that could be used for eating, used as desks, or maybe a card game. Two sofas, one loveseat, and two more lounge chairs made up the remaining ten seats. The loveseat and two additional lounge chairs were arranged around a good-sized TV in the rear of the plane. All the comforts of home seemed to be crammed into the small space.

Engine noise was hardly noticeable since the engines were in the back. Two people could carry on a conversation without having to raise their voices; normal voice-tones were all that were required, and the ride was as smooth as silk.

When they arrived at Ocean City, they saw the plane. It was solid white. Monty thought it was probably the most beautiful thing he had ever seen, and Joan just went on about it. He visualized the exterior trimmed with the same colors as the 707 with a large Staff on the tail. They took a thirty minute ride in the eighty-seven that wasn't really necessary. The ride from Chattanooga to Ocean City clinched the deal for Monty. Now, all they had to do was work out the price and arrange financing, which would be no problem.

On the way back to Chattanooga, Monty and Ted dickered on the price and had not come to a decision when they landed. Monty made one final offer, and told Ted if he wanted to sell him the plane, he

Redemption?

would have to let it go at his price. He told Ted to give him a call if he wanted to, and they shook hands and went their separate ways.

The next morning Ted called and when Monty answered the phone, Ted said, "I know where you got your training in bargaining. I didn't have to ask if you were David's son. I could figure that out for myself after trying to work out a price with you."

"I'll take that as a compliment."

"You should, because your Dad was one of the best. Look, Monty, I spent a long time last night trying to convince my boss to let you have the airplane for what you are willing to pay, and only after I threatened to choke him would he agree to your price, but he did agree to it. I was only kidding about choking him, but sometimes I feel like doing it. Monty, we're ready when you are. When do you want to take delivery of your new airplane?"

"I'm ready now. It'll probably take all day to get the financing worked out, so how about tomorrow? Can you arrange for a parking place or should I handle that? I'd like for it to be near the 707 if possible."

"I'll take care of that for you. What else?"

"I guess that does it, unless you can take it to Atlanta to get the exterior trim painted."

"That will have to be your job. Sorry."

 Are you coming here tomorrow?"

"Yes. Do you want to have lunch? I'm buying."

"Yeah, you'll have to buy because I probably can't after buying an airplane."

They joked a couple more minutes, then hung up.

****

The gynecologist's appointment was at two o'clock, and Joan arrived a few minutes early. New technology now made it possible to tell the sex of a baby while still in the womb, and Joan wanted to know. Monty preferred to wait and be surprised, but Joan outranked him and had the doctor do the ultra-sound. She was shocked and flabbergasted at what he found. Joan was going to have twin boys, and twins didn't run in either of their families, so it was really a surprise.

She was so excited, and she couldn't wait to get home so she could call Monty. Still in shock, she thought, *I've been wondering why I have been getting so big this early. I guess this is why.*

When she pulled into the garage, she almost jumped out of the car before it stopped running. She ran into the house and dialed Shepherd Apparel's number. "Hello, Connie, may I speak to Monty, please?"

"Okay, just one moment."

Monty picked up and Joan said, All right, Big Boy, are you ready for this?"

"Ready for what?"

"Remember, I had to go to the doctor today?"

"Yeah, is everything all right?"

"I would say so. Darling, we're going to have twin boys. Can you believe that?"

"Twin boys? How did you do that?"

"It wasn't me. It was you. You've been telling me you are a stud, so I guess I'll have to believe you now. What are we going to name them?"

"Let me think." He paused for a few seconds, then said, "Well, here's what I think; since they were conceived in Israel, why don't we name one of them Tel, and the other one Aviv. How does that sound?"

"Funneee. Get serious. We're going to have to come up with names."

"I know, Honey, but we've got plenty of time. We'll come up with two good ones. You had better call our Moms and tell them. I can already hear my Mom squealing."

"Okay, Stud. I'll let you go. Hurry home. I love you."

****

The following week, Tom and Monty were scheduled to go to Tel Aviv, and since Joan was getting pretty far along in her pregnancy, Monty asked her to go before she couldn't travel that far later. She gladly accepted the invitation, and she, Monty, and Tom left Monday morning for Israel by way of London.

This was Tom's first trip to Israel, and he was really looking forward to it. In the back of Monty's mind, he thought he would go with Tom to meet Myron and maybe work with them for the first half-day or so, then spend the rest of the time in Tel Aviv with Joan. He had enough confidence in Tom to let him do his thing without his looking over his shoulder, so he felt comfortable staying with Joan.

Tom missed Marlene and wished she was with him. He talked to her every day when he was in Chattanooga, but now he couldn't call her. He thought Monty wanted him to go to Munich the next week, and if he went, he was going to see if he could bring her home with him. While he was thinking of Marlene, an idea came to him. He was not very up-to-date on electronics, but he thought he would see if it would be possible to call Chattanooga from Tel Aviv, and have Connie patch it through to Munich. That would be wonderful if it would work.

When they arrived in Tel Aviv Tuesday, Myron picked Monty and Tom up at the hotel, and they went to the office where they spent the whole afternoon. Myron had an appointment canceled on him, and he wasn't able to book another for that time spot, so they had a beneficial *skull session* for two hours.

Monty offered to go with them the next day, but told them if they didn't need him, he would just stay at the hotel with Joan. Myron, not having worked with Tom before, was a little hesitant to agree with that, so Monty said he would go with them the next morning. During and after their first call Wednesday morning, Myron realized they didn't need Monty, and he said he would take him back to the hotel at lunchtime.

The rest of the week went well. Tom and Myron worked well together, and Myron was very glad that Monty had placed Tom in that position. He considered him a real asset to Shepherd's international picture. The week went well for Monty and Joan as well. They spent the better part of each day on the beach, soaking up the rays, and just enjoying each other. Tom joined them for dinner each evening, and the whole trip was a major success. The only drawback was that Tom wasn't able to call Marlene because Connie didn't know how to patch a call from one country to another.

At noon Thursday, the 707 took off for London on the way back to Chattanooga. They arrived in London around five o'clock, got a good night's sleep, and took off for Chattanooga at eight o'clock Friday morning, London time. The flight was an eleven-and-a-half hour flight, putting them in Chattanooga around one p.m., Chattanooga time.

Just as soon as they got off the plane and cleared Customs, Tom nearly ran to his car and headed straight to the Shepherd office to call Marlene. It was close to midnight in Munich, so he called her home. The phone rang and rang and finally a sleepy voice said, "Hello."

"Hello, Marlene, it's Tom. How are you, Honey? I'm sorry to call so late, but I just got home from Tel Aviv, and I couldn't call you from there. Are you all right?"

"Yes, I'm fine. I miss you. When are you coming back to Munich?"

"I thought I was coming next week, but things changed, and now it will be a week from Monday. Listen, do you still want to come over here?"

"Oh yes, I very much want to. Why?"

"Why don't you tell Gerhard you want to take some vacation, beginning the day we leave Munich to come back here. You can come over here and spend a week or so with me, and I'll buy your ticket to fly back to Munich. I'll take a week's vacation at the same time, so we can spend a whole week together, uninterrupted. Would you like to do that?"

"Yes, very much."

"Okay, then. That sounds like a plan. Let's do it. Listen, we have to hang up now. I don't want Monty to make me quit calling you because we talk too long, so go back to bed, and I'll call you again tomorrow. Sweet dreams."

"Goodnight, sweet Tomas. Ich liebe dich."

"What was that?"

"Ich liebe dich. In your language, it means 'I love you.'"

Stunned, Tom just sat there before responding, then said, "I love you, too, and I'll talk to you tomorrow."

He was on cloud nine when he got off the phone and couldn't believe Marlene had said she loved him. *When she gets over here in a couple weeks, I may just keep her.*

****

Before he left for Tel Aviv, Monty had the Gulfstream sent to Atlanta to have the exterior trim painted on it. He had it painted to match the beautiful colors on the 707, and it was scheduled to be back in Chattanooga on Monday, and he couldn't wait to see it. He called Joan and told her if she wanted to see it, to meet him at the airport at one o'clock.

When they got there, the plane hadn't arrived yet, so they stood inside and looked out the huge glass wall. In a few minutes, they spotted it making its approach and marveled at how beautiful it was. Joan said, "Honey, this is the prettiest airplane at the airport, don't you think?"

"It's pretty all right. Are you ready to take a trip in it?"

"I'm ready. Where are we going?"

"I don't know. The Dallas show is in a couple weeks. Maybe we can take it down there if you want to. In the meantime, I'm sure Charlie will be using it."

CHAPTER EIGHTEEN

Monty was on the phone, talking to Chuck Jacobs about hiring a flight crew for the Gulfstream, when Connie broke in and said, "Monty, I'm sorry to interrupt you, but your Mother is on the phone, and she sounds frantic. Can I put her through?"

"Yes. Chuck, let me call you back. Hi, Mom, what can I do for you?"

"Monty, I think your Dad has had a heart attack. I called an ambulance, and they are on the way. He looks terrible, Monty, and I'm afraid for him. I wish you were here. I haven't been able to get in touch with the doctor. Can you call him?"

"Yes, I'll try to get in touch with him. Where are they taking him … to Erlanger?"

"Yes, can you come?"

"Absolutely, I'll meet you there, and Mom, try to relax. Everything's going to be all right, okay? Did you call Joan?"

"No, she and Kathleen are out shopping, and I don't know how to get in touch with her."

"Okay, I'll call her later."

"Connie, call the sock plant and let me speak to Don, and when you do that, will you please call Chuck Jacobs for me and tell him what happened. I don't have time."

In less than two minutes, Monty's phone rang. "Monty, whatta ya need? This is Don."

"Don, Dad's had a heart attack. The ambulance is on the way to the house, and they're going to take him to Erlanger. I'm leaving to go right now. Do you want to ride with me or meet us there?"

"I'll just meet you there."

"Okay. Tell Tommy what happened and that you have to leave."

Monty had reached Doctor Strickland before he left the office and told him about his Dad, and since the doctor's office was near the hospital, he was already there with David when Monty and the others arrived.

The three of them—Thil, Monty, and Don—sat in the waiting room, anxious to hear something about David's condition. Finally, Dr. Strickland came out and said David had, indeed, had a myocardial Infarction, and he had called in a very fine cardiologist who should arrive at any moment.

Thil asked, "Doctor Strickland, does this attack look to be as serious as his first one?"

"Unfortunately, yes. Once the heart is damaged, each succeeding episode damages it further; therefore, each attack is a little more serious than the previous one. The EMT's did a wonderful job in the ambulance, and, thanks partly to that and the quick action by the Emergency Room staff, David is holding his own."

"When can we see him?" Don asked.

"It'll be a while, Don. He's connected to several machines right now to monitor him, and I would guess it will be a couple of hours. They'll move him to ICU a little later, and then you can see him, briefly. Look, why don't y'all go down to the lunchroom and get a cup of coffee or a Coke or something and come back up later."

They took the doctor's suggestion and went downstairs. Each of them got a soft drink and sat at a table, talking, and trying to get their minds off what they were going to have to face when they went back upstairs. After about thirty minutes in the lunchroom, they got up and went to the gift shop and browsed for a few minutes. None of the three could get their minds off David, so they caught an elevator and went back to the waiting room, just in case someone might bring them word earlier than Dr. Strickland had said.

Finally, Dr. Strickland walked into the waiting room and said, "Mrs. Shepherd, David's condition is stable now, and he's resting comfortably. It was touch-and-go for a little while, but then he began to respond to the drug therapy Dr. Robertson administered, and his vital signs stabilized. They are getting ready to move him to the ICU, so If you want to go up to the sixth floor waiting room, someone will come get you when you can see him."

Soon after they got to the sixth floor waiting room, a nurse came and told them they could go in to see David, but they could only stay for a couple of minutes. When they walked into where David was, they were stunned by the way he looked. He was as white as a sheet, and his eyes were closed. When Thil spoke to him, he responded, and he also responded when Monty and Don spoke to him, but he never did open his eyes. He didn't initiate any conversation, but responded weakly when spoken to.

Monty told Thil, "Mom, I think we should go now and let him rest."

"I guess we should, but I hate to leave him. I'm going to stay here at the hospital."

"But Mom, he can't have any more visitors for another four hours. Why don't you go home and come back when it's time to see him again?"

"I would rather stay here. You and Don go, and you can come back. I'll be all right by myself."

"Okay, I need to go back to the office. Let's see, it's two-twenty. We should be able to see Dad again around six or a little after. I'll be back in plenty of time. Don, are you going to stay here, or are you going back to work?"

"I guess I'll go back to work."

They walked to the parking lot together, and each got into his own car and headed toward Shepherd Apparel. Don had to stay in Monty's line of sight until they got there, but as soon as they pulled into the Shepherd campus and Monty went to the lot where he parked, Don turned and headed toward Ridgemont. Liz had taken a job at Shepherd Socks a week earlier, and things were not the same at Ridgemont when he went over there, but he had to see Brandon and not Liz, anyway.

J.D.'s truck was there for the weekly shipment when Don arrived, and he talked to the driver while it was being loaded. He tried to pick his brain without asking obvious questions. By the way he talked and answered the questions Don did ask, it was apparent that nothing scary was happening with Customs, or else he didn't know anything. He felt better when he left for his daily visit to Smokey's.

Pulling back a stool and sitting down at the bar, he ordered a beer as he looked around the room for somebody to talk to. Over in one corner were three guys he recognized that worked for one of the sock mills in town, so he walked over and spoke to them. They invited him to sit down, and they talked a lot about everything except what Don was interested in, Customs activities. Since there was no news about any of that, he got up, went to his car and drove to the hospital to see his Dad.

Arriving at the hospital just a few minutes before ICU visiting hours, he rushed from the parking lot to the sixth floor and caught up with Thil, Monty, and Joan just as they were going in. When they got to David's room, he appeared to be asleep, but opened his eyes when

176

they walked in. There were screens everywhere showing his heart rate, pulse, blood pressure and other things known only to the doctors and nurses. A nasal cannula was providing oxygen, and if the least thing went wrong or changed, the hospital staff would be at his side immediately.

Thil took his hand and asked, "How are you feeling, Darling?"

David didn't answer audibly. He just weakly nodded his head in the affirmative.

Don said, "Pop, don't try to talk. We just wanted to check on you and to make sure you're all right, and we can see that you are. You're going to be fine."

Again, David nodded yes.

It was a very uncomfortable time for the four. Monty didn't say anything to his Dad. He took his hand and held it for a while, but soon stepped back to let Thil take his place. She said a few things to David, but they were things that didn't require answers. The visit lasted for ten minutes, and the four got ready to leave, but before they left, Thil leaned over and kissed David on the cheek and told him she loved him. Then Monty took his hand and told him he loved him and would see him the next day. Joan took the back of his hand and told him she loved him, and David nodded and tried to smile. Don said, "Pop, I love you," as he walked toward the door.

As soon as they got outside and out of David's hearing, Thil broke into tears and Joan embraced her, trying to comfort her. Monty said, "Why don't we all go somewhere and get something to eat. That ought to help us."

Thil said, "I'm not hungry."

Monty said, "Mom, you've got to eat, or you'll get sick, and Dad is going to need for you to be healthy when he gets out of here. Let's go to the Cracker Barrel, and you can get as much or as little as you want, but you need to eat something, okay?"

"Okay, let's go."

"Atta girl," Monty said.

Don said, "Folks, I'm gonna take a rain check if you don't mind. I have something I have to do," and he left the others in the parking lot and went home to see Pat.

Joan had picked Thil up and drove her to the hospital, so they had two cars. As they were walking through the parking lot, they ran into Rev. Nathan Fowler, David's pastor, on his way in to see David.

They stopped and chatted a few minutes, and Rev. Fowler thanked Monty for calling him and went into the hospital.

Joan and Thil got into Joan's car, and Monty followed them to the Cracker Barrel where they all had a good meal. As it turned out, Thil was hungrier than she thought, and she ordered a full-blown meal.

After they finished eating, they all went home, and it was decided that Joan would spend the night with Thil, since she was so upset about David. Joan went into the house and got her night clothes and toothbrush and came back to Thil's. Monty kissed both women goodnight and walked back over to his house and watched TV until bedtime.

David's condition improved daily, and after three days in the ICU he was transferred to a private room. He continued to get better, and when he had been in the hospital eight days, he was released to go home.

Joan was a *lifesaver* for Thil. She was almost her constant companion. Thil was a strong woman and took good care of David, but where he was concerned, she was very fragile, so Joan stepped up and made sure she stayed strong. Monty went over every afternoon after he got home from work, and his presence helped both Thil and David.

Unbelievable was the only way to describe Shepherd's business. Monty had decided they needed to build another plant, but his Dad had a heart attack before he could talk to him about it, so he put it on hold until later.

Charlie had taken the Gulfstream to Toronto, and Tom took the 707 to Munich. Monty told someone about it, and he jokingly coined the term *Shepherd Airline*. Charlie was only gone for two days, but Tom was gone a full week, and when he returned, Marlene was with him.

Tom was able to take ten days' vacation while Marlene was there, and he entertained her royally. They went to see David the second day after they got in from Munich, and she and Thil had a conversation in which not one word of English was spoken; it was all in German. The next day, they went to Gatlinburg for a couple of days, where they had a very romantic getaway. When they returned to Chattanooga, Tom wanted to show Marlene all around his hometown, so they spent the rest of the time visiting areas of interest, and at night, he took her to some very fine restaurants.

The night before Marlene was scheduled to catch a plane back to Munich, Tom took her to eat, then they rode up on Lookout Mountain and parked where they could see all the lights of Chattanooga. It was very romantic. They sat in the car, holding hands, and in a few minutes, Tom asked, "Have you had a good time over here?"

"Oh yes. It has been wonderful. I'm just sorry I have to go home. I wish you were going with me."

"I do, too, but it won't be long until I will be back to Munich, and I don't think Monty will be with me, so I can stay with you."

"That will be good."

"Marlene, Honey, I've had something on my mind for quite a while, and your being here has made it impossible for me to keep it inside. You told me you loved me, and I told you I loved you, too, so what would you think about us getting married?"

"*Uberraschen.*"

"What did you say?"

"It means you caught me unaware."

"Well, what do you think? Will you marry me?"

"Tom, I love you, but before I can give you my answer, I need to think about it. I'm sure if we married, you would want to live here in America, right?"

"Yeah, we would live here. Is that a problem?"

"I don't know. I've never lived anywhere but Munich."

"You said you have no family, so what would hold you to Munich?"

"Tom, will you give me until in the morning to give you my answer? I love you, but leaving my home for a foreign country will take some thought. I'll tell you in the morning. Will that be all right?"

"Yes, that will be all right. I just hope you say yes."

Neither Marlene nor Tom slept very well. Marlene was trying to convince herself that she should marry Tom, but could not come to a happy conclusion. Tom knew he wanted her to marry him, and he kept trying to come up with points that would convince her. He woke up for good at four thirty, but stayed in bed trying to go back to sleep. When he realized it was no use, he got up at a quarter past five and put on a pot of coffee and a pot of water; the coffee for him and the water for Marlene's tea.

At fifteen 'til seven, Marlene came into the room, smiled and said, *"Guten morgen."*

"Guten morgen to you. Did you sleep well?"

"I'm afraid no. I had much on my mind."

"Are you ready for some tea?"

"Yes, please."

After Tom made her tea, he sat down with her, and they talked about her upcoming trip to Munich that afternoon and how much she hated to leave him.

"Tom, I have come to a painful decision."

"I'm afraid to ask. What is it?"

"First of all, let me say that this is by no means final. I may change my mind at any time if you still want me, but right now, my answer has to be no to your proposal, and here's why. You are traveling three weeks out of every month, and if I were to move here, I would not get to see you except for one week a month. If I stay in Munich, I can still see you one week a month. That's the same amount I would see you if I move here, and I would be at home and not in a foreign country. Can you understand that?"

"Yeah, I guess I can. Let me ask you this: what if we marry and you travel with me when I go on my business trips? That way, we could be together nearly all the time."

"Yes, but you would be gone all the time except for at night, and I would be alone in a strange country. I don't think so."

"Okay, here's one last thought. I have been working for the Shepherds for many years, and I have enough time in to retire with a good pension, but I'm not sure if I'm old enough. I'll have to check on that, and if I am, what if I retire, and you and I get married? Would that work for you?"

"That might be something we can think about. When would you retire?"

"I don't know. I'll have to get all the information from human resources before I can tell you that, but if you think you might want to marry, then I'll check it out."

"See what you can find out, and we'll talk about it. I really do want to marry you, but I just can't right now."

"Okay, I'll work on it and let you know. In the meantime, we need to get ready to go. It'll take us a little over two hours to get to the Atlanta airport, and you don't want to miss your Lufthansa flight to Munich."

Traffic was always a problem when trying to get somewhere in Atlanta, but it was relatively light when Tom and Marlene drove through. They arrived nearly an hour before Marlene's flight was to leave, so after she checked in, Tom went with her to gate four to wait on time to board. In a few minutes, the agent announced that it was time, and everyone stood up and got in line with their boarding passes. Before they opened the door, Tom kissed Marlene and told her how much he enjoyed having her in Chattanooga for the last few days. He told her to think about what they had talked about, and he would look into the retirement possibility. They told each other how much they loved the other, and the door opened, and Marlene left Tom to get on the airplane. She turned around once, and Tom blew her a kiss. She smiled and disappeared into the walkway leading to the plane.

Tom stayed and watched the big plane take off and thought, *Man, I sure do hate to see her go. I haven't felt this lonely since Mary Ann died.* When the plane lifted off, he held up his hand as if he were waving and wiped a tear from his eyes. Then he turned around and went to his car and headed north to Chattanooga.

****.

David's recovery was amazing. After about three weeks, he looked so good, that, unless one knew it, it was impossible to tell he had had a heart attack. Monty's duties and responsibilities were getting back to normal, and he was beginning to be able to relax a little. Between his job as President of the company and his concern for his Dad, he was almost stressed out, so David's improvement helped him greatly.

Charlie was making good use of the Gulfstream, and sales were up as a result. Tom made a trip to Brasilia and then to Tel Aviv before going back to Munich. He had settled into his new job as if he had been doing it for years instead of only a few months. When he went to Munich, he stayed with Marlene, but they still hadn't resolved the marriage proposal problem.

Monty finally felt the time was right to talk to David about building a new plant, and after presenting all the reasons why they should build it, David agreed that it was necessary. Monty was tickled about David's support, and he called Bob Martin that very day and asked him to come to his office the next day to discuss the new project.

On Friday of that week, David called Monty and said, "Son, I want you to come here to the house at one o'clock and meet with me and Ben Caldwell." Ben Caldwell was the Shepherd Apparel's attorney.

Puzzled by the request, he asked, "What's going on, Dad?"

David would only say, "I can't tell you over the phone. Be here at one, and we'll talk."

Monty's curiosity just about got the best of him, and he couldn't wait to find out what his Dad wanted. He called Joan. "Hey, Good-looking, wanna have lunch with a tall, dark, and handsome type?"

"Oh boy, would I? I would love to, if I knew one."

"Well, I know one, and I'm bringing him home to eat with you at noon. He said he would like to have a generous dose of hugs, topped off with delicious kisses. Is there anyone there that can handle that order, or should he go somewhere else for lunch?"

"I think I can find someone here, so bring him on. One question: do I need to get out some food?"

"Normally, no, but today is different. Mr. T. D. and H. has a meeting next door at one o'clock, so he will actually eat lunch today."

"Darn!! Always something to spoil the fun."

"I'll see you at noon, Sweetie. Bye. Love ya."

"See you. Bye."

When Monty walked into David's house, Ben Caldwell was already there. He had eaten lunch with Thil and David. After the greetings and the small talk that always accompanied it, David said, "Sit down, Son. There's something I want to talk you about."

"Is there a problem, Dad?"

"No, no, everything is fine; in fact, you're doing a wonderful job as President of the company, and that's why I wanted to have this meeting. After my first heart attack, I made you President, and that turned out to be a wise move. Now, after my second attack, I have decided to step down as CEO and transfer the title to you because I'm sure you can handle the job. As you know, I am on the Board of Directors, and I had a Board meeting, and this is what was decided.

There was some paperwork involved in the transfer, and Ben drew it up and signed as witness, so unless you have some objection, you are now the President and CEO of one of the largest apparel manufacturing companies in the world. The company has shown huge growth under your leadership, and I'm sure it will continue to grow as long as you are at its head."

"Dad, I don't know what to say except, thank you. I'll try to live up to your expectations. Does Mom know about this?"

"Yes, I told her, and she's so proud of you. She had a hard time keeping it secret."

"Have you told Don yet?"

"No, I wanted to wait until after I made the move. I think he'll be okay with it, though, because he was very supportive when I made you President."

The three of them talked for quite a while about Shepherd Apparel, its history and its future, and the feeling was unanimous that although the company had grown to mega status, there was still much room for additional growth.

Monty looked at his watch and said, "Gentlemen, I think I had better go. I don't want people to think the new CEO takes three-hour lunch times. Dad, thank you for your confidence in me, and Mr. Caldwell, it was nice seeing you. I'm sure we'll be in touch."

As he was leaving, he saw Thil, and she threw her arms around his neck and gave him a huge hug. "I'm so proud of you, Honey."

"Thanks, Mom. I'm really surprised. This is a big responsibility."

"I know it is, but I also know you can do it."

"Mom, I need to get back to the office, but I want to tell Joan first, so I had better be going. I'll see you later. I love you."

When he told Joan, she was flabbergasted. "Monty, ever since I used to see you in class at college, I thought you were something special. Then when you first asked me out and invited my parents to go with us, I knew for sure you were special. When you let me marry you and become part of your family, there's no way you could realize how special that made me feel. Now that you've been named CEO of one of the world's largest and finest companies, there's absolutely no limit to the positive influence you're going to have on the world. I can't express just how much I love you, and I'm so proud of you. It's beyond words."

"Does this mean I can come eat lunch with you without having to bring a tall, dark, and handsome man?"

"It means you can come eat with me anytime you want to. Of course, a tall, dark, handsome man wouldn't hurt."

"Okay, Sweetie, I've got to go. I just wanted to tell you about my new job. I'll see you after a while. I love you. Bye."

CHAPTER NINETEEN

Two weeks later

The group of men walked into the office of Ridgemont Hosiery, and their leader showed Ruth his badge and introduced himself. "I'm Agent Ron McNeal, United States Customs Service. Who's in charge here?"

Ruth answered, "Don Shepherd owns the company, but he's not here. Brandon Sterling is in charge when Don's not here."

"We'd like to see him."

Ruth called Brandon over the intercom and told him to come to the office. When he got to the office, Agent McNeal showed him his badge and asked if there was some place where they could talk. Brandon turned white and led the men to a vacant office.

Agent McNeal told Brandon they had received reports of *Fin* socks being manufactured there and asked to see their license authorizing the *Fin* production.

Brandon said, "Sir, I don't know anything about any of that stuff. I just work here."

"Aren't you in charge?"

"I'm in charge of the other plant workers. I'm like a foreman, and that's all. I don't have anything to do with policy or anything like that. I just work here."

"Who do you work for?"

"Don Shepherd. He owns the business."

"When will he be here?"

"I don't know. He just comes in every now and then."

"Where do you think I can find him right now?"

"Probably over at Shepherd Apparel. That's where he works."

"Does he own Shepherd Apparel?"

"His family does. They have the contract for *Fin* socks and sportswear, and it's my understanding they hired us to do contract work for them. Don is our contact with them."

"So you think you're doing work for Shepherd Apparel?"

"That's what I've been told, yes sir."

"Thank you very much, Mr. Sterling. We may be back in touch."

After the Customs agents left Ridgemont, they went straight to Shepherd Apparel. When they reached the Shepherd office, the routine was identical to that at Ridgemont. When they asked who was in charge, Peggy told them Chip Lowe was in charge, and she paged him. When Chip got up to the office, Agent McNeal asked if they could go somewhere to talk, and Chip led them back to his office.

"Mr. Lowe, it's our understanding that Shepherd Apparel has the license to produce *Fin* apparel and socks. Is that correct?"

"Yes sir. We have the license and a contract with All Conference Sports. Why?"

Ignoring Chips question, the agent asked, "May I see your license and contract?"

"I don't have the authority to do that. I'll have to get somebody higher than me to show it to you. Excuse me a minute." He picked up the phone and called Monty.

"Monty, there are some people here from the Customs Department wanting to see our license and contract for the *Fin* goods. I told them I don't have the authority to do that. Can you help me? Okay, thanks."

"Monty Shepherd is the head of the company, and he said he'll be here in a minute."

"Thank you."

No sooner had he got that out of his mouth than Monty was there.

Looking very serious, he said, "Gentlemen, I'm Monty Shepherd. What is it you need?"

Agent McNeal introduced himself to Monty and said, "We need to verify that your company has the rights to produce a brand called *Fin*, and we would like to see your license and contract authorizing the work, if you don't mind."

"Why are you people here all of a sudden? We've been making *Fin* for a long time, and we've never had any trouble. What's going on?"

"Mr. Shepherd, there have been shipments of counterfeit *Fin* socks seized and traced to Chattanooga. Undoubtedly, if you can present a license, your company is not involved in the counterfeiting. You do have a license, don't you?"

"Of course, we have a license. I'll give you the number of David

Brownlee, the CEO of All Conference Sports, if you want it. I don't appreciate you people coming here and acting like we're crooks or something." He picked up the phone and dialed Sam Armstrong's number.

"Sam, Monty. Look there are some people here from the Customs Department, and they want to see our authorization for *Fin*. Will you bring the license and contract to Chip Lowe's office right now? Thanks."

Sam arrived in about five minutes with the documents and handed them to Monty, who in turn handed them to Agent McNeal.

Chip received a call and was needed in the plant, so he asked Monty if he could be excused. Monty looked at Agent McNeal, and he said it would be okay, so Chip left Monty alone with the Customs agents.

"Everything seems to be in order, Mr. Shepherd. I'm sorry we had to bother you."

Monty gave the papers back to Sam, thanked him and told him he could go back to his office.

"By the way, Mr. Shepherd, just to be clear on everything, Ridgemont Hosiery is one of your contractors, isn't it?"

"Ridgemont one of our contractors? We don't have contractors, Agent McNeal. Where did you get that?"

"Ridgemont Hosiery is making *Fin* socks, and when we went there to question them, we were told that they were making the socks for Shepherd Apparel as one of your contractors. Do you have a Don Shepherd working for you?"

"Yeah, he's my brother. Why?"

"We were told at Ridgemont that a Don Shepherd owns that business, and the employees over there have been told, by him, that they are working as your contractor. Is Don Shepherd here? I want to see him."

"He's over at the sock plant," Monty directed him over there.

The four agents left Monty to go to Shepherd Socks. Monty told Connie he would be gone for a little while and followed them over there. They all arrived at the same time, so Monty told the agents to follow him to Don's office. Don wasn't in there when they got to his office, so Monty told the agents to wait, and he would go find him.

He found Don at the toe-seaming line and told him about the Customs agents wanting to see him. Don nearly fainted. He was scared to death, but Monty was with him, and that helped a little. They went to his office, and Monty introduced him to Agent McNeal. The agent questioned Don, and Don couldn't come up with any satisfactory answers. After about ten minutes, Agent McNeal said, "Don Shepherd, you're under arrest," and told him to put his hands behind him.

Monty intervened and said, "Look, Agent McNeal, we've all been cooperative, so could you please wait, at least, until you get outside to put handcuffs on my brother? That will save all of us a lot of embarrassment. If you will do that, I will appreciate it."

"Okay, we can do that."

"Where are you taking him?" Monty asked.

"We will take him to the Magistrate first, then the Magistrate will more than likely send him to the Hamilton County Detention Center. It will be up to a Federal Judge to decide where he will be taken from there, since this is a Federal charge."

"Can he be released on bail?"

"Possibly, but that's not up to me. The Magistrate will make that decision."

Don's office was located toward the rear of the plant, so he had to walk past most of the employees on the way out. As he passed Liz, they looked at each other, and Don shrugged his shoulders while Liz looked very concerned.

As soon as they got outside the plant and out of sight of the employees, Don was handcuffed and put in one of the agents' cars, but before they left for the Magistrate's office, Agent McNeal instructed the other agents on what to do when they got there. He told them to see one of the clerks and get the necessary papers to shut down Ridgemont Hosiery and seize their assets, and he also told them to get the necessary papers to seize all of Don Shepherd's assets.

Monty went into Don's office and called Connie. "Connie, we've got a small problem, and I probably won't be back today. Will you please connect me to Chip Lowe?"

"Hello, this is Chip."

"Chip, I probably won't be back today. My brother has got a problem, and he needs me. Take care of things, and I should be there in the morning."

When he arrived at the Magistrate's office, they hadn't got to

Don yet, so he waited with Don and Agent McNeal. Soon an officer came and got them and led them inside where the Magistrate was seated at a desk. A Magistrate's hearing is rather informal, so everyone except Don was pretty much at ease.

Don walked in first, followed by Agent McNeal and then Monty. When the Magistrate saw Monty, he followed him with his eyes all the way in. Before he asked Agent McNeal why they were there, he looked over at Monty and said, "Aren't you Monty Shepherd?"

"Yes sir, I am."

"Well, it's good to see you, Monty. I followed your football career from High School all the way through Tech. I watched you catch those two touchdown passes against Austin Peay for the win your senior year. Boy, you were a dynamo on the football field. I'm glad finally to meet you."

"Thank you very much, sir."

"Now, what have we got here?"

Agent McNeal presented the charges against Don and asked that he be held for trial.

The Magistrate looked at Monty. "Is this character related to you?"

"Yes sir, he's my brother."

"Monty, I'm sorry to have to do this, but there are rules, and I have to go by them. If I set bail, can you pay it?"

"I think so. It depends on how much it is."

"Normally, in a case like this, I would set bail at $100,000, but since he's your brother, and you're the one who will bail him out, I'll set bail at $25,000. Monty, that means you'll have to come up with $2,500."

"Thank you very much, sir. Will you accept a check?"

"Yes, we'll take your check. Are you prepared to pay it now? If you're not, he'll have to be held in the County Jail until you bring it."

"I can pay it now, sir."

"Good. Agent McNeal, release the prisoner to his brother."

The Magistrate was so taken with Monty, that when they finished with their business, and Monty started to leave, he asked him to step over to his desk.

When he did, the Magistrate held out a piece of paper and pen, and said, "Monty, would you mind signing this for my grandson?"

"I'd be happy to."

Bud Fussell

After they got outside, Don said, "Well, Little Brother, you saved my butt again. Thank you."

"Don, what's going on with you? You could have easily cost the company millions of dollars because of your greed. I think we need to have a long talk. What do you think Dad's going to do when he finds out about this?"

"That's the worst part of it. Maybe he won't find out unless you tell him."

"Are you kidding? Didn't you see that reporter in there? You'll be mighty lucky if it's not in the paper tomorrow. Those people check on every case that comes through, so he knows what just happened."

"What do you suggest I do, Monty?"

"I think you need to sit down with Dad and level with him. The truth sometimes hurts, but in the end it's easier than lying. Anyway, you can't get by lying to Dad; he's too smart. He'll know you're not telling the truth."

"You may be right, but I can't face him today. Maybe tomorrow, but not today."

"What are you going to do now, Don?"

"I don't know. I think I'll go home and fix myself a big, strong drink and try to think things through."

"How about coming to my office in the morning, so we can talk. I think you should get yourself a good lawyer because he might be able to keep you out of prison. I've heard of cases like yours where the courts imposed a big fine, but didn't put the people in jail, and hopefully a good lawyer can get you out of this. Man, you're something. Did you know that? You're really something."

Don's car was still at Shepherd Socks, so Monty took him to pick it up. On the way, Monty said, "Big Brother, I want to know something."

"What?"

"Remember awhile back, when Wayne Morris came because Customs had found some illegal *Fins?*"

"Yeah, why?"

"Were you involved in that?"

"No."

"But you knew something about it?"

"Yeah."

190

"Tell me what you knew."

"The guy who got caught was one of the men I have been selling to, but the socks they got weren't mine. They were made in Fort Payne and sent up here to be shipped out of a warehouse here."

"Is that all you know?"

"Yes."

The first shift had already left, but the office staff was still there when they arrived at Shepherd Socks. He wanted to see Liz, but hated to face the other office workers, so he went around the building and entered through the back door. He went to his office and called Liz. "Don, what happened this morning? I have been so worried."

"Don't talk so loud, Honey. I'm in my office. When you get off, how about coming back here?"

"Okay. I'll be there in a few minutes."

When she got to Don's office, they hugged, and she said, "I was so worried. Tell me what happened."

"Remember when I told you about the socks at Ridgemont being illegal? Well, the U.S. Customs found out about it, somehow, and raided the place. When they found out I was the one who owned Ridgemont, they came over here and arrested me. My brother bailed me out, and here I am. You're the first one I wanted to see. Thank you for coming back here."

"What will happen now, Don?"

"I'm not sure. Monty thinks I need to get a good lawyer, and I'll probably have to stand trial at some point. I just don't know. One thing I do know; it's serious when the Feds get involved."

"Is there anything I can do?"

"No, there's not anything. I'll keep you posted on what's happening. As bad as I hate to do it, I guess I'll be here in the morning. Go on home now, and I'll see you later."

****

It was David's habit to get up early and have coffee while he read the morning paper.

When he took the paper out of the bag that morning and looked at the front page, large, one-inch font headlines, right under the fold, read *PROMINENT AREA BUSINESSMAN ARRESTED*. Naturally, David wanted to see who the businessman was, and when he saw

Don's name, he began to have chest pains, and he yelled for Thil to bring him a nitroglycerin. She ran to him and placed the tiny pill under his tongue and leaned him back in the recliner in which he was sitting. In five minutes, she gave him another one when the first one didn't ease his hurting, and the second one began to conquer the chest pain.

"Call Monty," he said. "I want to talk to him."

"Darling, why don't we wait until your chest pains stop? I don't want them to start again."

"Call him now, Thil."

"Okay, I'll call him." She dialed the Shepherd number and asked for Monty, and when he answered, she said, "Monty, your Father wants to speak to you. Hold on a minute."

In the split second it took to hand the phone to David, Monty guessed what his Dad wanted. "Monty, what's going on with Don? Have you seen the paper this morning?"

"No sir, I haven't seen it yet."

"Well, it says that Don was arrested for counterfeiting a private brand of socks. What does that mean?"

"Dad, I know all about it. Don had a mill and was making *Fin* socks, and the Customs agents came yesterday and arrested him. I think he's planning to come talk to you today. I'm sorry you had to read it in the paper. I wanted him to talk to you yesterday, but he said he couldn't face you."

"Is he at work today?"

"I don't know. I've been busy ever since I got here, and I haven't checked to see, but I'll call over there now and have him get in touch with you, if he's there."

Monty was unable to reach Don at work, so he called him at home. "Don, are you sick?"

"No, I'm not sick. I'm just too embarrassed to face Tommy and the others at work."

"Listen, Don, you need to go talk to Dad this morning."

"I know I should. Will you go with me?"

"Don, you need to face him alone. Y'all need to talk, one on one. Will you go?"

"Yeah, I'll go but, boy, do I dread it."

Honesty was primary in Monty's life, and even though he hadn't done anything dishonest, his brother had, and it was so close to home, he felt he needed to clear up any misunderstandings from people that counted. He called the airport and talked to his Gulfstream pilot, Mike Taylor, and asked if the plane was free the rest of the week. When Mike said it was, Monty told him to stand by because he would call him back. They might be going to Seattle.

He told Connie to try to get David Brownlee for him at All Conference Sports in Seattle, and when she reached him, she transferred the call to his phone. "Hello, David, this is Monty Shepherd. How are you?"

"I'm fine, Monty. What can I do for you today?"

"I'm wondering if you would have time to see me one day this week if I come to Seattle."

"Why yes. Is there something wrong?"

"No, no, I just need to talk to you about something, and I would like to fly out there if you have time for me. Could I come tomorrow?"

"Yes, come on out. I'll be glad to see you."

"Okay. How about if I get there in time for lunch?"

"Sounds good. If you'll tell me what time, I'll have someone meet you."

"Let's see. You're three hours behind us, so if I leave here at nine o'clock my time, that's six your time, and if it takes four hours flying time, I should be able to arrive out there around ten o'clock. Will that be convenient?"

"That's fine, Monty. I'll have someone at the airport at ten o'clock, and I'll look forward to seeing you."

He called Mike back and told him to get ready to go to Seattle tomorrow, and to be ready to take off at nine o'clock. He hoped to only be there until shortly after lunch, so they could fly back home tomorrow afternoon.

****

As promised, a very nice young lady met Monty's plane when it arrived at ten o'clock and took him to All Conference Sports headquarters. It was a very impressive layout, and Monty was glad he had come, if only to see such a grand place.

The young lady took him to David Brownlee's office and left him in the outer office with David's secretary. She said David was on the phone and would be off in just a minute. Sure enough, he hung up almost immediately and came to the door and gave Monty a very warm greeting.

The two spent the usual first five minutes talking about nothing important: the weather, Monty's new plane, and other miscellaneous things. Then David asked, "Tell me what's so important that you flew three thousand miles to tell me."

"I don't know exactly how to start, but here goes. David, I'm sure you remember sending Wayne to our place awhile back because a truckload of counterfeit socks was found and traced to Chattanooga. We didn't have anything to do with it, but there's a connection to what I'm going to tell you next. Day before yesterday Customs agents came to our place wanting to see our license and contract with you. It seemed that they had found more *Fin* socks. We showed them what they wanted to see, and as they were leaving, one of the agents mentioned this other sock mill making *Fin* socks, and he said he understood they were our contractor. When I told him we didn't have any contractors, it really hit the fan."

"They then went to the other mill and shut it down; then they arrested the owner, and David, here's where I'm heartsick: the counterfeiter and owner of the other mill is my older brother. I had no idea he owned another mill and certainly didn't know he was involved with anything illegal, especially *Fin* socks. David, honesty is very important to me, personally, and our company was founded with integrity as its bedrock, and I felt I owed it to you to come here and tell you about it. Again, we weren't connected to any of this, but since my brother was, I hope you won't hold that against Shepherd Apparel."

"Monty, you're quite a remarkable young man, and I can't tell you how much I appreciate you coming all the way out here to tell me this. I didn't know anything about it until you told me. What are they going to do with your brother?"

"I don't know. I hope they will just fine him and not send him to jail. David, all this is very serious, but let me tell you something funny that happened at the Magistrate's office. You know, they took Don there first, and I went with them. When I walked in, the Magistrate recognized me, and said he had been a fan of mine from the time I was in high school all the way through college. He not only reduced Don's bail from $100,000 to $25,000, but before we left, he asked me for my autograph. Can you believe that?"

"Are you serious? That's funny."

"David, are we in any trouble?"

"Not a bit. I know what kind of company you have. Don't you think we checked you out before we signed on with you? Man, we checked you out from A to Z. No, you're not in any trouble. We love working with you, and the quality of the garments you turn out is excellent. I'm just sorry about your brother. If I can help him, let me know, and I'll try to do something."

"Thank you so much, David. That really means a lot."

They finished up by talking about several more unimportant things, then went to lunch. When they got back to David's office, the nice young lady that picked him up earlier drove him back to the airport where he boarded the Gulfstream and got ready to take off for Chattanooga.

The flight was as smooth as silk. They landed in Cheyenne, Wyoming, to re-fuel and made it home by a little after eight o'clock. Monty thought, *Isn't this something? We leave at nine, fly thirty-five hundred miles, work half a day, and fly thirty-five hundred more miles, and get home in time for a late supper. Man, what a world we live in.*

CHAPTER TWENTY

Early the next morning, Monty went next door to see his Mom and Dad. He wanted to find out if Don went to see David, and what kind of conversation they had. David said that Don had come by, and they had talked at length about what he did and the possible consequences. He said Don tried to put on a good front, but he could tell that deep down, he was depressed. Don told him that he had talked to a lawyer, and the lawyer told him that he would more than likely get fined a substantial amount, but it was possible that not only could he get fined, but he could get up to five years in prison. It's no wonder he was depressed.

"Son, when he was confessing his wrong-doings, he mentioned something else he had done, and he said you knew about it and would tell me what it was if I ask you. What was he talking about?"

"Dad, I'd rather not tell you. I promised Don I wouldn't."

"But he said if I asked you, you'd tell me, and I'm asking."

"Well, all right. About a week or so before you had your first heart attack, I uncovered some shocking things involving Don. If you recall, you put me in charge of Shepherd Apparel while you were in the hospital. When you went home, and I felt safe in leaving, I went to Munich, and one day when I called the office, I was told that Don had moved into your office and declared himself as the new head of Shepherd Apparel. I knew that wasn't supposed to be, so when I got back, I confronted Don about it, and I showed him figures I had gathered about the bad deeds he had been doing."

"What bad deeds?"

"Dad, Don was leasing the company plane and having the people pay him instead of the company. As close as I could figure, he embezzled over three hundred thousand dollars and had it deposited in a bank in the Cayman Islands. I showed him what I had, and he pleaded with me to not tell you about it, so I came up with a conditional offer, which he accepted in lieu of going to jail. Sam Armstrong was brought in, and at my direction, he set up a payroll deduction for Don at the rate of five hundred dollars a week until the full amount is paid back. I felt like he should have gone to jail, but he's my brother and I love him, so I caved and gave him a second chance.

"That's the reason I was hesitant to offer him something when the *Fin* contract came up. I was afraid of what he might do, and it looks like I was right."

"Monty, that's my Son we're talking about. It's unbelievable that he would steal from his own father. I have to rest now. Thank you for telling me, Son. I'm thankful that you have stood by me. I love you."

"Are you okay, Dad?"

"I'm all right. Now, you go to your office and try to have a good day."

****

One week later

Thursday, 11:30 p.m.—"Hello, is this Mr. Monty Shepherd?"

"Yes it is. Who's calling?"

"Mr. Shepherd, this is Trooper Ron Hiatt, Tennessee Highway Patrol. I'm sorry to have to tell you, but there has been an accident, and your name was in the victim's wallet as the contact in case of an emergency. Mr. Shepherd, Don Shepherd was the driver of a vehicle that crashed into a bridge abutment on Interstate 75, and I regret to tell you that he was killed in the crash."

"Oh, my. Where did this happen?"

"At Exit one at the Georgia line. Mr. Shepherd, the Medical Examiner is on the way, and when he finishes, where would you like to have the body taken?"

Monty had to think for a minute. "You can take him to the Chattanooga Funeral Home on McCallie Avenue."

"Thank you, sir, and I'm very sorry for your loss."

Monty asked, "What should I do now?"

"There's nothing for you to do, sir. Someone will be in touch with you a little later. Again, I'm sorry for your loss."

The phone woke Joan, and she put the pieces together while Monty was talking, but he filled her in on the details after he hung up. They both put their robes on and walked next door to give the news to David and Thil.

They rang and rang and rang the doorbell, and finally a light came on upstairs, then on the stairs and lastly at the back door. Thil was standing there in her robe looking scared to death, and she was

197

shocked when Monty told her the news. "Come upstairs, and I'll wake David. Wait a minute while I get his nitroglycerin pills. This could give him another heart attack."

They walked upstairs, and David was awake. Thil woke him when she got up. "What's wrong? Monty, Joan, why are you here?"

"Dad, I'm afraid I've got some very bad news. I just got a call from the Highway Patrol, and Don was killed in a wreck about an hour ago."

David winced, and as tears came to his eyes, he asked," What happened?"

"The Trooper said he crashed into a bridge abutment on I-75 at the East Ridge exit, and that's all I know."

"Was he drinking?"

"I don't know, Dad. The Trooper said someone would be in touch later."

First thing Friday morning, Monty called Connie and told her about the accident and asked her to announce it on the speakers in all the plants. He said he would call her back later, when they had made the funeral arrangements, and he wouldn't be in today.

With heavy hearts David, Thil, Monty, and Joan made the trip to the funeral home to pick out a casket and make the funeral arrangements. Since the body wouldn't be ready until late Friday afternoon, they decided to have visitation from four to nine Saturday and the funeral at two o'clock on Sunday afternoon. When they finished making the arrangements, they went home and started calling friends to tell them about Don.

After lunch, friends began coming to both their houses, bringing food and best wishes. Don didn't actually have too many friends, but David and Monty had hundreds.

Reverend Nathan Fowler conducted the service, and he did an exceptional job considering Don was not a Christian. That hurt both David and Monty more than Don's death itself.

Monty went to work Monday and sat in on the regular weekly staff meeting. Chip Lowe was now conducting the meetings since Tom was promoted, and Monty thought he did a great job. Around eleven o'clock, Joan called and when he answered, she said, "Monty, I hate to bother you, but the mail just ran, and there is something strange in it. It's something from Don addressed to you. What do you think it is?"

"I don't know. Tell you what. I'll come home at lunch and see what it is, okay? Can you have me a sandwich ready, because I'll have to eat and run? I've got a million things to do today."

When Monty picked up the envelope, he noticed the postmark was Friday. He thought about that and decided that Don must have mailed it shortly before his accident. He opened the envelope, and it contained a letter folded around two large Cashier's checks drawn on a Cayman Island bank. One check was for $250,000., payable to Shepherd Global Apparel Group, and the other was for $350,000., payable to Monty Shepherd.

The letter read:

Dear Monty,

Well, Little Brother, I guess it's time to settle up while I still can. The check to Shepherd Apparel should take care of what I still owe them, and the one made out to you is for you to do whatever you want to do with it. You probably make enough to not need it, and if I'm right, why don't you set up some kind of foundation to give scholarships or something. I don't care what you do with it—it's yours.

Monty, you probably don't know Liz Patterson, but she works for you, and I think I might love her. We've been out several times, and would you believe, Little Brother, I never did sleep with her. That's the kind of lady she is. I sent her a check, too, so if she says anything about it to you, tell her I want her to have it.

I'm sorry I screwed up my life. I wish I could have been what Dad wanted me to be, and I'm sorry you looked up to such a first class screw-up for an example. I never did tell you, but Monty, I'm very proud of you. I wish I had been a better son and big brother, but I really do love you both and hope you won't think too badly of me.

It's getting late, so I had better go. Just remember: I love you, and I love Dad, dearly.

Your Big Brother, Don

"Joan, do you know what this means?"

"What does it mean?"

"It means Don killed himself."

"Are you going to tell your Dad?"

"I don't know. I'm going to have to think about that. What do you think I should do?"

"I don't know either. Maybe you should ask your Mom what she thinks."

"Good idea. I'll do that when I get home tonight. Gotta go. Love you." He put the letter back in the envelope and carried it with him.

When Monty got back to the office, he called personnel and asked if a Liz Patterson worked for the company. They checked and told him she worked at the sock plant, so he called over there. He told the lady who answered the phone who he was and that he wanted to speak to Liz Patterson.

In a couple minutes Liz answered, "Hello."

"Liz, this is Monty Shepherd, Don's brother. I wonder would you mind coming over to my office? I would like to talk to you."

"Yes sir. When do you want me to come?"

"Right now, if you can."

"All right, I'll be right over."

When Liz walked into Monty's office, he stood up and introduced himself and invited her to sit down. They talked for a few minutes, mainly about Don, and then Monty took the letter out of the envelope and read the part about her. She cried when he came to the part where Don said he might love her, and she said softly, "I think I loved him, too."

When they ran out of things to talk about, Monty said, "Liz, that's all I wanted. You can go back to work if you want to, but I want you to remember something. If Don loved you, then you must be a lovable person, and I would like for you to stay in close touch with me and my wife. Maybe we can all go out to eat one night. Would you mind giving me your phone number?"

"That would be wonderful, Monty. I'd love to meet your wife."

"Right now, she's a big girl. She's carrying twins."

"Oh, my. I bet she is a big girl. Here's my number, and I'll look forward to your call."

"You'll get one. I'll see you. Thanks for coming over."

The next morning, Liz was at Monty's office waiting for him when he got there. "Good morning, Liz. You're here bright and early. Is there something I can do for you?'

"Monty, Can we go into your office?"

"Yes, of course."

When they got inside, she pulled a check out of her purse and said, "I just wanted to show this to you. When you said Don sent me a check, I didn't dream of anything like $350,000. Should I keep it?"

"Well, Liz, I don't know for sure where Don got all his money, although I have an idea, but it was his money, and he said he wanted you to have it, so yes, I think you should keep it. I don't know how much money you have, but when you add this to it, you'll have a pretty nice nest egg. With a check that large, I suggest you see somebody at your bank, or maybe an accountant, if you know one, and get some advice on what would be the best way to handle it."

"That's a good idea. I'm going to ask my boss if I can be off for a while this morning, because I hate to carry this around."

"I feel sure they'll let you. Good luck. Bye, Liz."

Two nights later, Monty had Joan call her and set up a dinner date for Friday night. They would meet at the Town and Country and get better acquainted.

Dinner went well, and Liz and Joan really hit it off. They had a lot in common, and Monty wound up being more of a spectator than a participant in the conversation.

On the way home, Joan said, "Honey, I'm glad we met Liz. She seems awfully nice. I think I'll stay in touch with her."

"That's good. She does seem nice. I can see why Don liked her. It's a shame he didn't find her earlier. Maybe she could have changed him enough to save him."

****

Three months later

Around midnight, Joan began having pains. "Monty, Monty, wake up. I think it's time."

Monty jumped out of bed like a wild man and started grabbing clothes and suitcases. Joan told him he needed to call the doctor, and he settled down enough to do that while Joan finished getting ready. They rushed to the car and sped toward Erlanger Hospital. Monty pulled around to the Emergency Room entrance and got out with Joan, and went inside to find someone to help them. He then went out and parked the car. When he got back in, they were getting ready to take Joan up to the maternity floor, and they held hands on the elevator ride. Joan asked Monty if he called their parents, and he sheepishly said, "No, I was so excited, I forgot to."

"Well, you had better go call them."

After they put Joan in a birthing room and things slowed down,

Monty called both sets of parents, getting them out of bed. All of them were excited, but Joan's mother was especially so. The maternity people said it would probably be a few hours, at least, and Monty passed that information on to the parents. Charles and Kathleen said they would be right there, but Thil, fearing for David's health, said they might wait until a little closer to time.

At four forty two a.m., two beautiful, healthy boys came into the world. Joan put her foot down when Monty kidded, and said they should call them Tel and Aviv, since that's where they were conceived. Instead, they decided to name them John David and James Montgomery. They were named James and John after two of Jesus' disciples, and their middle names put together made Monty's name. David was also their grandfather's name. Their names took some special thought, and they were very meaningful to Joan and Monty.

Both sets of grandparents couldn't have been happier. Thil and Kathleen had been buying baby clothes ever since they found out that they were going to be boys. They not only bought plenty for the twins to wear as newborns, but there were so many, the babies would probably outgrow some of them before they ever had a chance to wear them.

****

Tom Ratcliff had been making his monthly trips to Brasilia, Tel Aviv, and Munich, and he just returned from Munich the previous Friday night. Monday morning, he went to Monty's office and asked to talk to him about something. Monty invited him in, and Tom told him about his dilemma with Marlene: how they wanted to marry, but they couldn't as long as he was traveling so much.

"Monty, is there someone else who could replace me, and let me stay here and work? Marlene will move over here if I'm home every night. I don't want to put you in a spot, but if you say no, then I'm afraid I'm going to have to retire. I've been working here since before you were born, but Monty, I've been alone ever since Mary Ann died, and I need someone. How about seeing what you can do?"

"Okay, Tom, I'll see. I don't want to lose you, and I really hate to give up your dealing with our overseas offices, but let me see what I can do."

He sat at his desk and tried to figure out how to keep from losing Tom. In a few minutes, he got up and went to Charlie Crawford's office. "Charlie, I've got a problem, and I hope you can help me with it."

"What is it?"

"I'm going to lose Tom if I don't bring him back in and find someone else to do his job. Do you have anybody working for you that would be good doing what he does? Preferably a single guy who's a great salesman with a lot of charisma."

"As a matter of fact, I have the perfect person. You know Jeff Ellis, don't you?"

"Yeah, I know Jeff."

"Well, Jeff might be the best salesman I've got, but he's got some problems. His wife ran off with another man a couple months ago, and he's about to go crazy going home to an empty house every night. He sees her everywhere he looks, and I'll bet he would love to have something like Tom's job. You want to talk to him?"

"Yeah, where is he?"

"He had a dentist appointment, but he'll be back in a little while. I'll send him to see you."

"Thanks, Charlie."

In a little while, Jeff knocked and stuck his head in Monty's door and asked, "Can I come in?"

"Yeah, boy. Come in, Jeff."

"Charlie said you wanted to talk to me."

Monty went over the whole thing with Tom and Marlene, and how he was going to have to have somebody to replace Tom. He explained the travel necessary to all the neat places, and Jeff jumped at the chance to take the job.

While Jeff was still in his office, Monty told Connie to call Tom and tell him to come to his office. When Tom came in, Monty told him that Jeff would be replacing him with his travels, but he was going to have to make as many trips with him as necessary until he felt comfortable letting him do it on his own. Tom was thrilled, and he invited Jeff to his office to talk about what was involved with the job. Before they left, Monty told Tom to come back to his office a little later, so he could tell him what he was going to be doing. He smiled at Tom and said, "All right, Lover Boy, you had better call Marlene and tell her the news."

"Thanks, Monty, I will. You're the best."

Four people were made happy before lunch that day: Monty was happy because he didn't lose Tom, and Tom was happy because he was going to be able to stay home with a new wife. Marlene was happy because she was going to marry Tom, and Jeff was happy because he didn't have to go home to an empty house every night. God has a way of working things out, and those are four good examples.

When Tom came back to Monty's office a little later, he asked Monty, "All right, Boss-man what's my new job, cleaning bathrooms?"

"It's a little better than that. I've been thinking about this ever since you came in here this morning, and here's what I've decided to do. As you know, we have four large apparel plants plus a sock mill, and we're building a fifth apparel plant. You've had the job of looking after everything in the company, and you know that it's really too much for one person to look after, so here's what we're going to do. We're going to split Chip Lowe's job up. Each one of you will be in charge of three plants, and since you both have several years' experience, there shouldn't be any problem for either one of you. What do you think?"

"I think you're a genius. Who but you could come up with such a wise plan? Thank you, Monty, from the bottom of my heart. Oh, and I called Marlene, and she's beside herself. She can't wait to get over here. I told her that when I come to Munich the next time, I'll bring her back with me, and we can get married over here. Thank you again, Monty."

****

Ever since Monty received the check that Don had sent him, he had been trying to decide what to do with it, and finally, he made the decision to do what Don suggested in his letter. With Ben Caldwell's help, he put the entire $350,000 into a foundation and named it *THE DONALD ALEXANDER SHEPHERD MEMORIAL SCHOLARSHIP FUND*. He created a board to manage the fund, and some deserving boy and girl would receive a $10,000 scholarship each year to any college in the University of Tennessee system. If the recipients went on to graduate, they would be guaranteed a job with Shepherd Global

Apparel Group if they wanted it.

Monty was delighted with the foundation, and he reasoned that, although Don's life was a mess, the foundation named for him would help deserving students for years to come. He knew God's requirement to get to heaven, and he knew in his heart that Don didn't meet that requirement. Although he knew that, still, he secretly hoped that since so many kids would benefit from his legacy, maybe, just maybe the Lord would give that some consideration.

****

All was well with the Shepherds. Shepherd Apparel was flourishing, and everyone in the Shepherd family was doing fine. David was feeling really good, and he and Thil were spending time at their place in Florida when they could break away from the twins. Monty was utilizing the Gulfstream to reach more places and more people with his witness for the Lord, and he and Joan seemed to be happier with each new day. Joan was staying in touch with Liz and including her in some of the Shepherd family activities. The babies were growing and very happy, and they definitely were not lacking for love, so from a human standpoint, everything Shepherd was just about perfect. God is so good.

**Also available from Indigo Sea Press
By Bud Fussell**

In his first novel, Bud Fussell has penned an epic: a struggle between two very different brothers; a pioneer man of the early 19th century building a family and an empire; a troubled soul far from home encountering travel and grace. Jake is the Scoundrel, an unforgettable character living out a saga that remains in the reader's mind and heart long after the book is finished.

In his second novel, Bud Fussell moved from historical fiction to modern settings and modern problems—that are eerily reminiscent of the most timeless themes: men of power and hubris forced to face the consequences of their actions and the cunning, resourceful women who must cope with their machinations. *Shepherds* is a page turning read.

www.ingramcontent.com/pod-product-compliance
Lightning Source LLC
Chambersburg PA
CBHW060922250626
47159CB00008B/3123